DIG
TWO
GRAVES

DIG TWO GRAVES

GRETCHEN MCNEIL

HYPERION
Los Angeles   New York

First Hardcover Edition, March 2022
First Paperback Edition, February 2023
10 9 8 7 6 5 4 3 2 1
FAC-029261-22357
Printed in the United States of America

This book is set in AGaramond, Melior/Monotype; Badhouse Light/House Industries
Designed by Marci Senders

Library of Congress Cataloging-in-Publication Control Number for Hardcover Edition: 2021010154
ISBN 978-1-368-07387-5

Visit www.HyperionTeens.com

To the Firestones, real best friends forever:
Roy, Michael, Jacob, Trevor, and Noelle

Any kind of person can murder.
—*Charles Anthony Bruno,* Strangers on a Train

SPRING

PROLOGUE

NEVE STOPPED AT THE END OF THE DRIVEWAY AND STARED UP at the brightly lit Spanish-style McMansion with a mix of loathing and trepidation. "I really don't want to do this."

Yasmin rolled her eyes, a signature move. "We've been over it, like, a bazillion times."

"I know, but . . ." Neve let her voice trail off as the front door flew open, flooding the street with the rhythmic, booming bass of house music. A group of La Costa Canyon High School students—most of whom Neve recognized, but whose names she couldn't have come up with if there was a gun to her head—spilled out onto the front lawn, each holding a red plastic Solo cup.

"But what?" Yasmin threw up her hands. "Marisol's spring break party is supposed to be, like, *the* event of the school year. We *have* to show."

Neve was pretty sure she didn't *have* to show up at a party she hadn't actually been invited to, but she knew voicing that opinion would only lead to another overdramatic Yasmin Attar eye roll, so instead, she stood with her hands wrapped around her waist, unwilling to move.

"You *promised*," Yasmin whined, a hint of a threat in her voice. "You're my best friend. This is what best friends *do*."

"Go to boring parties full of people we don't even know?"

"Go to *awesome* parties full of people we *want* to know." Another eye roll. Neve wondered if they gave Yasmin headaches. "Stop acting like the first half of an antidepressant commercial and let's go."

Neve sighed, feeling like a very bad friend. She didn't understand why Yasmin was suddenly so hell-bent on going to this stupid party. They never went to these things—Yasmin always declared that San Diego parties weren't as cool as the ones she used to go to back in Chicago—which was just as well since she and Neve were never actually invited to any.

Then suddenly, Yasmin's stance had changed. They'd been at Starbucks "studying"—which was more like people-watching while sending snarky texts back and forth—when Marisol Arenas and her boyfriend, Brian Leaf, breezed through the entrance accompanied by Marisol's BFF Luna Krupkin and some tall, muscular guy with striking hazel eyes. Yasmin had gone silent, her attention fixed on the unknown hottie. The group sat at a nearby table, either ignoring LCC social outcasts Neve and Yasmin or else not even noticing their presence, and discussed the upcoming beach bash. When they left, Yasmin decided that she and Neve were going to crash it, and Neve had decided that they absolutely were not.

They were an odd BFF couple: Neve Lanier, the weird Bay Area transplant with a penchant for black-and-white film noir and its accompanying fashion, and Yasmin Attar, the suburban Chicago princess who'd done beauty pageants as a kid and who loved to have all eyes on her. But when Yasmin transferred to LCC at the beginning of junior year, she'd had difficulty making friends and had eventually sought out the mutually friendless Neve, who ate her lunch alone in the hallway of the science building.

Neve had been skeptical at first: She'd been at LCC for two years already and the only reason anyone at that school ever talked to her was to make fun of her retro clothes and hairdos, taunting her with the nickname "I Love Lucy," and challenging her I-don't-give-a-fuck-what-you-think attitude by trying to get under her skin. But Yasmin didn't give up, and Neve appreciated that. After all, she'd been the new girl once, and she knew firsthand how hard it was to make friends at LCC. That initial lunch had been chilly, but Yasmin had showed up again and again in Neve's lonely hallway, and much to Neve's surprise, they'd bonded over a mutual dislike of the über-wealthy, painfully snobby San Diego suburb of Carlsbad they'd both been forced to move to by their families. And they'd never had a single argument until that day at Starbucks when Neve refused to go to the party.

Except Yasmin had begged and pleaded and threatened and cajoled, and eventually Neve had given in, a decision she was currently regretting with every antisocial fiber of her being.

Yasmin watched her closely, her lips pressed together in an ugly sneer as if she was about to unleash one of the nasty zingers she usually reserved for Marisol, Luna, or their exclusive clique, but then she appeared to change her mind. The sneer vanished, replaced by a tiny pout of her full lips. Yasmin clasped her hands in front of her chest and batted her impossibly long eyelashes. *"Please?"*

It was a lethal combination, the pout and flutter. Every time Yasmin used it, Neve's heart thumped heavily in her chest, reminding her of the growing attraction she felt toward her best friend. And every time, Neve caved.

"Twenty minutes," Neve said. A peace offering, not a capitulation.

"Thirty?" Yasmin begged, tugging on the puff sleeve of Neve's forties-inspired black-and-gray housedress. "Then we can go if you still hate it."

I will. "Fine."

Yasmin squealed with glee as she dragged Neve up the driveway. The outdoor partiers cast cursory glances in their direction, and Neve was grateful that most of their faces were lost in shadow, because she was pretty sure every single one of them would have registered the same thought: *Why are* they *here?*

Once inside, Neve understood why the group outside had relocated. The interior of Marisol's house was packed with barely dressed bodies dancing, leaning against one another, lingering on the stairs, making out in the hall. There were faces she recognized but also plenty she didn't, and she wondered if this "social event of the year" was actually famous enough to attract students from all over San Diego County.

She huddled close to Yasmin, who led her through the crowd, snaking around the soccer team and apologetically cutting through a half-dozen conversations. Yasmin kept her eyes moving, almost as if she was searching for something, while Neve tried to make a mental note of all the exits in case a fire broke out or something equally catastrophic occurred. *Death by house party* was not what she wanted in her obituary.

After a circuitous route that seemed to drag them through every room on the ground floor, Yasmin made a sharp turn, then stopped so abruptly that Neve ran into her, knocking her forward.

Recessed lighting illuminated a kitchen so huge that Neve was pretty sure both her bedroom and her sister's could have fit inside with square footage to spare. The countertops and cabinets were blindingly white, especially after the darkened rooms in the rest of the house, and the far wall was one giant glass accordion door, which was wide open, revealing an expansive deck. Neve could hear the waves crashing on the beach below.

She knew Marisol was rich, but she didn't realize she was *this* rich.

The kitchen, like everywhere else, was swarming with high school students, most wearing swim trunks or bikinis and little else, and Neve realized how conspicuous she must be in her dark vintage dress, reddish-brown hair pinned up in a pompadour. It was kind of hard to blend into the background, especially in these painfully white surroundings, and Neve zeroed in on the microwave's clock, hoping by some time-warping miracle that their thirty minutes was up.

No such luck.

She turned to Yasmin to tell her that she was going to wait outside on the deck—in the dark—but her best friend stood frozen, her stare fixed on something across the room.

No, not some*thing*. Some*one*.

He was tall and handsome like every other cookie-cutter suburban douchebag in that house, pouring a rum and Coke from the bar with the ease of someone who did that sort of thing all the time. He wore a blue slim-fit tank top and swim trunks, and a strand of pukka beads around his neck. He would have blended into the beachy upper-middle-class miasma of the party if it hadn't been for his eyes. Large and hazel, staring right at Neve.

The guy from Starbucks.

Brian stood behind Hazel Eyes with an obviously intoxicated Marisol hanging off him, arms caressing his bare neck and chest as if there was no one else in the room. Hazel Eyes finished pouring the drink, then handed it to a blond girl beside him. Neve couldn't see her face, but she must have said something funny because Hazel Eyes laughed, then leaned down and whispered in her ear.

Yasmin stiffened, her gaze locked on Hazel Eyes and the blond, and suddenly Neve knew exactly why they were at that party: Yasmin had a crush on Hazel Eyes.

"You've seen him once!" Neve blurted out, feeling irrationally peevish at the blush she saw creeping up Yasmin's neck. "You don't even know his name."

Yasmin squared her shoulders. "I don't know who you're talking about." Then she nudged Neve toward the bar. "Come on. I want a drink."

Neve followed Yasmin to the bar, where she unabashedly angled her body between Hazel Eyes and the blond girl. Neve was begrudgingly impressed with her friend's ballsiness, but flirting with a dude you didn't know at a party you weren't invited to in front of the blond he had clearly been putting the moves on was more than just bold. It was rude. And in addition to the sort of nebulous rage over the whole evening she was feeling, Neve was suddenly ashamed of her friend's brazen self-interest.

"Hey!" Yasmin said to Hazel Eyes, using the same combination of fluttering eyelashes and pouty lips that had worked on Neve earlier. "What's good here?"

The blond snorted. "I'll catch you later," she said before sauntering away. She moved like a girl who was hot and knew it.

Meanwhile, Hazel Eyes hadn't responded to Yasmin's question. Not that it stopped her. "Pinot? IPA? The hard stuff?"

"Oh!" Hazel Eyes seemed surprised she was talking to him. "Um, I don't drink."

Yasmin's approach shifted instantly. "Cool! Neither do I. Funny, right? That we'd both be here in front of the bar but neither of us drinks? I'm Yasmin, by the way."

Neve tried to lose herself in the house music and white noise of the crowd so she didn't have to listen to her friend's bullshit. She felt like an accessory, tossed aside and forgotten as soon as her purpose had been served. Yasmin was at that party for one reason: to meet Hazel Eyes. And she hadn't wanted to show up alone, so she'd dragged Neve along, telling her it would be good for both of them.

Meanwhile, Yasmin flirted shamelessly with her crush, her hand on his arm. It looked as if he was being polite by humoring her, but twice his eyes strayed toward Neve. She may not have totally understood Yasmin's instalove for this guy, but she couldn't deny that the dude's eyes were beautiful. Still, checking out one girl while he was talking to another after being ditched by a third? It made Neve think of one of her favorite movie quotes.

"You're about as romantic as a pair of handcuffs," she said out loud with a gruff laugh.

"Wha?" a slurred voice said at Neve's shoulder. She turned to find Marisol pointing at her, a sneer of disgust elongating her collagen-enhanced lips.

Neve could have explained that it was a line from *The Big Heat*, a classic of hard-boiled film noir from the early 1950s, but she was pretty sure that would be too much information for the intoxicated hostess to process. Better to just disappear.

"Nothing," Neve said, and turned toward the door.

Marisol grabbed her shoulder. "Wait, who're you?"

Nobody. "I'm sorry?"

"Who. Er. You." Marisol hung on to Brian for support with one arm while jabbing the other in Neve's general direction, punctuating each syllable.

Neve was about to say her name when someone answered for her.

"*I Love Lucy,*" Luna said, blue eyes cold and narrow. She looked significantly less drunk and more pissed off than her bestie. "She and her skank friend were definitely not invited."

Normally, Neve was pretty happy to float under the radar. Not that she was an intentional loner, more like a loner by circumstance—because who wanted to be chummy with these rich assholes? It hadn't been like that in the middle school up north that she'd attended before her family relocated to Carlsbad. She hadn't exactly been popular, but she'd had a few friends and, more importantly, didn't hate the place with every fiber of her being like she did LCC.

But staying in the Bay Area to start high school wasn't an option after her dad's breakdown. He'd tried to go back to his old job after his hospital stay and some extensive outpatient mental health maintenance, but he couldn't handle the stress. Down to one income, her parents couldn't afford their mortgage, so they'd moved to Carlsbad, California, Neve's mom's hometown, to live in Grandma K's old house, rent-free.

She was a poor kid in a rich town, and she hated the privilege that oozed from Luna and Marisol like toothpaste from an uncapped tube. Maybe all that pent-up resentment finally boiled over or maybe Neve's anger at Yasmin needed an outlet, but instead of avoiding a fight that wasn't worth the added negative attention, Neve squared her shoulders and looked Luna dead in the eyes.

"*I Love Lucy* ran from 1951 to 1957, and this shirtwaist day dress is clearly World War Two–era, so if you're going to insult me, I suggest you at least get your references straight."

Luna blinked, too shocked to totally process Neve's rebuke. "What the fuck did you say?"

"You wouldn't understand if I drew you a Venn diagram."

"Hey!" Marisol pushed herself off her boyfriend and staggered over to Neve, swaying dangerously close. "Don't be a bitch to my friend. Don't come to *my* party, at *my* house, and act like a fucking bitch!"

Her volume escalated with each word until Marisol was screeching in Neve's face. Slowly, everyone in the kitchen turned to look at them.

Neve was about to counter this drunken shriek fest with a well-placed *I guess with you and Luna around, the bitch quotient is all full up,* but before she could open her mouth, Yasmin caught her eye. She looked horrified, disgusted, desperate not to be associated with Neve, and when she silently mouthed *What the fuck?* as she edged away, Neve wanted to melt into the floor.

"You!" Marisol said, pointing an accusatory-though-unsteady finger at Yasmin. "Yer her friend."

Yasmin looked at Hazel Eyes. "Um . . ."

Seriously? Was Yasmin going to get all Peter at the Crucifixion?

"Get out," Marisol sneered, lunging toward Yasmin. "Don't get your weirdo loser stench all over my friends."

The color drained from Yasmin's face. "But—"

"Out!" Luna parroted. "Get out or I'll make you get out."

A look of rage washed over Yasmin's face, and for a moment Neve thought she might launch herself at Luna, but when she grabbed Neve's arm with a grip so fierce Neve almost cried out in pain, she realized Yasmin's anger was directed entirely at her.

SUMMER

ONE

NEVE FELT A KNOT OF ANXIETY TIGHTEN IN HER STOMACH AS her dad eased the Lanier family minivan off the main road, the only budget car in a never-ending stream of luxury hybrids and SUVs that crawled up the semicircular driveway of Oakland Hills College, where Neve would be spending the last two weeks of her summer.

As they reached the top of the hill, they were directed to a parking lot by a squad of pink-vested girls who exuded enough perky self-confidence to power an entire cheerleading squad. Draped across the entrance of the imposing stone-facade dormitory was a giant banner that read WELCOME TO GLAM in matching bubblegum-pink letters.

Neve cringed, an involuntary full-body clench that stretched from her toes to her forehead.

I can't believe I'm at freaking GLAM Camp.

Her parents—well, her mom—had been pushing the Girls Leadership and Mentorship camp since they moved to Carlsbad her freshman year, insisting that it would help her to fit in at her new school, but Neve had never been able to get past the eye-rollingly horrible name that sounded like a conversion racket for normcores.

According to Neve's mom, an alumnus, the GLAM experience was about forging solid friendships, unearthing life-altering personal discoveries, and opening oneself up to "the vulnerabilities of female strength." Like a feminist ayahuasca trip. To Neve, it sounded like a touchy-feely rah-rah *Go team!* place for rich kids that she would loathe with every fiber of her being, where she'd stick out like Wednesday Addams at a Barbie convention in her vintage black dresses and black heels and blacker mood. Neve would rather endure a bout of food poisoning than get stuck at GLAM for even twenty-four hours, let alone two long weeks.

Yet here she was, coerced into attending by Grandma K, who offered Neve the one thing she couldn't refuse: freedom. In the form of college tuition. Neve knew her parents could no longer afford to send her to college since her dad's mental health problems and subsequent unemployment, and Grandma K had agreed to pony up an entire year's worth of tuition, as well as room and board, if Neve would keep the family legacy alive and attend GLAM.

"We," her grandmother had begun during an ambush family meeting the first week of summer, "think that it might be the reset you need going into senior year." She turned to Neve's mom, who'd nodded dutifully.

"Maybe give you the confidence—"

"I'm not lacking confidence, Mom," Neve had snapped.

"Right," her mom had said, her smile sickly sweet as she shifted into her professional PR executive mode. "We just want you to have the tools to deal with . . ." She'd paused, grasping for the right words.

"To deal with the fact that I'm a social pariah?" She shook her head. "The only thing that's going to prevent everyone at LCC from hating my guts is if Yasmin Attar moves out of Carlsbad."

At the mention of Yasmin, Neve's dad, who'd sat silently throughout the intervention, twitched. His already pale face had turned a translucent shade of white, and his foot had begun to bounce violently, shaking the dining room table with its force.

Neve cursed herself for using that name in front of him. Yasmin's betrayal had enraged Neve's dad to a degree that was actually kind of scary. She'd never seen him that angry, and the ensuing confrontation— where her dad had shown up at Yasmin's house and threatened her parents—had resulted in a police intervention.

Which only made Neve's situation at school worse.

Fucking Yasmin.

Neve gritted her teeth, forcing thoughts of her ex–best friend from her mind. That was the past. She wasn't going to let the drama of the last four months follow her to Northern California. The one good thing about GLAM camp? No one knew who she was.

Her dad eased the minivan into a parking spot between a Tesla and a Mercedes hybrid. As girls disembarked around them, filing into a grassy quad where a check-in line snaked out of the main entrance to the dorm, the all-encompassing sense that Neve was out of place swelled within her. The upper-class stench—an expensive mix of Jo Malone pomegranate-scented candles and new-car leather upholstery—was so prevalent, Neve might as well have been back in Carlsbad, where almost everyone had too much money, everyone got a car when they turned sixteen, everyone had the latest iPhone, and nobody had ever set foot inside a Walmart.

Strutting across the asphalt with their matching wheelie bags and laptop carriers, these girls looked about as in need of an empowerment camp as the Skull and Bones society. A few even seemed to be repeat offenders, waving at girls they knew or calling them by name before scurrying across the grass to exchange cutesy hugs.

Barf.

"Are you ready for this?" her dad asked, his voice crackling with anxiety.

Neve looked at him out of the corner of her eye. The lines across his forehead were deeply entrenched and the sandy-blond hair that peeked out from below his ever-present green tweed Trinity cap was now decidedly gray. He looked significantly older than he had three years ago after he'd been released from the hospital, unsteady and underweight. He'd shuffled around their old house for months, an elderly shadow of his former self, and though his emaciated form had gained back some of the weight and vitality since then, as Neve looked at him behind the wheel of the minivan, she was suddenly struck by the difference between this dad and the one she remembered from her childhood. Before his breakdown, he'd been a strong, robust guy. The dad who had shared his love of black-and-white movies and '80s synth pop, who'd always had time to play with his daughters after he picked them up from day care, who was ready with a hug and a smile when words weren't enough, and never showed them anything but positivity and love.

Now he looked tired all the time. He jumped at loud noises, slept away the afternoons, and got unreasonably agitated by small things. And then there was that green tweed cap he only took off when he slept or showered, like it was a helmet that would protect him from the world. Neve's dad was frail, inside and out, and as he rubbed his thumb and forefinger across his brow with a shaky hand, Neve wondered if she'd ever see the old version of her dad again.

"Neevy," he said slowly, trying and failing to control the tremor in his voice. "What's wrong?"

Neve knew his agitation was a direct result of her pissy mood, and she felt simultaneously guilty and annoyed. She wanted to say something to soothe him, like *I'm great! Let's do this!* but she knew it would have come across as false at best, sarcastic at worst, and as the charged silence swelled between them, Neve didn't know what to say that wouldn't result in a panic attack.

Thankfully, she was saved by her twelve-year-old sister, Deirdre, who sat up in the bench seat at the back of the minivan where she'd been lying down, engrossed in one of her video games. "Are we there?" she asked, pulling out an earbud.

"We made it, Erdried," her dad said quickly. His voice was more chipper than it had been moments before, using Deirdre's PlayStation ID—her first name, backward—to sell the lightheartedness. The taut features of his face contorted into a smile, and again, Neve felt irrationally resentful. Her dad shielded his younger child from the full impact of his mental health crisis, while Neve got the brunt of it. She felt personally responsible for his daily happiness—a self-imposed task she'd failed at miserably the last few months.

"Good. That drive made me carsick." Deirdre gazed out the window at the bustling parking lot and wrinkled her nose. "Neve's gonna hate all these rich bitches."

"Language!" her dad snapped. Then he opened the car door with more force than was absolutely necessary and slid out of the minivan.

Neve sighed. His moods were difficult to gauge, impossible to predict. "Be nice to him, okay?" she said to Deirdre under her breath. "Talk to him. No video games all weekend."

Deirdre narrowed her eyes. "What'll you give me for it?"

All negotiations with this one. Just like Grandma K. "I won't tell Mom about your secret PlayStation ID."

Deirdre winced, clearly unaware that her sister was onto the user profile she used to play games that were not exactly age appropriate. Her sister had gotten too used to having both of her parents checked out. Someone had to be on top of her shit.

Neve opened the door. "Deal?"

"Fine."

"Good."

She hopped out of the car, but before she closed the door, she heard Deirdre call her name.

"Neve?"

The smallness of her voice reminded Neve of when Deirdre was little, always chasing around after her big sister instead of hiding herself in video games like she did now. She wished her sister, like her dad, could go back to what she used to be.

"Yeah?"

"I'll miss you."

The response caught in Neve's throat. "I'll miss you, too."

Neve sighed as she trudged to the back of the van, where her dad had already popped the trunk and removed her wheelie bag, a beat-up black hand-me-down with a wonky rear wheel that made it almost impossible to maneuver, a far cry from the designer luggage she saw some of the other girls toting.

"I shouldn't have agreed to this," Neve mumbled.

Her dad took a slow breath, trying to gather up the energy for a meaningful talk. "I know this must seem pretty gnarly," he began, using the kind of Gen-X slang her parents mistakenly thought was still applicable. "But it won't be all bad."

"I guess." She reminded herself why she'd accepted this deal in the first place: College was worth it. College was worth it. *Wasn't it?*

"That film class looked interesting, didn't it? Maybe work on that neo-noir project we've always talked about?"

"I guess," she repeated, kicking some loose gravel with the pointy toe of her lace-up boot. Neve and her dad—who had introduced her to the films of Billy Wilder, Robert Siodmak, Fritz Lang, and Hitchcock and Preminger and George Cukor—had always talked about shooting their own modern film noir, a dream that had been derailed, like so many others, when he was hospitalized.

"Okay, well, we'll be at the hotel until checkout Monday. . . ." He allowed his voice to trail off as he closed the rear door of the van. He wanted Neve to fill in the rest.

"In case I freak the fuck out?"

"Language."

"Sorry."

"But yes."

That gave her twenty-four hours of safety net. Though as much as she wanted to get back into the car right now, she knew she needed to stay. To try. If not for herself, then for her dad. And for Deirdre.

TWO

NEVE PECKED HER DAD ON THE CHEEK, GRABBED HER BAG, AND joined the gaggle of girls streaming toward the dorm. Most of them looked like mini adults heading to a spa weekend, waving off their parents' tearful good-byes and hurrying away, pulling their fancy overnighters behind them. There was even one girl who had driven herself, no parents in sight. The gleaming paint of her white BMW 3 series was marred by a thick layer of road-trip dust, and the windshield was a veritable insect graveyard—just like the Lanier minivan after seven hours on I-5—but despite the long drive, the girl who stepped out from the driver's side looked like she'd emerged from the salon.

Her blond hair, a radiant corn-silk yellow that was a popular shade in San Diego, bounced with shampoo-commercial body as she strutted around to the trunk. She wore white skinny jeans that looked as if they were painted directly onto her legs, beaded sandals, and an electric-blue tank top that hugged her chest just enough to accentuate its volume. Most of her face was covered by an enormously oversize pair of white-rimmed sunglasses, and Neve pictured the perfect, easy-breezy makeup she probably wore underneath.

Blondie hauled a Coach patterned wheelie from the trunk, then slammed the door with an emphatic shove, and as she swung around toward the dorm, she paused. Neve detected a glint of a smile on her face, which then broke into a full grin, and for a heart-stopping second, Neve thought Blondie was smiling at her. Something tightened in Neve's stomach at the idea that this hot chick had noticed her, and she was about to smile awkwardly back when Blondie's arm shot into the air.

"Charlotte!" she cried, waving at someone behind Neve.

Neve watched as she hurried over to a girl with waist-length wavy brown hair, throwing her arms around Charlotte's neck in a warm hug before they walked to the check-in line together.

She fought against the fluttery emotions uncoiling in her gut. Blondie was the epitome of what Neve was hoping *not* to encounter at GLAM: a princess, driving a luxury car and carrying a designer bag, a gleaming, shimmering white against Neve's guarded, protective black. LCC teemed with girls like this—the Marisols and Lunas of the world—and though Neve envied Blondie's calm, self-assured demeanor, she made a mental note to stay the hell away from her for the next two weeks.

Unwilling to let Blondie and the rest of her ilk know how apprehensive she was about starting her GLAM experience, Neve did her best to mimic Blondie's swagger as she cut across the quad. Shoulders back, chin up, a hint of a smile on her face. She stepped into the registration line behind Blondie and Charlotte, wheelie bag in one hand and her phone in the other, trying to look busily preoccupied while the line crept forward. Not that her phone offered any real distraction. Neve had no friends to text, and she'd had to lock down her social media accounts since April to prevent the steady stream of abusive posts and messages. Instead, she scrolled through a film-buff subreddit, rereading old posts and trying to look as busy as humanly possible.

"I'm sooooo glad you're here," Blondie said to Charlotte, dragging out the vowel with notable relish, as if voicing the elongated *o* gave her an infinite amount of pleasure. "We're going to have so much fun."

"Um, sure," Charlotte said.

"Did you know I was going to be here this summer?" Blondie asked. "Did I mention it at school? It's, like, toooooh-tally okay if you followed me."

"F-followed you?" Charlotte sputtered.

Blondie giggled. "It's cool. I'm flattered."

Holy shit. The ego on this chick.

"Diane," Charlotte said, her voice shaky, "I had no idea you were going to be here."

"Uh-huh." Blondie dropped her voice. "Our little secret."

Neve braved a glance at the two girls in front of her. Blondie, whose name was apparently Diane, had the thumb of one hand hooked on a belt loop of her white jeans while she brushed Charlotte's long hair behind her shoulder with the other, a move that signaled an intimacy Neve hadn't picked up on from their conversation alone. Diane had pushed her sunglasses up to the top of her head, and as Neve had imagined, her eye makeup—a glittery champagne shadow, thin black liner on the top lid only, and light coating of mascara—was flawlessly applied to a singularly attractive face.

While she was perving, Diane flashed her eyes toward Neve, who instantly turned back to her phone, fighting the blush that she felt rising up from her chest. But if she'd caught Neve checking her out, she didn't acknowledge it.

"This is the registration line, right, Char?" she asked her friend.

"I—I guess," Charlotte said by way of an answer. "I've never been to GLAM before."

"Me neither!" Diane exclaimed with more enthusiasm than was strictly necessary. She may have been hot, but Diane seemed like a total airhead. "I have no idea what I'm doing."

Neve fought hard to suppress a snort. Diane looked so comfortable, Neve had assumed she was a repeat GLAMster.

Charlotte looked confused. "O-kay."

The line moved more quickly and Diane's pace of conversation picked up accordingly. "I mean, I've been to camp before, just not this one. Most of them are pretty cool, but I haaaaaaaated all the outdoorsy stuff at Brown Ledge. And not having a car, that part sucked ass. So I pitched GLAM to my mom and stepdad this year because I could drive up." She paused, sucking in a dramatic breath. "Oooooooh my God! If I'd known you were going to be here, I'd have offered you a ride from San Diego!"

San Diego? This time Neve couldn't stop her head from snapping up to look at them, instantly betraying her eavesdropping. Diane was eyeing her, head tilted to the side, probably formulating a cutting remark about weird retro goth chicks who listened in on other people's conversations, but a sudden quickening of the line saved Neve from the confrontation as

Diane had to turn and grab her wheelie bag. The line fanned out at the entrance, and Neve took the opportunity to dash inside, leaving Diane and Charlotte behind.

The interior looked more like the entry hall of an English manor house than an aging private-school dormitory. Hardwood floors stretched the length of the room, gnarled and warped like arthritic old hands but still lacquered to a gleaming shine that felt out of place beneath the sun-faded chesterfield sofas and purple velvet settees thoughtfully arranged in conversational clusters. Six-foot-tall casement windows lined both sides of the room, flooding the dark decor with enough natural light to make a dungeon seem cheerful, while an almost comically large fireplace dominated the far end of the room. The wide, carpeted staircase beside it disappeared to the upper floors, hosting a steady stream of campers dutifully lugging their bags up to their rooms.

Registration stations had been set up at a series of folding tables along the east wall, and each had an alphabetical sign taped above it. Neve hurried toward G THROUGH L, desperately hoping that neither Diane nor Charlotte had a last name that fell within the same alphabetical swath. She was socially flustered and out of breath when she reached the desk, which was manned by a smiling Black woman with tightly spiraled braids and the longest eyelashes Neve had ever seen.

"I'm Kellie!" she said as Neve approached. Her megawatt smile was almost blinding. "With an *i-e*. I'm one of the senior counselors here at GLAM. Can I get your name?"

"Neve Lanier." She almost added *Also with an* i-e but decided that would come off as a dig, and despite her loathing of the eternal perkiness of GLAM, she really didn't want to start off on the wrong foot with one of the counselors.

Kellie flipped through a box of paperwork, divided by letter, and paused at *L*. Her face lit up even more, a feat Neve wouldn't have thought possible if she hadn't witnessed it for herself. "You're a legacy!"

Neve wasn't entirely sure how she should respond and settled on a noncommittal shrug.

"Well, Miss Legacy, we're *so* excited to have a second generation here at GLAM camp." She slipped a thick manila envelope into a pink tote bag and handed it across the desk. "There's a full itinerary in your welcome packet, which Pam will go over at orientation after lunch. Here's your dorm room key and your ID badge, which is good for all meals, so try not to lose it." She gave Neve a conspiratorial wink as if losing her ID badge was not only inevitable but somehow a planned sabotage.

"I'll try?" Neve replied feebly.

Kellie pointed to a door on her left, opposite the main entrance. "Lunch starts at noon here in the cafeteria, and you might want to get there right at the crack of, because orientation is at one and you don't want to be late. It's in the Magdalen Theater, ground floor of the Fillmore Building across the quad. There's a campus map in your packet. But that still gives you some time to settle in, unpack, and meet your roommate!"

"Great," Neve said, suppressing a sigh. Her roommate. That was the part of GLAM she was looking forward to the least. Kind of hard to keep your emotional distance from someone she'd be bunking with for two whole weeks. Neve's eyes strayed to bubbly Diane, currently laughing with the counselor at the next registration desk, and prayed she wouldn't land her as her roomie. Two weeks might feel like two years, shacked up with all that forced giggling and those elongated vowels.

"So nice to meet you, Neve!" Kellie wiggled her fingers as a wave good-bye. "Happy GLAM Day!"

Barf.

THREE

"SO WHAT'S YOUR ROOM NUMBER?"

It was Diane's voice, right behind Neve as she headed across the entry hall to the grand staircase.

Neve started to turn around to answer when she heard Charlotte respond. "Three-ten."

Right, duh. Of course Diane would be be talking to the friend she actually knew from home rather than the complete stranger she'd just caught eavesdropping. Twice. Neve kept her eyes forward as she dragged her bag up the carpeted stairs, bracing herself against the smooth oak banister and trying to pretend as if she couldn't hear every word of their conversation. Again.

"Bummer." Diane sighed with disappointment. "I'm in two-twelve. Wouldn't it have been *hil-air* if we were roomies?"

Neve discreetly cast a glance at the enormous key ring in her hand: 304. Phew, she hadn't gotten stuck with either of them.

"Heeeeeeeey," Diane continued despite Charlotte's silence, "if I end up in a solo, maybe we can make that happen!"

"I don't think—"

"Kidding. Catch you later?"

"Um, okay." Charlotte didn't actually sound okay about anything.

Neve struggled up a second flight of stairs, then strode quickly down the third-floor hallway, ensuring that she put some distance between herself and Charlotte. Three doors down on the left, she found room 304, and she took a deep breath as she inserted the comically large key into the lock. So far, attendees like Diane and counselors like Kellie-with-an-*i-e* fit Neve's GLAM stereotype to a T, and she had no reason to believe her roommate would be any different. She was pretty sure she'd find a teen version of Taylor Swift pinning boy band photos on the wall beside a bed decorated in a rainbows-and-narwhals comforter set she'd brought from home. The worst.

As she attempted to open the door, struggling with the old-fashioned key and her unyielding bag, the solid oak wouldn't budge. She leaned into it, jiggling the key in case the dead bolt was wonky, and just as she was about to give up and go back downstairs to the registration desk for help, the door gave, swinging violently into room 304. Neve barreled through the doorway and landed in a heap on the warped wooden floor.

Neve's roommate lay reclined on the nearest twin bed, head propped up by several pillows, and despite Neve's chaotic entrance, she hardly moved a muscle. She casually flipped a page of the *Ms. Marvel* issue she was reading, one combat-boot-clad foot crossed over the other on top of a fluffy plaid comforter.

Her roommate's bedding wasn't the only plaid in the room. Girlfriend was literally awash in it.

She wore a plaid flannel tied around the waistband of her frayed cutoff jean shorts, and her long dark hair was swept up into a messy topknot, secured by a scrunchy in yet another color combination of plaid. The pillowcases, the socks peeking out from above her boots, the metallic water bottle on the nightstand, hell, even the frames of her sunglasses that sat beside said water bottle: all plaid. It was like a kilt supply store had exploded, spraying the room with tartan.

But at least it wasn't rainbows and narwhals. Neve could work with this.

"Hey," Roomie said, once Neve had extricated herself from her luggage and clambered to her feet. She hardly glanced up from her comic book.

"Hey," Neve panted, trying not to sound as mortified as she felt.

"Name's Inara Escobar. Yes, the parents really, really loved *Firefly*. Into girls. No Spanish. Don't ask about the plaid."

Neve blinked, attempting to simultaneously process all of Inara's information while deciphering her roommate's mood as she continued to focus on her comic book. Inara was brusque, not overly friendly, but not exactly hostile either.

Kind of like me.

"Neve," she said, heaving her bag on top of the empty twin bed. It bounced heavily, hinting at a tightly coiled mattress. "Neve Lanier. I've never seen *Firefly*, but I also have to explain my name a lot, so I get it."

Inara's eyes peeked around the side of her comic book, large, brown, and alert. They scanned Neve from head to toe, and Neve waited for a look of confusion to pass through them as her roommate digested Neve's simple black A-line skirt and vintage tie-neck blouse, but instead of asking an unspoken question about her style, Inara narrowed her eyes, as if trying to decide whether or not Neve was being an asshole. Neve wasn't really sure herself.

"How so?" The words sounded like a challenge, but once again, Neve didn't detect actual malice in her roommate's tone.

"Well, the pronunciation for starters. 'Neve like in Sleeve' has been my mantra since kindergarten."

"Irish?"

Neve nodded, reluctantly impressed. "I'm named after a fairy queen."

Inara dropped her comic book to the bed. "Learn something every day."

"You're welcome."

"Need help?" This time, Inara almost sounded chummy.

"I'm good."

"Sweet." She picked up her comic book. "Heading to lunch in ten."

Neve hustled to unpack in the ten minutes Inara had allotted her so they could head down to lunch together. Or at least, she thought it had been an invitation to join. As Neve unzipped her bag, she wasn't entirely sure. Inara's style of speech was so stilted and weird, it was hard to really know what she was suggesting. *Heading to lunch in ten.* It certainly sounded like a statement rather than an offer, but then there had been something about her delivery that had felt . . . inviting?

Neve's social anxiety hit her hard. Ugh, why was she so bad at reading people? She'd trusted Yasmin, thought they were friends, and then . . .

Neve squeezed her eyes shut, trying to wrestle down the memory, but it punched her in the gut with the force of a runaway train, stripping away any self-confidence she had been able to scrape together for her first day of camp. Once again, she was back at spring break, naively unaware of what Yasmin had in store for her.

The day after the disaster at Marisol's house party, Yasmin acted as if she'd already forgiven Neve for their embarrassing exit, though Neve expected her best friend to pout all week. Things had gone back to normal, and Yasmin never even mentioned her infatuation with Hazel Eyes. For the rest of spring break, Yasmin was only focused on two things: Marisol and Luna, and what total fucking bitches they were.

Yasmin texted about them all the time, calling out Marisol's supposedly loose sexual morals as a source of her popularity and insinuating that Luna's family made all their money through the Russian Mafia. Neve had never experienced this level of vitriol from her friend, and though confused, she couldn't help chiming in with one joke—just *one*—at Marisol's expense.

Marisol spreads faster than the plague.

It wasn't until days later that Neve realized she'd been played, realized that Yasmin had been baiting her into making a rude comment that called out Marisol by name.

The morning of their first day back at school, Yasmin posted an out-of-context screen grab of Neve's text across her social media platforms. *After* she'd managed to get hold of Neve's phone and deleted all of her own texts in that conversation. Now Neve had no proof that a cold-blooded Yasmin had instigated the whole thing.

Neve arrived at school that morning totally oblivious to Yasmin's betrayal, her blissful ignorance obliterated when Marisol and Luna confronted her in the hallway, flanked by their new best friend, Yasmin Attar.

And why had Yasmin gone through all of this trouble? To ingratiate herself with Marisol and Luna. To claw her way into their friend circle. To get closer to Hazel Eyes. She'd thrown her friend under the bus over a guy.

Yasmin had been a friend, Neve's *best* friend, and someone she thought she could trust.

So maybe Neve shouldn't rely on her own judgment with new people like Inara. Maybe her statement about lunch wasn't an invitation at all, and Neve should go down to the cafeteria by herself.

"Ready?" Inara announced, swinging her combat boots to the bare wooden floor.

Neve let out a slow breath. *Not everyone is Yasmin Attar.* "Yep."

"Sweet."

Neve followed Inara down the hall to the stairs, moving briskly to keep up with her roommate's long strides. She moved with the certainty of someone who had been to Oakland Hills College before, and when she waved at Kellie-with-an-*i-e* as they passed through the registration area, Neve was pretty convinced that Inara was a GLAM repeat offender. "I take it you've been here before?"

"Second year," Inara said without breaking stride. "Older sister came, too."

Suddenly, Neve realized why Inara's speech felt so stilted and odd: She didn't use any personal pronouns. Interesting choice. "Any insider info to share?"

"Sign up for film for the focus module," Inara said immediately, "or art."

"I was thinking film."

"Good," she said with a nod. "Just avoid theater. That's Kellie's domain."

"Noted." She wasn't sure how much of Kellie's perkiness she could stomach before she *actually* barfed. "Thanks."

Inara peeled off as they entered the cafeteria, leaving Neve to wander around, examining the various options. Every dietary need had been accommodated: vegetarian, vegan, gluten-free, dairy-free, gluten- *and* dairy-free. Neve eventually settled on a grilled-cheese sandwich, fries, and a bowl of fruit salad, and she was delighted to find the refrigerated section stocked with bottles of her favorite chocolate blended coffee beverage in both the regular and sugar-free varieties.

She found Inara waiting for her near the cash registers. They each swiped their ID cards through a scanner and were waved along by the cashier. Without a word, Inara headed straight for a long table beneath a wall of stained-glass windows on the opposite end the dining hall.

There were four girls already seated and Inara greeted two of them— one white and one Black—who wore *almost* matching boho floral baby-doll dresses and *definitely* matching hair, done up in two little pom-pom buns on either side of their heads. They looked relaxed and comfortable in their too-odd-to-be-a-coincidence coordinated outfits, which gave Neve the impression that, like Inara, these were GLAM veterans.

On one side of the Twins sat a pale redhead with wildly curly hair and an award-winning resting bitch face. On the opposite side, a nervous-looking girl with a long, thick mane of wavy brown hair whom Neve immediately recognized—it was Charlotte.

"Quince. Sequoia." Inara nodded at the Twins, then jutted her head toward her roommate as she straddled a chair. "Neve."

Quince and Sequoia looked up from their lunch trays in unison. "Hi, Neve!" they said together.

"Hey." Oh shit. Stepford GLAMsters.

"This is my roommate, Rachel," the Black twin said—Sequoia, Neve decided for no reason—leaning into the redhead, who gave Neve a half wave that felt utterly dismissive.

The other twin, who was now Quince in Neve's mind, piped up immediately, dovetailing onto her friend's words. "And this is *my* roommate, Charlotte."

Charlotte glanced up quickly by way of acknowledgment, then returned her attention to the phone in her lap as quickly as possible. If she recognized Neve as the perv who was listening in on her conversation with Diane during registration, she didn't acknowledge it.

"Quince and Sequoia were roommates last year," Inara explained.

"And," Sequoia added, "we discovered that we're basically the same person."

The Twins high-fived.

"Sister from another mister," Quince said.

"Sib from another crib."

This was going to get very old, very fast.

Inara agreed with Neve's unspoken reaction. "Cut out the creepy, dudes."

The Twins deferred to Inara without protest—she had that kind of personality—and Neve smiled at her non-gendered use of the word *dude*. The California pronoun.

"Neve, you'll want to avoid theater class," Quince said, leaning across the table like a conspirator.

Sequoia finished the thought. "And take film or art instead."

"Yeah, you've only mentioned that a dozen times," Rachel said, hardly moving her lips. Like a ventriloquist. Maybe her resting bitch face had actually frozen that way like parents always threatened?

"A dozen plus one," Sequoia said. "Trust us."

Suddenly, Neve was caught by the pattern. Three veterans, three newbies. She glanced around the room and noticed that almost every table had an even number of people. Roommates, two-by-two: one relaxed in her environment, the other jumpy and excited like a new puppy right out of the crate.

"They pair up noobs like me with returning GLAMsters."

She said it out loud, not meaning to, and immediately felt the heat rise in her face at pointing out such an obvious fact to a bunch of people who were already aware of it.

Instead of rolling her eyes like Yasmin would have done, Inara smiled. "GLAMsters," she said. "Dig it."

"Pat," Sequoia began, "she's the director. She likes to make sure everyone feels welcomed and included."

"So they try to put the old and the new together," Quince added. "This is actually my third year, if you can believe it!"

I totally, totally can.

Sequoia grinned at her. "Quincy was the best roomie *ever.*"

Neve gave herself a mental high five at picking the right name for the right twin. Quince was about to respond, most likely to tell Sequoia that no, *she* was the best roomie ever, thus igniting a Möbius strip of compliments, when her attention was suddenly distracted by something behind Neve. Neve was about to turn and look when she heard a familiar voice.

"Hey! Mind if I join?"

Then Diane bounced into an open seat at the end of the table. Alone.

FOUR

"I'M DIANE," SHE SAID, SETTLING INTO THE CHAIR AFTER NO one responded to her question.

The silence that met her arrival was unnerving. Diane must have sensed the instantaneous chill, because she didn't let go of her tray. "Iiiiiiis it okay if I sit here?" Her eyes landed on Charlotte, who didn't look up from her phone and appeared not to have noticed Diane's arrival.

Neve didn't feel any personal affinity to Diane, but in that supremely awkward moment, she definitely internalized her embarrassment and, much to her own surprise, jumped in to assuage it.

"Of course," Neve said, hoping she wasn't pissing anyone off by answering. "Chair's open."

Diane let out a slow breath, then relaxed her grip on the lunch tray. "Thanks!"

Inara tilted her head to the side. "Diane . . ." She left the question unasked, but Diane was quick to answer.

"Diane Russell." She beamed at Inara as if they were old friends. "Have we met?"

"Don't think so," Inara said, shaking her head.

Quince and Sequoia still seemed thrown by Diane's presence, eyes wide in confusion. "Where's your roommate?" Quince and Sequoia asked as one. *Quinquoia? Sequince? Sequince, definitely.*

Diane winced. "In bed, poor thing. I don't think she's feeling well."

"Oh no!" Sequoia said, hand to her face. "Who is it?"

Diane scrunched up her face, trying to remember. "Annabelle. I think that's what she said. She was kind of out of it."

"Oh, we *love* Annabelle!" Sequoia laced her fingers together.

"*So* love her. And she looked fine when I saw her at registration this morning." Quince's confusion deepened, etching across her forehead in long, wrinkled lines. "She loves eating lunch."

Sequoia bit her lower lip. "And people."

Rachel arched an eyebrow. "She loves eating people?"

"Eating lunch *with* people," the Sequince Twins replied, rolling their eyes in eerie unison.

Inara rested her elbows on the table, interested. "Annabelle is sick?"

"Mmhmm," Diane said, taking a bite of her pizza.

Inara eyed her closely, and Neve couldn't tell if it was from general interest or suspicion. With Inara, maybe those were the same thing. "How?"

"Not sure. She seemed fine at first, then got all sweaty and had to use the bathroom." Diane contemplated the pepperoni slice in her hand. "Food poisoning maybe?"

"Came on suddenly?" Inara pressed. Why was she so interested in Annabelle's health sitch?

Diane shrugged. "I guess so." Then she shifted her gaze to Neve for the first time, eyes twinkling. Neve fought against it, but felt her heart thump in her chest anyway. "So, what's the lowdown on GLAM? Can you returnees give Charlotte and me some hints?"

The mention of her name had an effect similar to sending three thousand volts of electricity racing through the arms of Charlotte's chair. She jolted in her seat, sliding the chair across the old tile floor with an ear-shattering screech. Her fingers lost their grip on her phone, she fumbled with it, and eventually knocked the device to the floor, where it skittered to a stop next to Neve's foot.

Neve reached for it, inadvertently glancing at the screen. She caught a fragment of a text exchange with the all-caps words *I WANT TO COME HOME.*

"Here you go," Neve said, trying to sound friendly as she handed the phone back to Charlotte. She totally understood the sentiment.

Charlotte flashed a quick smile. "Er, thanks."

Inara pointed one index finger at Charlotte, the other at Diane. "Know each other?"

"Yeah," Charlotte muttered. Her eyes scanned the room from windows to other tables to the cafeteria entrance, resting at last on the nearest exit. Was she planning an escape?

"From camp?" Inara pressed.

Charlotte dragged her chair back to the table and tucked her chin to her chest. "No."

She might be the only person less happy to be here than I am.

Diane's light laughter rang out from the other end of the table. "Char and I go to school together, but I didn't know she was going to be at GLAM this summer until I saw her out on the quad this morning." Then she leaned closer to Inara, fluttering her long eyelashes as she dropped her voice. "She's a little shy."

Inara seemed drawn in by Diane, meeting her gaze with steady attention. "Been to other camps?" she asked in her brusque, pronounless manner. Neve wasn't sure whether the missing-pronoun thing was charming or irritating, but she had to appreciate Inara's full commitment.

"A few."

"Such as?"

Diane shrugged. "Vega. Timber Lake."

"Brown Ledge," Neve blurted out before remembering she only knew that because she was perving on someone else's conversation.

Inara stiffened. "Brown Ledge? Really?"

"Have you been there?" Diane asked quickly.

Inara shook her head in answer.

"Oooo!" Quince cooed. "Brown Ledge! The grounds are supposed to be beautiful."

"Do you really get to ride horses every day?" Sequoia added.

Quince bit her lower lip. "I heard the lead horse trainer guy there is hot *as fuck*."

"I guess," Diane said quickly, waving off the mention of that specific camp as if it meant nothing. "I didn't really like it there."

More silence as Inara stared out the window, eyebrows knitted together, the fingers of one hand absently twirling a loose strand of black hair. Annabelle's sudden illness and the mention of Brown Ledge seemed to darken her mood, though how those two things could possibly be related, Neve had no idea. She was about to ask if her roommate was okay, when Inara abruptly pushed her chair away from the table. "Time to go to orientation."

Neve was pretty sure that was an order.

Everyone else took it that way as well, and the table was quickly vacated. Trays were bussed; garbage, recyclables, and compost separated; and then everyone hurriedly followed Inara's long strides out of the dining hall and across the quad to the theater.

It was an older building, in need of some repair. The burgundy velvet chairs were worn at the edges, exposing glimpses of white fabric beneath the furry exterior, and the wooden armrests were lightened by friction in the places where decades of hands and elbows had rested. Neve could even discern a pink pathway down the middle of the red-carpeted aisle hinting at the thousands and thousands of feet that had treaded this path, and she wondered if the same crimson nylon had been there since her mom's visit to GLAM. Because it sure the hell looked like it.

Despite the wear and tear, there was something homey about the small theater—like going to your grandma's house filled with scarred, ancient furniture, where each piece had some story to tell—and Neve wondered if the consensus warning against theater class was overblown. She could almost picture herself spending a lot of her time in this cozy space over the next two weeks. Not acting, of course. No spotlights or attention for her. They must need crew. Painting sets. Or maybe even as a playwright? She'd already contemplated writing a screenplay for film class—wasn't playwriting kind of the same thing?

"It's too bad the theater class is supposed to be a nightmare," Diane said to Charlotte as they filed in behind Neve. "I kind of like this place."

On the surface, it had seemed like Neve and Diane had absolutely nothing in common, and yet her words could have come from Neve's mouth. Maybe they weren't so different after all?

"Come on down! Don't be shy!" A heavy voice boomed through the speakers as a tall, lithe woman strode across the stage, microphone in hand, and took her spot dead center, perfectly lit. Her air of authority meant this must be Pat, CEO of GLAM camp. "Let's fill in the front rows first so I can see all your smiling GLAM faces."

A nervous ripple of laughter undulated through the assembling girls.

Pat had short cropped hair, heavily styled in the front to give it wave and bounce despite the super-short length at the sides and back. It was the kind of haircut Neve's mom, who spent thirty-five minutes giving herself a salon-worthy blowout every other day of her life, would have referred to as an I-give-up mom-do, but the rest of Pat's appearance bore no hint that she'd given up on anything. Her clothes were casual but expensive: tailored jeans tapered at the ankle above mustard-yellow point-toed Rothy flats, and a sleeveless wrap shirt in a graphic blue floral print looped around her teensy waist with an elaborate kimono-style knot. Her arms were toned, a clear sign that she spent a lot of time in the gym, and her face, though not young, had a vibrancy that hinted at someone who was fueled by a bottomless tank of personal energy.

"I can't wait to get to know each and every one of you," Pat continued as Neve sat down next to Inara. She sounded like she meant it, too.

Diane took the seat beside her. "I'm so excited to get started." Like Pat, she sounded one hundred percent committed.

It took a few moments, and a little bit more prodding from the junior counselors, to get all the GLAMsters into their seats. Pat waited center stage until she felt every single pair of eyes in the theater was firmly fixed on her, then she raised the microphone to her lips again.

"Welcome to the forty-fourth year of GLAM camp summer session!" Pat cried, eliciting a rumble of applause and cheers from the theaterful of raucous girls. "And though I've said this at the beginning of every summer session for the last dozen of those years, I mean it as much today as I did the other eleven times: This year is going to be the Best. GLAM. Ever!"

An ecstatic roar filled the theater, punctuated by several taxi-stopping whistles piercing the chaos. While Neve tried to muster enough enthusiasm for a clap that registered somewhere between "sarcastic golf" and "polite yet forced" on the applause-o-meter, beside her, Diane sat erect in rapt attention, her clapping a rapid flutter, excitement radiating from her every pore. On her other side, the stoically cool Inara was practically losing her mind, hands cupped around the sides of her mouth as she hooted like a hyped-up fan at a football game. Even Charlotte at the end of the row sat forward in her seat with her watery eyes fixed on Pat, her lips parted in awe.

Inara and Diane especially surprised Neve. Didn't cool people generally not want to show enthusiasm for, well, anything? Yasmin sure the hell wouldn't have clapped if she'd been there. She and Neve would have been huddled together, arms folded across their chests, rolling their eyes at the ridiculousness of it all.

Then it's a good thing she's not here.

Pat held out her hands, palms facing the floor, calling for silence as she pantomimed tamping down the noise. "Two announcements before we begin. Number one, we've had to cancel the film module this summer. Ms. Mendez had her baby six weeks early, so she won't be able to join us."

Damn it. The one thing Neve was looking forward to.

"Mom and baby are doing fine," Pat continued, "and there will be several congratulations cards out in the lobby lounge over the next few days if you'd like to sign one." She paused, and then a sly smile spread across her face. "Now I want you to get all of your groans out at once for this second announcement: There are no cell phones allowed outside your dorm room. If a counselor finds that you've broken this rule, your phone will be confiscated for the remainder of camp."

The predicted groan swelled from the campers. Behind Neve, someone wailed, "But what will I put on my Instagram?"

"And that," Diane said, giving Neve a gentle nudge with her elbow, "is why I don't have any social media."

"Wow, none?" Neve was impressed. Even she had Instagram and Facebook accounts, though since her social life imploded, she'd had to lock both down.

"None," Diane said. "I'd rather actually live my best life than try to make everyone else think I did."

Those might have been the wisest words Neve had ever heard.

Pat raised her arms like an orchestra conductor, signaling that she wanted more volume, and the campers obliged, enhancing the verbal protest with boos and fake crying. Then Pat called for silence once again, and the protest stopped on cue.

"Good," Pat said with a laugh. "I'm glad we got that out of our system. Sounds like we have a fantastic group this year and I can't wait to get started! So without further ado . . ."

The orientation was more pep rally than informative meeting, with clap-worthy lines about feminism, girls supporting each other, and toppling the patriarchy. Or something. Neve wasn't entirely paying attention. She found herself distracted by her fellow camp-goers and counselors, who all sat perched on the edges of their seats, hanging on Pat's every word even though many of them had probably heard this speech before. Was everyone having the same religious experience except Neve? It felt like they were all about to get raptured.

This was how cults happened.

Yet, as the orientation wound down, and Pat gave her parting words about the empowerment and self-efficacy she wanted to instill in each and every camper over the next two weeks, there was a little piece of Neve—unjaded, innocent, hidden away deep inside of her—that felt a shiver of excitement. Just a teensy tiny bit of her soul that made applauding a little less painful, smiling a little less forced.

She glanced at Diane, whose striking blue eyes were wide with excitement, and for the first time all summer, Neve thought that maybe GLAM wouldn't be so bad after all.

FIVE

"PAT'S PRETTY RAD," INARA SAID TO NEVE, WALKING BACKWARD up the aisle like a tour guide as they filed out of orientation. There was a skip in her step and her voice was energized, her contemplative mood from lunch forgotten. "Sets a badass tone for the session."

Neve nodded. She was starting to get a little swept up in the rah-rah community aspect of GLAM, the one thing she swore she'd never do. "So what's next?"

"Module sign-ups. In the lobby. Get a move on!" Inara laughed as she turned and fell into step beside Neve. It was more of a hearty guffaw than Diane's tinkling princess giggle, but it also felt more genuine.

"That sounds like something my grandma K would say."

"Compliment or dig?" Inara asked with an arch of her left eyebrow.

"Compliment," Neve said without hesitation. "We don't usually agree on shit, but her old-fashioned sayings always make me smile."

"Sweet."

"She's actually the reason I'm here," Neve continued quickly as they stepped into the lobby. "Grandma K, I mean. She paid for me to come to GLAM."

Inara whistled. "Nice gift. Rich or just—"

But before she could finish, Diane appeared at Neve's other side. "Your grandma paid for GLAM?"

Ugh, Neve hadn't meant to tell the whole world. "Er, yeah."

"That," Diane said with a demure smile, "is a nice gift." Without waiting for a response, she skipped ahead, linking her arm with Charlotte's. "Come on, let's get in line before everything fills up."

"Meet up after," Inara said as she watched Diane walk away. "And remember . . ."

"No theater!" Neve said with her in Sequoia-Quince-style unison. Then Inara peeled off toward the sign-up line for photography.

Neve took a moment to look around the lobby, which had been rearranged since check-in. There were more tables now, and instead of one neat little row they were spread evenly throughout the lounge. Gone were the plain alphabetical labels, replaced by fancy poster boards on easels beside each station, all advertising the exciting options for GLAM's two-week classes.

They were each supposed to sign up for one focus module, though they'd spend time rotating through the other options. Their focus module would be like their own little sorority and they'd spend every afternoon with the same group.

GLAM offered everything from creative writing, to botany, to coding, to art, for which the Sequince Twins were in line. Scanning the lobby, Neve was overwhelmed by the possibilities as girls chose quickly, minds decisively made up, filling the limited spots in each module.

But there was one class that had almost no line, and Neve was unsurprised to find Kellie's smiling face at the theater table, joined only by Diane and Charlotte.

"Come *on*," Diane was saying as Neve edged closer to them. "It'll be fun."

"I think you and I have different ideas of fun," Charlotte mumbled, almost too low to hear over the cacophony of voices in the lobby.

Neve felt for her. Diane, the extrovert, trying to push her introverted friend into doing something new and intrinsically uncomfortable reminded Neve of Marisol's beach house party. It hadn't been the first time Yasmin had nudged Neve out of her social comfort zone, but it had certainly been the biggest shove. And it had ended in disaster.

She really hoped theater wouldn't have the same result for Charlotte.

"Oh, hey!" Diane said, waving at her. Neve hadn't realized she'd been staring at them.

"Hey." Ugh. First Diane had caught her eavesdropping, and now this.

Diane tugged on the arm of Charlotte's shirt, dragging her over to Neve. "Sorry, I didn't catch your name at lunch."

"Neve."

"Cute!" Diane said. Neve hated that a single word ignited a small flutter inside her. "What are you signing up for?"

"I, uh, was thinking about creative writing." Neve tried not to let her growing desperation creep into her voice.

Diane tilted her head to the side, scanning Neve's face. Neve wasn't sure what she was looking for, but it made her feel insecure about her own insecurity.

"Sounds kind of boring," she said at last. "Why don't you sign up for theater with us?"

Charlotte stepped away from her. "Oh, I'm not—"

"It'll be fun!" Diane added, cutting her off. "And you need some fun in your life."

It was almost as if Yasmin were speaking through Diane, and for a brief moment, Neve contemplated signing up for theater just to protect Charlotte.

"Ladies!" Kellie-with-an-*i-e* cried out to them. She was holding up a clipboard and pen. "Come on, you know you want to."

Charlotte winced. "But this is the class everyone said to avoid."

Diane rolled her eyes. Another classic Yasmin move. Were those two related? "Yeah, but why? Because of Kellie? She doesn't seem that bad."

Neve looked over Diane's shoulder to where Kellie was still waving at them enthusiastically with her clipboard. "I'm not too sure about that."

"Come on." Diane flashed her kajillion-watt smile. "Even if it's terrible, at least we get to hang out in that cool theater. Plus, the three of us will have each other."

Three of us. As much as she hated to admit it, being grouped into a friend clique felt a little comforting at this camp where Neve knew almost no one. And though she was worried about offending Inara, whose advice she was about to completely ignore, she found herself nodding at Diane in agreement.

"Awesome!" Diane squealed, then linked her arms through both Neve's and Charlotte's, leading them back to the theater table. "See, Char? You can't back out now. Neve will be so disappointed."

Neve snorted at the idea, but neither she nor Charlotte protested.

Kellie's face lit up the moment she realized that Neve, Diane, and Charlotte were voluntarily approaching her table. "Ladies! Are you ready to get down with some 'dramatic'"—she used air quotes to emphasize the word—"empowerment this summer?"

The pun plus perkiness was almost enough to make Neve change her mind. "Um, what does the theater module entail exactly?"

"I'm so glad you asked." Kellie pushed a tablet toward them and started a slide show. The first image showed a group of girls in conversation onstage, dressed in workout clothes with a set that consisted of an exercise bike and a couple of chairs with loose weights beside them. "We work collaboratively to present a collection of monologues and scenes for the Activism in Art showcase on the last night of camp. Last year's theme was Body Beautiful, thus the gym set, and this year's is My Eyes Are Up Here. Don't the possibilities sound exciting?"

Neve wasn't entirely sure there were more than one or two possibilities inherent in that theme, but she nodded her head in agreement, unwilling to ask Kellie to elaborate.

"Does everyone have to act?" Charlotte asked.

"Only those who want to," Kellie said as the first image dissolved into a new one. This photo showed the gym-rat actresses out of focus in the background, photographed through a half-closed curtain while two girls dressed head to toe in black—one wearing a headset, the other holding a yoga ball—stood in the wings, poised for action. "We also need stage crew, writers, someone to operate the light board."

"Sounds fun!" Diane said. She picked up the pen and printed her name on the sign-up sheet. "I'm in." Then she handed the pen to Neve.

Neve hesitated. It was easy to get swept up in Diane's enthusiasm, but what exactly was she getting herself into? Theater? What if she got stuck acting in a scene? What if she was horrible and everyone laughed at her? What if she actually had a good time hanging out with Diane and Charlotte and then neither of them wanted to maintain the friendship when they left camp?

Neve tensed. That was the real issue. She was worried she might enjoy herself, might actually believe that these girls were her friends, which was setting herself up for another major disappointment.

But you loved that theater, she told herself. *And it's only for two weeks.*

Only two weeks. Right. And at least she was going into this forced friendship with eyes wide open. She needed to prove to herself that Yasmin hadn't broken her.

With a deep breath, she took the pen from Diane's hand and added her name to the theater list.

"Whoa!" Inara appeared at Neve's shoulder, silent as a ninja. "Theater?"

"Yes!" Diane said, moving aside to let two girls behind her sign up. Neither of them looked quite as enthusiastic as she did. "I know you said not to, but we got a good feeling from that space, so we thought, *What the hell?*"

Inara arched an eyebrow at Neve. "Really?" It was a question and an accusation.

Neve bristled. While she liked Inara's vibe and appreciated her advice as someone who had been to GLAM before, she certainly wasn't a child who needed to have her hand held through this process. She was picking a stupid class for summer camp, not choosing her college major. She was pretty sure she could make her own decision.

Instead of saying all that, she merely shrugged. "I like to figure things out on my own."

Diane bounced up and down while clapping like an excited eight-year-old at a birthday party. "This is going to be so much fun."

Inara's second eyebrow joined the first as she watched Diane closely. Neve wasn't sure if she was going to laugh at her or punch her in the face. She did neither.

"Diane might be right," Inara said slowly, as if saying the words took every ounce of strength in her body. And then, without another word, she marched up to Kellie and added her name to the theater list.

Neve was confused. Was this part of Inara's task as the roommate of a newbie—to shadow Neve through her every moment of the next two weeks? Couldn't be. The Sequince Twins had signed up for creative writing while their roommates picked art and theater, so why had Inara broken one of her GLAM cardinal rules? Neve couldn't believe that it was because she was just so awesome and her new roomie wanted to hang out more.

There was something odd about the way Inara watched Diane so carefully, as if she were a Russian spy intent on undermining the democracy of the United States one girls-only summer camp at a time. Maybe Inara was attracted to Diane? That might explain it.

But as Inara wandered back to the photography table to remove her name from that list, she turned back toward Diane. Eyes narrow, brows low. Inara didn't look like someone who had a crush.

She looked suspicious.

SIX

NEVE COULD FEEL THE EXCITEMENT RIPPLING THROUGH HER dorm floor the next morning as she groaned and hit the snooze button on her phone alarm. Outside in the hall, a high-pitched squeal mixed with low rumblings raced back and forth across her doorway, as if a herd of squeaky-voiced bison were stampeding through the building. It was the quintessential "electricity in the air" that Neve had always thought was some kind of weird poetic analogy, but was now experiencing firsthand as she attempted to go back to sleep.

On the first "real" day of camp, everyone but Neve was raring to go.

There was no tangible reason other than apprehension to prevent her from rising and shining like everyone else. They'd all partaken of the same campus tour the day before, the same pizza-and-ice-cream karaoke party, the same reasonable bedtime. But Neve was probably the only one who had tossed and turned most of the night, unable to sleep.

GLAM had already pushed her way out of her comfort zone. She was tepidly buying into the group mentality, enjoying the company of her roommate, and getting to know some of the other girls. She'd even contemplated—but not actually pulled the trigger on—singing karaoke in front of a bunch of strangers. The song list on the tablet didn't have many entries she knew, certainly not any Cold Cave or the Soft Moon or any of her other favorites on Bandcamp, but she did recognize some of the oldies her dad had gotten her into—Depeche Mode, Joy Division, and a freaking Ministry song—that she could have performed in a pinch. Everyone at GLAM seemed down with the karaoking, even Inara, who had shocked her with an impressively pronounless rendition of "This Is What You Came For" and the Sequince Twins, who had shocked no one with the "Sisters" duet from *White Christmas*—Grandma K's favorite holiday movie—complete with two-part harmony and well-rehearsed choreography.

In the end, Neve wasn't quite brave enough to invite the spotlight. She was having a difficult enough time feeling comfortable in a large group of strangers. And she wasn't the only one. Charlotte looked positively miserable. Her face was tense, her shoulders so tight they practically touched her ears, and during the karaoke portion of the evening, she sat on a floor cushion with her knees tucked up to her chin and her long black hair draped around her like a protective shield. Even Diane, who was flitting around like a social nursemaid, wasn't enough to soothe her, and Neve felt a fresh wave of empathy as she internalized Charlotte's discomfort, dredging up bittersweet memories of the early days of her friendship with Yasmin.

"Just getting up?" Inara burst into the room, dressed in a green plaid robe with her hair wrapped up in a matching bath towel.

"Yeah." Neve yawned, stretching out her back. GLAM might have been a fancy summer camp, but it certainly didn't have fancy summer camp mattresses. Her eyes fell on her phone display, which showed eight o'clock. "What time do you usually get up?"

"Six." Inara nodded toward the running shoes at the side of her bed. They were, surprisingly, not plaid. "Fun Run every morning. Wanna join?"

Neve laughed. She was possibly the least athletic and outdoorsy person on the planet. "The words *fun* and *run* should never be used in conjunction with each other."

"Fair enough," Inara said with a smile, combing out her long brown hair. "But there's a nature hike at nine." She pointed at Neve's assortment of black Victorian-inspired ankle booties and chunky Mary Janes with a raised eyebrow. "Got shoes for that?"

"Don't you know?" Neve replied, pushing back her comforter. "Fluevog makes an excellent hiking boot." Which was probably true, though Neve couldn't afford a pair of Fluevogs unless she sold a kidney. But despite her joke, she'd actually brought a pair of flat, rubber-soled booties that were supposedly made for the kinds of outdoorsy things advertised on the GLAM website, so she hoped she would still be able to walk by the end of the morning's hike.

"Gotta take care of a few things." Inara twirled her hair up into a bun and pulled on shorts and a plaid tee. "Meet up in the lobby for the hike. Five to nine."

"Will do." Inara's lack of pronouns was rubbing off on her.

Neve managed to shower and dress in the most athletic clothing she'd packed—a pair of black high-waisted pedal pushers with a sporty-ish gray sailor top—with enough time left over to get down to the cafeteria for a leisurely breakfast, but as she was about to leave, she saw Grandma K's name pop up as an incoming call.

Neve sighed. There was only one rule in the Lanier household: *Always take calls from Grandma K.* She kissed her relaxing breakfast good-bye and picked up the phone.

"Hi, Grandma!" she said, managing to sound perky. Grandma K could read tonal subtext better than most people could read body language.

"Did you just wake up?" her grandmother said, words quick and sharp like they came from someone who drank entirely too much caffeine. "You sound as if you didn't sleep much last night."

Neve closed her eyes, wondering exactly how Grandma K could have inferred that from literally three syllables, but refrained from asking. "All the excitement, I guess."

"Hmm." Grandma K didn't sound convinced. "You arrived on time for orientation yesterday? *Your father* didn't make you late, I hope."

Something about the way she said *your father* set Neve's teeth on edge. It was no secret in the family that Grandma K had hoped her only daughter would marry someone wealthy, famous, powerful, or a combination of all three and had been gravely disappointed when Neve's mom fell in love with lowly environmental-studies major Scott Lanier. Her attitude toward her son-in-law had been chilly at best, but since his recent troubles, Grandma K had been outwardly dismissive of Neve's dad, a move that hadn't exactly endeared the old lady to either of the Lanier girls.

But Neve was cognizant of the fact that she needed to stay on Grandma K's good side, as mercenary an attitude as that was, not only because she'd offered to pay for Neve's first year of college, but because Neve and her family were living in one of Grandma K's rental properties for free. So instead of telling her grandmother to kiss her ass, Neve donned a plastic smile and behaved.

"We arrived on time," Neve said. "I didn't miss a thing."

"Hmmmm." Again. Longer this time, which seemed to imply she thought Neve was lying. "I take it you're miserable?"

Neve rolled her eyes. And the family wondered where her natural negativity came from.

Grandma K continued, not even pausing for Neve to answer. "Wishing you were home and counting down the moments until GLAM is over?"

"I'm having a great time, actually," Neve said, aware as she spoke that she wasn't even lying.

"Really?"

"Yep."

Neve's truthfulness must have come through in her tone, because suddenly Grandma K sounded less salted. "Well, that is wonderful to hear, Neve. Wonderful!"

Take that, Grandma K! "But I really have to go," Neve said—again, not even a lie. "I need to eat breakfast before the nature hike."

"Of course, of course. The morning constitutional. Your mom loved those!"

Neve found it difficult to reconcile her face-forward, PR-executive mom with a nature lover who hiked every morning, but whatever. "I'll talk to you l—"

"Neve," her grandma said, cutting her off. "Remember: There is only one person in this world who controls your destiny, and that is you. Don't ever let someone else dictate the terms of your life."

It took a minute for the words to sink in, and though Neve wasn't sure if Grandma K was referencing her recent trouble at school or simply giving her basic life advice, the sentiment behind the words caused Neve to choke up. "Thanks. I'll remember."

As Neve placed her phone back on the nightstand, she was pretty sure that was the realest moment she'd ever had with her grandmother.

Neve had just enough time to layer some rubbery scrambled eggs and a slice of cheese between two halves of a bagel and shove them in her mouth before she dashed to the lobby. All of GLAM was gathered, outfitted appropriately for the morning's outdoorsy activity in brightly hued athletic gear and sturdy footwear. Neve's Wednesday Addams fears seemed to be coming to fruition: In her black and gray, she looked like an unintentional inkblot on an Andy Warhol painting.

She had a moment of flailing panic where she once again fought the urge to run upstairs, call her dad, and flee back to San Diego with him and Deirdre, but then she spotted Inara on the stairs scanning the lobby. As soon as she saw Neve, she waved, and whatever social anxiety Neve had felt melted away.

With a broad smile, Inara cut through the mass of girls, heading right for her. "Breakfast?" she asked, eyebrows raised in concern.

Neve nodded as she swallowed the last of her bagel sandwich, then pointed to her feet. "Even managed to put on functional shoes."

"Sweet."

"Inara!" Sequoia scampered across the lobby, Quince in tow. "Did you talk to her?"

Quince didn't wait for an answer. "How is she?"

"Why did she go home?"

"Is she coming back?"

The Sequince Twins panted in unison as if this was merely an extension of their karaoke choreography from last night.

"FaceTime," Inara said, holding her palms up in front of her as a signal for them to calm down. "Annabelle is feeling better but not coming back to camp."

Annabelle . . . that name was familiar. "Is that Diane's roommate?"

"Was," Quince replied with a grimace. "Pat had Kellie take her to the ER last night."

"She couldn't stop barfing. Even after her stomach was empty." Sequoia's hand flew to her lips as if merely discussing vomit was enough to induce it.

"Is she still at the hospital?" Quince asked, returning to the rapid-fire questioning.

"Is she contagious?"

"Are they going to shut down camp?"

"Are we quarantined?"

Instead of answering, Inara gazed off into the sea of GLAMsters, distracted from the Sequince Twins' interrogation by something in the crowd. Neve followed her eyes and found them locked onto Diane, who was weaving around the perimeter of the lobby with her arm linked firmly through Charlotte's, per usual.

"Diane!" Inara cried.

Diane turned, scanning the lobby for the source of her name, but instead of finding Inara, her eyes rested on Neve. She said something to Charlotte, then half dragged her across the lobby.

"Hey!" she said to Neve. "Wild second day of camp, am I right? I heard theater is paired up with creative writing for the nature hike. Maybe we'll all find inspiration!"

"Yesterday morning," Inara began as if Diane's comments had been directed to her, "before lunch. How did Annabelle seem?"

Diane blinked, processing both the question and the source. "Um . . . barfy."

"Before that."

"Oh." Diane's eyes arced up toward the beamed ceiling. "Okay, I think? She was unpacking when I arrived. Not super chatty."

"That doesn't sound like Annabelle," Sequoia said.

"Maybe she was already feeling sick?" Quince offered.

"Could be," Diane said, nodding. "I went to the bathroom and when I got back, she was lying down and said she didn't feel well. And then when I got back to my room last night, she was gone." Her eyes widened. "Oh my God, is she okay?"

"Fine," Inara said slowly. "But the ER doctors commented on how strange the vomiting was. Like, there was no cause. Came out of nowhere. Annabelle wasn't even running a fever."

"That's so awful!" Diane cried. "Poor thing."

"Annabelle was tested for norovirus."

The Sequince Twins gasped. "What. Is. That?"

"Gastrointestinal," Inara said. "Like a stomach bug."

At the mention of norovirus, Charlotte perked up. "A gastrointestinal virus? Is she sure?" Weird that a mention of the flu would inspire the most animated response Neve had seen from her, but whatever. Maybe she was a science nerd at heart.

Inara shook her head. "Waiting on test results."

"That sucks." Diane shrugged. "But probably something she ate. Shall we get our hike on?"

SEVEN

THE BLAZING SUN BEAT DOWN FROM A NEARLY CLOUDLESS SKY, baking Neve in her dark-hued outfit as they headed out of the lobby and through the north edge of campus.

There were about thirty of them, the theater and creative writing modules along with a guide, and they were the last group to leave the lobby. As they crossed the main road north of campus, Neve could see the groups ahead of them disappearing into a leafy copse of trees, and she breathed a sigh of relief. At least they wouldn't be exposed to the brutal sun all morning.

They climbed a short hill into an abandoned, overgrown parking lot where weeds pushed through cracks in the pavement and the paint that once delineated car boundaries had chipped and faded into oblivion. At the end of the lot, a dirt trail snaked down into the trees, whose shade brought instant relief from the morning sun. The unexpected wooded oasis felt like a totally different world from the college campus and the suburban sprawl that surrounded it, and as the roars of cars faded away, replaced by chirping birds and the gentle whoosh of swaying trees, Neve could almost forget that she was in a city at all.

The trail hugged a trickling creek that was flanked by enormous slabs of granite coated with soft moss. The whooshing trees—"coast live oaks," according to their guide, Samantha, from which Oakland derived its name—arced over the ravine like flying buttresses in a medieval cathedral.

Samantha was one of those nature enthusiasts who probably could have survived a month on Mount Everest if she was dropped there with only a flask, a roll of duct tape, and fishing line, and she pointed out the flora of the area with a full-throated enthusiasm that hinted at her comfort and familiarity with the subject matter. Thimbleberries, wildflowers, and something about redwood growth jumbled together in Neve's head as she struggled to keep up with Samantha's pace in her more-practical-than-heels-but-less-practical-than-hiking-boots choice of footwear, and before long, she had drifted to the back of the group, where Diane and Charlotte brought up the rear.

They'd been talking quietly, separated a bit from the pack, but as soon as Neve joined them their conversation stopped.

"Hey," Neve said, almost apologetically. She kept her eyes on the trail, carefully picking her way around rocks and holes. "Sorry to interrupt."

"Not at all!" Diane said cheerfully, homing her megawatt smile on Neve. Girl put out more energy than a supernova. "We were enjoying the scenery. You can see more back here without all the people."

"Oh, cool."

Silence again, and Neve wondered if they were still pissed about her apparent eavesdropping while they were in the registration line. That might explain the tension Neve detected. Only one way to find out.

"Sorry about yesterday." Neve spoke quickly, trying to get her apology out before her nerve failed. "At lunch, when I told everyone you'd been to Brown Ledge. I'd accidentally overheard you and Charlotte talking in the registration line and I—"

"Ooooooh my God!" Diane laughed. "Don't even worry about it."

Neve felt her tension melt away. "Thanks."

"I was soooooo excited to run into Charlotte, I was probably talking at ten decibels anyway." She grinned sheepishly, her blue eyes twinkling. "I do that when I get excited."

"So do I." It felt odd to have another something in common with the princess. "What a weird coincidence that you'd both be at the same camp."

"Weird. Yep," Charlotte said, under her breath.

"Neve!" Inara called. She had stopped at the back of the main hiking group, now several yards ahead of them on the trail. "Catch up."

Diane shrugged. "Guess we should follow orders." She tugged at the sleeve of Neve's sailor top, then jogged ahead, bridging the gap to the main group. Diane ran with an easy, loping stride, like someone who was no stranger to athletic activities, which made Neve horribly self-conscious about her own awkward gait. And the fact that she was out of breath by the time she reached Inara.

"Catching up on old times?" Inara asked once they were all together. The question was directed at Charlotte, but Diane answered instead.

"Just admiring nature." She gestured to the canopy of leaves and tree branches.

"So, what school?" Inara asked.

Diane paused, momentarily thrown by Inara's conversational tic. "What school do I go to?"

"Yep. And Charlotte."

"Holy Name Academy," Charlotte said, her tone morose. She sounded as if she hated her school as much as Neve hated LCC.

"That's in La Jolla," Diane added. "Which is, like, basically San Diego in Southern Califor—"

"From Oceanside," Inara said, cutting her off.

Neve was surprised that her roommate lived, like, fifteen minutes away. "And I'm in Carlsbad."

"Carlsbad?" Diane said, genuinely shocked. "Wow!"

Inara shrugged, unsurprised. "Pat tries to pair up local GLAMsters. For support when summer is over. Annabelle's from Poway. Quince in the OC."

"GLAMsters!" Diane laughed again, bell-like and airy. Her voice sounded like a Disney princess but less cloying. "I love it!"

"Can't take credit." Inara jabbed her thumb toward Neve. "That was Neve."

"Cute." Diane shifted her smile to Neve. "So you've been to GLAM before?"

The question caught Neve off guard as her brain was still fixated on the fact that Diane had called her cute for the second time in as many days. "Oh, hell no."

Charlotte glanced over her shoulder, suddenly interested. "Don't you *want* to be here?"

Shit. Neve needed to remember that she was probably the only person here under duress. "Sorry, just meant that, uh, my decision to come here was last-minute."

"How is that possible?" Diane asked. "They send out acceptances in the spring and GLAM is notoriously hard to get into. I heard there's a wait list a mile long."

A wait list? Damn, how many strings had Grandma K pulled—or how many donations had she made—to get her reluctant granddaughter this spot?

"Neve is a legacy," Inara said slowly.

Diane's eyebrows shot up. "Is that how you got in?"

"I . . . I guess?"

"Guess?"

Neve sighed. There was no point in lying. "My grandma did it," she said, realizing how privileged and childlike the words sounded as they tumbled out of her mouth. It was too late to gobble them back up, so instead she kept going. "She and my mom applied for me. I, uh, had some trouble at school last year, and they thought that I needed a reset." Fuck, she was making it worse.

A painful silence hung over the group, punctuated by the crunch of gravel beneath their feet, before Diane piped up. "What kind of trouble?"

"Um . . ."

"Save it," Inara said, before Neve could answer. "The story. Save it for Confessional tonight."

"Confessional?" Neve asked. She didn't like the sound of that at all.

"Bonding exercise," Inara said as the trail began to open up, trees thinning. "Each GLAMster makes a confession. Usually something never shared before."

"Perfect!" Diane cooed. "You can tell the whooooole Carlsbad story, then."

The crunch of gravel beneath Neve's feet slowed, her legs suddenly leaden weights. "Yeah, perfect."

Diane linked her arm through Neve's, the same move she'd done with

Charlotte a half-dozen times, and guided her forward into the bright sunshine. "Maybe it's not about *wanting* to do something as much as it is about *needing* to do it."

Neve blinked. For the second time that day she'd heard a soul-piercingly poignant comment from someone whom she'd thought totally devoid of deep thought: first from her über-practical grandmother and now from the bubbleheaded Diane. Maybe Neve had been too quick to judge both of them.

By the time they filed into the theater for the afternoon module, Neve almost felt comfortable. She wouldn't go so far as to say she was *happy* her mom and grandma had gone behind her back and applied for this camp, but there was certainly something about the vibe of GLAM that was thawing her icy armor.

"Good afternoon, everyone!" Kellie strode across the stage with less aplomb and more timidity than Pat had shown the day before. She seemed to have lost some of her cheerful confidence, and Neve could have sworn she saw Kellie's hand shake as she shielded her eyes from the spotlight.

"First time running a group," Inara whispered to Neve, reading her mind. "Just an assistant last year."

"Ah." So that's why they were all supposed to avoid theater. Kellie didn't really know what she was doing.

"I'm so excited to see all these smiling faces," Kellie said, sitting on the edge of the stage and allowing her legs to hang down. "Are you gals ready for the best theater experience of your lives?"

A round of *Yeah!*s erupted from the fourteen other girls around Neve, a response that she heartily joined. It was as if she *wanted* to enjoy herself.

"We've got exactly twelve days before the Activism in Art showcase, which means this is going to be a whirlwind for everyone. Me included!"

She laughed as if it was scripted—a little higher-pitched and more forced than was totally natural. "We have thirty minutes of showcase time to fill on the theme My Eyes Are Up Here, and what I'd like to see is a mix of monologues and scenes. Original or not, whatever you guys come up with! That's the funnest part of theater—the creativity."

Neve was pretty sure that Kellie's biggest leap of creativity was in using *funnest* as a word, but like she'd successfully been doing all day, she pushed that snarkiness to the back of her brain and focused on staying positive, a feat that was working out better than she could have anticipated.

"What I'd like to do today is get all the roles filled. Figure out who is doing what and get this show moving forward. So . . ." She clapped her hands. "Does anyone have an idea of how they'd like to participate?"

I'd like to hide backstage were the words that immediately came to Neve's mind, but she wasn't about to blurt that out and hoped Kellie wouldn't put her on the spot. Thankfully, Diane piped up.

"I have an idea."

Kellie let out a breath through pursed lips. "Diane Russell, right?"

"That's me!"

"What would you like to do?"

Diane laced her fingers together and slowly twisted them. Neve had never seen her look so unconfident. "I wrote this, like, scene kind of a thing. Last semester. But it's never been performed."

"Impressive!" Kellie cried. "It's completed?"

Diane nodded.

"And does it fit with our theme?"

"I think so," Diane said slowly. "It's about personal boundaries and how men use both their environment and the conventions of social norms to make women feel uncomfortable and violated."

Inara turned to her, blinking. "Wow."

"It's for two characters," Diane continued. "A guy and a girl, but I think it's on theme."

"Sounds like it!" Kellie said.

"I'll direct and Charlotte can stage manage," Diane said, volunteering her friend. "Is that cool, Char?"

"Sure," Charlotte replied, though she looked far from it. Neve instantly felt some empathy for her inability to stand up for herself. Not that Neve was a pushover. She'd always been the kind of person who, when she sensed she was being manipulated into doing something she didn't want to do, would dig her heels deep into the dirt, fold her arms across her chest, and stubbornly refuse to yield. She had no interest in an audience for her failures. It was, perhaps, the reason she understood Grandma K better than anyone else in the family: They were cut from the same cloth.

But as Diane looked at Charlotte with a warm, trusting smile, her thick lashes low over her blue eyes, Neve felt her own resolve fail, as if Diane was volunteering her for a role she didn't want to play instead of Charlotte. She smiled to herself, thinking of one of her favorite lines from *The Big Heat*: *"We're sisters under the same mink."*

Neve wasn't sure she'd do any better than Charlotte had done when faced with those eyes.

Kellie clapped her hands. "Great! Now for a cast. Who would like to play—"

"The guy," Inara said, raising her hand to claim the role. She seemed like the last person in the world who'd enjoy acting.

"Excellent!" Kellie squealed. "And for the other part?"

Diane grabbed Neve's hand and raised it high in the air. "Neve is going to play her."

EIGHT

THEY WERE BACK IN THE THEATER AFTER DINNER FOR THE evening's Confessional event, and the excitement was palpable. The ambient background noise of a hundred side conversations seemed louder than it had during orientation, more frenetic, and girls were flitting around the rows, checking in with friends and figuring out where they wanted to sit. Inara and Neve had changed into something a little bit dressier for the big event, which for Neve meant a black Kitty Foyle–style dress instead of pedal pushers and top, and for Inara meant a nice pair of plaid Chucks and jeans.

Neve was nervous as they threaded their way down the aisle, her stomach twisting in knots, her mouth bone-dry. Her tongue felt two sizes too large, like it barely fit in her mouth, and if she tried to verbalize words, they would come out as a series of incoherent grunts and groans instead of actual intelligent communication. She wasn't sure she'd be able to get up on that stage and confess anything to anyone without falling on her face in a panic, and if she couldn't even get through a five-minute Confessional with all eyes on her, how was she supposed to perform an entire freaking scene in front of the whole camp in two weeks?

Maybe it was time to call her dad and get the hell out of there.

Inara had spotted Quince and Sequoia in the crowd, sitting with the lemon-faced Rachel and a surprisingly un-tense Charlotte, who looked happier and more relaxed than Neve had yet seen her, and slipped into the row behind them. Neve followed, disappointed that Diane was nowhere in sight.

"Ready?" Inara said to no one in particular.

"Always," Sequoia said. She raised her fists to either side of her face and shook them like an excited eight-year-old. "This is, like, the best night."

"*So* moving," Quince added.

"I'm totally going to cry."

"Me too!"

Inara snorted, rolling her eyes. "Don't get snot on the plaid." The words were playful and good-natured, and even though Neve sensed that the Sequince Twins' routine was just as annoying to her roommate as it was to Neve herself, she recognized that it took some maturity not to make comments that were cutting or rude. It was a skill Neve certainly didn't possess, and her tendency to make fun of situations where she was uncomfortable had been encouraged by Yasmin.

"So, um, what are the rules of this thing?" Neve asked, surprised that her tongue actually functioned.

"Pat will explain," Inara said, "but basically, open mic night. A place to shake off intrusive thoughts."

"Ah." *Intrusive thoughts* pretty much defined Neve's life these days. Everything seemed to be weighing on her, from her dad's health to her mom's avoidance of it, from Grandma K's controlling influence to the nagging fear that Deirdre was going to grow up to be some kind of sociopath due to the emotional unavailability of her family members. Not to mention her biggest secret of all: the attraction she felt toward other girls sometimes. That was something she'd never told anyone.

And maybe it was the confession she needed to make?

"Heeeeeeey!" Diane's tinkling voice broke Neve from her thoughts. She took the aisle seat beside Neve and directly behind Charlotte. "Are you excited for this?"

Neve felt a definite pang of jealousy when Diane leaned forward and folded her arms on the back of Charlotte's seat, clearly addressing the question to her high school friend.

Charlotte hardly looked at her. "I guess."

"What are you going to confess?" Diane pressed. "Some deep dark desire of your soul? Something horrible you've done? Or something horrible you *want* to do?"

"I've never done anything horrible," Charlotte said. Then she turned around, eyes sharp. "Have you?"

"Me?" Diane laughed. "No way. I'm a boring goody-goody."

"Doubt that," Inara said under her breath. It seemed uncharacteristically snarky, especially since Inara had gone out of her way to be kind to the Sequince Twins, even while teasing them. What did Inara have against Diane?

As she had yesterday morning, Pat took the stage and quieted the room with her commanding presence, shushing some lingering whispers from the crowd before she explained the rules of the evening. Which were pretty simple. There was a microphone on the stage, and it was available to any GLAMster who wanted to use it. Each of them would have two minutes, and during that time they could share a secret, tell a story, share an experience, or whatever they wanted so long as every word of it was true. If it was something that the person had never shared before, great, but not necessary.

"The point," Pat said, "is to get rid of whatever is weighing you down before we move forward. In order to get the most out of your GLAM experience." She smiled, slowly pivoting from left to right so every girl at GLAM might feel the warmth of her expression. "We don't want past anxieties holding you back. So tonight is where you drop them. Permanently."

Neve wasn't sure she could.

It was no surprise that the first girls to storm the stage once Pat opened things up were Quince and Sequoia, who went to the microphone together but spoke separately. Sequoia confessed to lying to her parents about the guy she was dating because she was afraid they wouldn't like that he was white. She felt so much shame over it that she broke up with him and still had anxiety spirals about her own cowardice. Quince admitted to cheating on a huge project for school, borrowing the bulk of her oral presentation from an early TED Talk on the same subject. She said that she knew she had to ace the assignment in order to keep her GPA up for college applications, and the fear of failure overshadowed her good judgment. And the worst part? She'd gotten a B on the assignment anyway, not the A she'd hoped for.

Neve watched both of these Confessionals, mesmerized. The Sequince Twins were so confident on the surface, so comfortable at GLAM with their matching outfits and dovetailing conversation, yet here they were admitting to having the same fears of rejection and failure that plagued Neve on a daily basis.

The floodgates were open. Girl after girl took the microphone and shared something about their life. Something they liked about themselves. Or hated. Something they'd done or wanted to do. Something they were proud of. Ashamed of. A dream. A failure. A success.

It was amazing how open and raw the confessions were. Some girls cried while others seemed to get the words out through sheer force of will, fighting for each syllable. Even Inara managed to surprise Neve again with her matter-of-fact confession that she was still in love with her ex-girlfriend. It was such a brave thing to do—show vulnerability in the face of rejection—and it made Neve's own problems seem less overwhelming.

That said, Neve was still on the fence about whether or not she was going to share anything, let alone slice open a vein and spill the blood of her emotional pain all over the stage in front of an audience of strangers.

Until Diane took the stage.

"My life is pretty cushy," she began, one hand gripping the microphone like a rock star, the other pressed against her stomach. "My mom and stepdad have plenty of money. I drive a nice car. I don't have to work." She swallowed and a pinched look crept onto her face, her brow tense and lined. "But my life is actually kind of like . . . a nightmare?"

Neve sat up in her seat as Diane's voice faltered. Her grip on the microphone tightened, her knuckles bright white beneath the glaring follow spot, and she squared her feet, as if afraid she might lose her balance.

"There's this guy. I'm not interested in him and I've never pretended to be. But he's, like, very aggressive in his attention." She paused again, this time for a steadying breath. "At first it was just comments. A look. He'd say something about my clothes or my body. He'd call me baby. Tell me that I'm pretty when I smile."

The entire theater groaned at that frequent male sin, but Diane didn't pause, barreling on as if she might run out of time before she got everything out.

"Then we were at a friend's house one night in a big group, and while we were hanging out on the sofa, he slid his hand up my skirt."

Was this the inspiration for the theater scene Diane had written? Could it have been based on personal experience?

Diane shifted her legs, visibly uncomfortable. "And my friends—well, my former friends—they told me to stop complaining about it because he's hot and popular and the captain of the baseball team."

Charlotte's head shot up. They went to school together, so she must have realized who Diane was talking about.

"My 'friends'"—Diane used air quotes to emphasize the word—"told me I should be honored that he was trying to get with me. Super empowering, right?"

An undercurrent of jeers against Diane's friends rippled through the audience.

"This guy found out I'd complained about him, then turned around and told everyone that I was crazy. That he wasn't interested in me at all. That I was making it all up. And I've only been at that school for, like, a year, so it's not like anyone knows me well enough to believe my side of the story."

Neve was shocked by what she was hearing. So similar to her own alienation at school. She'd never have pegged the calm and confident Diane as a school pariah.

"Anyway," Diane said with a shake, throwing off the emotion that had overcome her and resuming her cheerful demeanor. "He's not going to win. I'll figure out a way to expose who he really is, or at least get him out of my life." Then with a short nod, she left the stage.

Something about Diane's confession affected Neve, and before she could even register what she was doing, she'd stepped into the aisle and was walking determinedly toward the stage.

The spotlight seared Neve's eyes, which wasn't necessarily a bad thing since it completely obscured her view of the faces smiling up at her from the theater. She might not have been able to say what she was going to say with all those eyes upon her.

And what *was* she going to say?

"I tried to sabotage my best friend."

Those weren't the words she was expecting. She'd been planning to talk about how she was bisexual and had only been able to admit that to herself recently, let alone tell anyone else, and besides, if she *was* going to tell them all about Yasmin, hadn't Neve been the victim of Yasmin's social climbing? Not the other way around.

"We went to this beach house party last spring," Neve continued, her words slow and calm despite the roiling emotions in her chest. "I didn't want to go. I hate parties and being surrounded by people who don't know me and don't like me, but Yasmin said it would be good for us to be seen at a party like this. Once we got there, I realized we'd only come so she could introduce herself to this dude she had a crush on. . . ."

Neve felt the tears welling up and paused, waiting for the wave of emotion to crash over her and ultimately recede.

"Well, I was angry. Really fucking angry. She'd lied to me and then as soon as she started talking to him, she forgot that I existed. So I picked a public fight with the drunk-ass hostess and her best friend to make sure this guy would want nothing to do with my friend. And it worked."

She paused again, not from emotion this time but from indecision. Did she want to justify her actions? Explain her feelings toward Yasmin and then lay out what Yasmin did to her in retribution?

Neve shook her head. No, this was a Confessional. What happened to her might have been brutal, and she certainly wasn't giving Yasmin an out for her betrayal, but this was the first time Neve had admitted to anyone that she had intentionally picked that fight with Marisol and Luna, and that she'd done it to make sure that Hazel Eyes would never speak to Yasmin again.

That was all she wanted to say. She stepped away from the microphone and down the stairs, away from the blessedly blinding spotlight. She kept her eyes glued to the threadbare carpet, oblivious to the applause of support around her as she slipped past Diane to her seat.

"That was unexpected," Inara said under her breath. "Feel okay?"

Neve nodded, not trusting her voice. Beside her, Diane shifted in her seat, and Neve glanced up to find Diane facing her.

She was smiling.

NINE

INARA WAS GONE ON HER DAILY FUN RUN BY THE TIME NEVE'S phone alarm went off the next morning. She hadn't really gotten a chance to talk with her roommate after last night's Confessional, since Inara headed up to bed as soon as the evening's official activities were over, whereas most of the other girls hung out in the lounge until almost midnight. Neve was hoping to catch Inara at breakfast. For some reason, she really wanted to know that Inara didn't think badly of her after her confession.

She showered and dressed quickly, then headed down to the cafeteria.

Groups of girls were clustered at tables, but there was no telltale plaid in sight. Neve loaded up a tray with cereal, fruit, and her favorite blended coffee drink. Then, despite plenty of open chairs at the occupied tables, she decided to sit by herself. The GLAM openness was seeping in, but it hadn't yet made her brave enough to sit down at a table of complete strangers like Diane had done that first day.

It must have taken a tremendous amount of self-confidence—or a total lack of social anxiety—for Diane to have done that. And on the first morning of camp, no less, where she hadn't met anyone yet. Sure, she knew Charlotte, but Diane's friend from school wasn't exactly a bucket of fun. She always looked as if she had a gun pointed at her head when Diane was with her, and though Neve thought it was sweet that Diane was trying to help Charlotte overcome her shyness by shepherding her through the opening days of GLAM, it certainly appeared as if Charlotte wasn't interested in the effort.

Meanwhile, Neve would have killed to have someone like Diane— outgoing, friendly, bold—holding her hand at GLAM. Charlotte should have been more appreciative.

"Hi." A tray hit the table beside Neve with slightly more force than was necessary, and Charlotte sat down behind it. At first, Neve thought the dropped tray was an aggressive move until she realized that Charlotte's hands were shaking as she picked up her bagel.

"Are you okay?" Neve asked.

"Yeah," she said, then sucked in a breath through puckered lips. "Yeah, I'm fine. Is . . . is it okay if I sit here?"

"Totally." Diane sure was right about Charlotte's shyness. Her face was unusually pale as she pulled her chair closer to the table. Neve waited, wondering if Charlotte would open up the conversation, but she didn't. Normally, Neve would have been content to sit there in silence, but this was GLAM and she needed to be more GLAM-like. Or at least more Diane-like. "So, you live in La Jolla?"

But instead of answering with a yes or a nod or even some color commentary about the northern area of San Diego, Charlotte blurted out: "Maybe you should switch out of theater and into a different module."

Neve reared back her head as if Charlotte's words had bitch-slapped her. "Wait, what?"

Charlotte took a deep breath, preparing again. "Maybe you should switch out of theater and—"

"*Neve!*" Diane rushed over to their table, coffee sloshing out of her cup and into the saucer on her tray. "Char! I'm so glad you're both here!" She placed the tray on the table, pushing it aside as if she was no longer interested in eating, and pulled out two stacks of paper from her bag, setting one in front of Neve and one in front of Charlotte, whose face had gone from pale to bright red in the course of thirty seconds.

"I printed these this morning," Diane said, her voice bubbling with excitement. "Copies of the scene I wrote for Theater!"

Neve stared at the thin stack of pages before her, three-hole punched and secured by brads, as icy-cold dread replaced the warmth of Diane's arrival. This was the scene she was supposed to perform at the showcase. In front of people. Why the fuck hadn't she told Diane no? Maybe she *should* take Charlotte's advice.

"You're playing Ryanne," Diane said to Neve. "I've already highlighted aaaaaaall your lines."

"Wow." Neve flipped through the pages, noting all the yellow highlighter.

"I know it seems like a lot," Diane said, reading the look on Neve's face, "but I promise it's not. Just looks that way because there are only two of you in the scene. It only runs for about twelve minutes."

Which was exactly eleven minutes and fifty-nine seconds longer than Neve wanted to be in the spotlight. "Okay."

Charlotte turned the pages quickly, scanning them from top to bottom like a speed reader. "Neve is playing Ryanne," she said absently. Neve half expected her to add that she thought Neve should drop out of Theater altogether, but Charlotte seemed to have forgotten that she'd made the comment. "Which rhymes with Diane."

"Guilty," Diane said. "I guess I'm not very good at disguising my own trauma."

"And Francisco is Javier?"

Diane blinked. "I'm sorry?"

"The character of Francisco," Charlotte said, nodding at the page. She didn't look up. "That's based on Javier Flores, right?"

A faint blush of pink rose up Diane's pale cheeks as a similar shade drained out of Charlotte's. A teeter-totter of embarrassment, which meant Charlotte's guess was spot-on.

"I've seen him with you," Charlotte continued. "At school. Behind the gym." Then without another word, Charlotte grabbed her tray in one hand and the script in the other, and stood up. "I'll see you later."

As soon as Charlotte was out of earshot, Diane pressed a hand to her chest, counting to ten in a muted whisper. Neve waited, not wanting to interrupt whatever calming exercise she was doing and not really sure what she would say anyhow, but when Diane reached ten, she saved Neve the trouble of trying to wrestle up a platitude.

"Sorry about that," she said, wrapping a hand around her half-empty coffee cup. "Charlotte just reminded me of a particularly nasty encounter I had with Javier."

Why the fuck would Charlotte bring it up like that? "I'm sorry."

"He had me pinned against the side of the gym after school. No one was around. His hands . . ." She swallowed and her fingertips drifted from her throat down over her chest and then to her stomach, where they slipped up underneath the hem of her shirt as if she was reliving the moment. She shuddered, then sighed; her shoulders sagged forward in defeat.

"Can't you tell someone?" Neve asked. It was ridiculous that Diane would have to endure this kind of harassment, especially in a post-#MeToo world. "Teacher? Parents?"

Diane shook her head. "It's . . . complicated."

"Oh." Neve wanted to ask but recognized that she didn't really know Diane well enough to pry.

"That's why I wrote this scene," Diane said, shaking off the shadow that had passed over her mood. "My way of taking the power back."

Once again, Neve was awed by her strength. "That's amazing."

"Yeah." Then Diane leaned forward, her eyes twinkling as she smiled. "And that's why I wanted you to play Ryanne."

"Huh?" Neve had no idea what she meant.

"On the hike, you mentioned some trouble. At school. I know there's more to the story you told at Confessional. More about what happened with your best friend."

"I . . ." Had Diane guessed that she'd had a crush on Yasmin? Or had word of Neve's epic social disaster reached all the way down to La Jolla?

Whichever it was, Diane didn't explain. "And I thought maybe we could both work through our traumas." Then she slid her hand across the table until her fingers rested against Neve's. "Together."

TEN

"WHAT'S WRONG?" INARA ASKED, BACKING NEVE UP AGAINST THE wall. "Don't you like me?"

"Not like that." Neve pushed Inara away, creating an arm's length of distance between them.

"Wearing that little dress, showing off your curves." Inara scanned her from head to toe. "You want me to look."

"Stop it. Please."

Inara pressed closer. "Your body is sixty percent water, and I'm thirsty."

Her eyes narrowed and met Neve's, then without warning, Inara snorted and broke into laughter. "Oh, come on!"

Kellie stood up from where she'd been crouched down on the stage, watching their rehearsal. "Inara, you need to try and stay in character through the whole scene."

"Hard when the dialogue is this unrealistic."

Diane, who'd been watching the rehearsal from the wings, stepped out onto the stage. "Um, this actually happened to me. Javier *actually* said those exact words."

"'I'm thirsty'?" Inara rolled her eyes. Even though they'd been working on this script for almost a week, it still felt odd when Neve heard Inara use pronouns in her dialogue. "No one *actually* said this."

"Yes, he did."

"Uh-huh."

Diane lowered her chin, frustrated. "He *did*."

"Sorry," Inara said with a dismissive shake of her head. "Sounds like dialogue from a church-group PSA video warning against short skirts and the wrong crowd."

"Okay, okay." Kellie held out her hands like a referee in a boxing match. "I'm sure we can find some middle ground between the two of you."

Inara wandered downstage. "Cheesy-ass straight people."

Neve had to admit that Inara was right—the line was awful, the kind of thing guys think is funny and smart but comes off as smarmy—but she didn't like that Inara was questioning Diane's truthfulness about her experience. GLAM preached that girls needed to have each other's backs, and since their rehearsals on this scene began, Inara had done nothing but challenge Diane about both it and the real-life experience that inspired her dialogue.

It had been a weird week.

Something had changed after Confessional. Once Neve opened up about her behavior the night of Marisol's party, Diane seemed different. Not that she'd been unfriendly before—quite the opposite—but her bubbly personality and energy had been primarily focused on Charlotte. Then, suddenly, Diane was seeking out Neve's companionship more and more.

In art class the next day, their easels had ended up side by side, and then at lunch, Diane and Charlotte joined the table with Neve, Inara, and the Sequince Twins, but again, Neve felt as if Diane's focus was fixed on her, and as she got caught up in Diane's animated conversation, it was as if everyone else at the table faded into the background.

They had more in common than Neve would ever had thought possible, from their mutual love of Dorian Electra to the fact that they'd both hated *Romeo and Juliet* when forced to read it for English lit class. Diane was smarter than she looked, or at least smarter than Neve had supposed her to be based on her physical attractiveness (honestly, it wasn't fair that Diane was hot *and* smart), and despite her ever-present bubbliness, Diane had a depth of feeling and understanding about people that Neve found both awe-inspiring and mind-boggling.

Yes, she came from a privileged background, but Diane wore it more as an ideal she needed to live up to than a gift she was entitled to. She wanted to help others, to lift them up, and especially to empower girls by sharing the story of her abuse by her classmate Javier. Having been through her own tough year, Neve appreciated the way Diane discussed her situation without bitterness, and the more time they spent together, the more Neve wanted to put her fist right in that guy's nuts for the harassment he'd doled out to her new friend.

By the fourth day of camp, Neve and Diane were the new Sequince Twins, and Neve realized that her initial impression of Charlotte had been misplaced: It was Neve and *Diane* who were sisters under the same mink.

Charlotte seemed utterly unfazed by the sudden lack of Diane in her life. She'd been hanging out with two other girls in the theater pod who were doing all the stagehand duties for the upcoming showcase, and she looked really happy with her new friends. In fact, the only person who seemed bent out of shape by Neve's new friendship was Inara.

Her attitude toward Diane, though rather tepid from that first day, had gotten positively chilly. She watched Diane constantly, her eyes quick and suspicious, and whenever she overheard Neve and Diane having any kind of personal conversation about school or family, Inara would intervene and change the subject. It was as if she didn't want them to get to know each other at all, and the jarring negativity of her attitude felt completely at odds with the inclusivity of GLAM.

"Let's take a break," Kellie suggested. "And then we can try the scene again?"

Inara shrugged, then jumped off the edge of the stage. "Gonna grab a soda."

"Sorry about that," Neve said, her voice low even though Inara was already halfway up the aisle and couldn't possibly hear her.

"About what?" Diane tilted her head in confusion. "I thought your performance was great."

"I agree," Kellie said as she carefully picked her way down the steps into the house. "I'm really impressed with your acting, Neve."

Neve did a double take. "Really?" She'd been trying to channel a bad-girl mash-up of Anne Shirley in *Murder, My Sweet* and Mary Astor in *The Maltese Falcon*, which seemed more like a real person than a traditionally angelic Madonna figure, but she wasn't sure if she was getting that idea across at all with her fledgling acting skills.

"Absolutely!" Kellie beamed. "Keep up the good work."

"See?" Diane laughed as Kellie stepped away to give some notes to the stage crew. "No reason to apologize!"

"Not my performance," Neve said. "I'm sorry about Inara."

"Unless you're responsible for her opinions I don't think you should have to apologize for them."

Neve appreciated her practicality. There was no drama in Diane, not a mean bone in her body, which gave Neve a sense of security in their friendship, something she'd never really had with Yasmin. She never felt off-balance with Diane, never felt that she had to pretend to be someone she wasn't, and it made her want to be a better friend. "I want you to know that no one doubts your experience."

"Thank you." Diane smiled, and the entire theater suddenly got warmer. "I don't think Inara wants to be negative. That's the jealousy talking."

"Jealousy?" Neve had never even considered that word in conjunction with Inara. She was so confident and self-assured—what could Inara possibly be jealous of?

"Yeah. I mean, I think she's definitely interested in you. . . ."

It took Neve a hot minute to process what she meant. Interested romantically? "Me?"

"Absolutely! You're cute. Funny. Girlie in a vintage goth kind of way."

Neve was relatively sure that no one other than her parents had ever referred to her as cute and now Diane had done it three times.

Not that Neve was counting.

Except she totally was.

"Of course Inara's interested," Diane continued, "and since you and I have been spending so much time together, it's natural that she's jealous."

Romantic interest from Inara. Huh. Neve knew that Inara was queer, but it had never occurred to her that her roommate would harbor anything but platonic feelings for her.

"If it stresses you out," Diane said, placing a hand on Neve's shoulder, "rooming with her, I mean, you could ask for a transfer."

"Transfer rooms?" That seemed extreme.

Diane smiled and gave Neve's shoulder a light squeeze. "Oh, it's cool if you don't mind. I just thought that since I have an empty bed in my room . . ." She shrugged. "No biggie." Then she walked away to discuss some aspect of the scene with Kellie while Neve was left onstage feeling jelly-legged and light-headed.

That night, Inara seemed unusually agitated. It had been a long day, ending with movie night in the theater, where they showed *Hidden Figures* followed by a Q&A with one of the screenwriters, and though Neve was ready to fall asleep the second she crawled into bed, Inara, who was usually sound asleep by the time Neve got into the room, tossed and turned.

Neve should have asked if something was wrong and she and Inara might have talked it through, but after Diane's comments that afternoon, Neve wasn't sure what to say. It wasn't that she didn't have feelings for Inara—she really liked her—or that she had a problem if her roommate had a crush on her—she'd have been a hypocrite if she did—but mostly Neve wanted to avoid the initial awkwardness of a conversation about their feelings and the continued awkwardness such a conversation would bring into their room for the last week of camp.

So Neve said nothing and hoped that Inara would want to avoid the weirdness, too, and do the same.

"Be careful with Diane Russell."

No such luck.

"What do you mean?" Neve asked more sharply than intended.

"Diane is trouble."

Inara sounded like Grandma K, who didn't approve of anyone unless they were Catholic or Irish, and Neve was immediately defensive. "You barely know her."

"Diane was . . ." Inara stopped, brows low over her brown eyes. She took a breath as if she was going to complete the sentence, then thought better of it and snapped her mouth shut.

"What?"

"Nothing."

Neve was tired of the secrecy. "I know you don't like Diane. What I don't know is why."

"Not about liking or disliking."

"Then what the fuck is it about?"

"Trust!" Inara wielded the word like a knife, slashing at Neve's soft underbelly. Judging whom to trust and whom not to was definitely one of Neve's biggest weaknesses, and she was still suffering the ramifications of mistakenly placing her trust in Yasmin Attar. When she'd decided to come to GLAM, the idea of trusting someone again had seemed utterly impossible, but now with Diane, Neve felt as if she'd met someone who really saw her, not just as a social life raft the way she'd been for Yasmin, but as a whole person. And it felt good to be seen.

"Diane has been nothing but open with us," Neve said.

"So?"

"So why shouldn't I trust her?"

Inara reached for her phone. She scrolled through as if looking for something, and just when Neve thought she was going to flip it around and reveal the fruits of her search, Inara quickly locked the screen and put the phone facedown on her nightstand.

"Be careful, okay?" No explanation, no elaboration on why Diane was trouble or what, exactly, Neve should be careful of. It was an instruction, the kind Inara was prone to giving to everyone around her, and though Neve wanted to be indignant at being preached at, there was a kindliness in Inara's tone that she had never heard before and that instantly defused her temper.

"It's not like we go to school together," Neve said, deflecting. "I'll probably never see Diane again after GLAM." A lie, Neve hoped. *La Jolla is only half an hour from Carlsbad.*

Inara lay back in bed, pulling her plaid comforter up to her chin. "Good."

She was signaling that she was done with the conversation, content with Neve's response, but the kindliness had vanished from her tone and all Neve got from it now was an abrasive, know-it-all attitude that rubbed her the wrong way. Neve should have swallowed her pride, realized where Inara's tone was coming from, and rolled toward the wall to go to sleep.

But she didn't.

"This is bullshit," Neve said, swinging her legs around to face her roommate. "You don't get to tell me who I should and shouldn't be friends with."

Inara lay utterly still. "Didn't say that."

"You're telling me not to trust Diane without offering any reasons why. That kind of sounds like you're trying to control me."

"Protect, not control."

Seriously? Like Neve was some kind of neophyte without any experience with people or judging character. "Thanks, *Mom.*"

"Be thankful." This time, Inara pushed herself up and leaned on her arm. "Mom died four years ago."

Fuck. Neve didn't know about Inara's mom, but though she felt horrible for scratching at that scab, it didn't change the crux of her argument. "I'm saying that I can choose my own friends."

"Yeah?" Inara simply raised an eyebrow. She knew enough about Neve's problems at school.

"Yeah. And just because I chose Diane instead of *you* doesn't mean you get to act like such a bitch." Then, without another word, Neve turned to face the wall.

Silence fell between them. Neve strained her ears listening for a hint of movement from Inara: walking across the room, reaching for her phone, inhaling to renew the conversation. But all Neve heard was Inara's mattress creak lightly as she lowered herself back down.

ELEVEN

AND THEN THINGS GOT AWKWARD IN ROOM 304.

Neve was simultaneously furious with her roommate and embarrassed by her own behavior. She'd barely known Inara a week and already they weren't on speaking terms, a situation that Neve could only kind of sort of justify in her mind. Yes, Inara had been rude to Diane and, when confronted about her behavior, had been unable or unwilling to explain it. But Inara had also gone out of her way to make sure that Neve felt comfortable at GLAM, even signing up for the theater module she had warned against. It was enough to make Neve feel painfully guilty whenever she saw her roommate.

Thankfully, Neve didn't have to confront that guilt very often. Mornings, Inara was up and out of the room for her daily Fun Run before Neve's phone alarm chimed, and at night, Neve hung out in the lounge with Diane until she was pretty sure Inara was already asleep. The cycle repeated itself in an unspoken avoidance of their argument during all of week two, which meant the only time Neve and Inara actually needed to spend together was in rehearsal for their showcase scene.

They avoided chitchat in Theater and sat on opposite sides of the house when Kellie was presenting workshops or running class exercises. Neve felt the cold shoulder of rejection even if she and Inara had never broken up as friends: On the rare occasion that Neve allowed her eyes to stray to Inara's face, she always found her roommate's gaze to be fixed pointedly on something that wasn't Neve. And somehow, even though Inara had been the one to provoke the fight with her rudeness, Neve felt as though she was to blame for the iciness between them.

Fine. Whatever. Neve didn't need Inara's friendship, had never sought it out in the first place. They were just roommates who had been thrown together due to the proximity of their hometowns. It wasn't kismet or some complicated mathematical algorithm designed to help Neve find her new BFF; it was random. She didn't need to feel like a horrible person for not being friends.

Besides, Neve *had* made a friend.

And Diane was pretty awesome.

Also, just pretty.

And maybe she and Neve would be more than friends.

Or at least Neve hoped so.

If Diane felt the same way, she certainly hadn't mentioned it. Though the two of them were now inseparably close, Diane never crossed the line from platonic to romantic, and as the last day of camp approached, a knot tightened in Neve's stomach at the thought of their impending separation. She was going to miss seeing Diane every day, sharing jokes at meals, rehearsing their scene, talking about life and music and all of Neve's favorite film noirs Diane had promised to watch when she got back to La Jolla. Those deep, energizing conversations they had while curled up on a tufted sofa in the dorm lounge were Neve's favorite moments of camp, especially after her months of social isolation, and on the night of the Activism in Art showcase, Neve wasn't sure what she was more nervous about—performing her scene in front of people or moving out of Oakland Hills College the next morning.

Both were pretty terrifying.

"Stop fidgeting," Diane said, pulling away from Neve's face. She held a compact of powder in one hand and a Kabuki brush in the other, and had screwed up her mouth in mock anger. "Or am I going to have to strap you to that chair to finish your makeup?"

"Sorry," Neve said, letting out a slow breath to steady her nerves. She focused on sitting still in the diva chair while Diane dabbed at her face, even though the idea of being tied up by her friend made her heart flutter around in her chest like a caged butterfly.

"You're going to be great." Diane lifted Neve's chin with her middle finger, admiring her own handiwork in the flat light of the makeup mirror. "You've been totally killing it in rehearsals."

"Thanks." Neve wasn't a good enough actress to keep a little sigh of resignation out of her voice.

"What's wrong?"

"I'm anxious."

"About what?"

Neve swallowed. "The scene?" She was pretty sure Diane would be able to detect the interrogatory inflection in her voice.

Diane stepped in front of her, right eye crinkling playfully as a lopsided smile pinched her cheek. "Bullshit. You know your lines and blocking backward and forward. You could pass out, hit your head on the stage, forget who you are and what you're doing, and *still* be able to finish the scene."

Neve laughed. Though prone to exaggeration, Diane was probably right.

"So what is it?"

Neve opened her mouth, unsure what to say. *I'm going to miss you. I want to see you again. I think I might be in love with you.* All true and all too terrifying to admit. She thought of Grandma K's advice: There is only one person in this world who controls your destiny, and that is you. Was this one of those times where Neve needed to show the universe exactly who and what she wanted?

You did that before, and look what happened.

Another conversation, another friend, another face that made Neve's heart go all conga beat in her chest.

"Okay," Yasmin had said, sitting cross-legged on her queen-size bed. "Tell me who it is."

"Who *who* is?" Neve was on the floor, unlacing her boots, having arrived at Yasmin's house the morning of Marisol's party after an urgent *OMG YOU HAVE TO GET OVER HERE RIGHT FREAKING NOW AND TELL ME WHAT'S GOING ON* text from her best friend.

"Who *he* is." She'd handed her phone to Neve as she joined Yasmin on the bed. On the screen, Neve saw her own Instagram feed, which had exactly twenty-seven followers, making it practically a private account.

Yasmin had pulled up Neve's latest post from a week ago—a photo of a Starbucks napkin with a doodle drawn on it of two overlapping hearts with the word *evermore* written in the shared oval.

It had been a stupid thing to do. Neve had been hiding her feelings for Yasmin for as long as she'd recognized that she had them, but that afternoon at Starbucks as she was listening to Yasmin go on and on and on about the guy with the gorgeous hazel eyes they'd seen with Marisol and Luna, it was as if Neve's feelings needed to find an outlet before her heart exploded. She hadn't even realized what she'd drawn until Yasmin used the restroom before they left, when her eyes had trailed down the napkin, the pen still in her hand, and the telltale drawing.

Why had she taken a photo of it before shoving the napkin in her empty grande cup? Why had she then posted that photo on her Instagram page?

The answer, of course, was that she'd wanted Yasmin to know the truth, but was too terrified of actually saying *I love you* to her face, so Neve had found a work-around.

But as they'd sat facing each other on the bed in Yasmin's room, Neve realized that her passivity had failed. *Who he is*, Yasmin had said. She thought the second heart in Neve's doodle was a guy.

"Is it Hazel Eyes?" Yasmin had said quickly. Too quickly and with an almost hysterical edge to her voice. "Tell me! You have to. We're best friends, for fuck's sake."

There it was. Neve's chance to tell Yasmin how she really felt. She'd looked up at her best friend with a shy smile and their eyes had met.

Yasmin's emotions had passed across her face so distinctly that Neve could discern the exact moment each one morphed into the next. Confusion. Then questioning. Realization. And finally, revulsion.

Without a single word, Yasmin had rejected her.

"Y-yes," Neve stuttered, her eyes faltering to the floral duvet cover. The pink-and-red roses mocked her shame. "Hazel Eyes. I didn't want to tell you I have a crush on him."

Neve desperately wanted to take their friendship back in time sixty seconds to when Yasmin hadn't known the deep, dark secret of Neve's soul, hadn't looked so utterly disgusted by the idea that Neve was attracted to her, and so she'd grasped at the low-hanging fruit. Hazel Eyes. He was attractive; Neve could see the pull.

"He's gorgeous," she'd added, trying to sell it. Which wasn't even a lie. He was an objectively hot guy, but Neve wasn't an instalove kind of girl. Not like Yasmin.

"Oh," Yasmin had said slowly. "I . . . yeah. Of course. Makes total sense. Sorry if it's been awkward listening to me talk about him so much."

Yasmin had decided to accept the lie. And a week later, their friendship exploded.

Was that what would happen if Neve told Diane the truth?

"I just don't want camp to end," Neve said, chickening out.

"Oh yeah. Me neither." Diane forced a smile, though her eyes dropped in disappointment. She turned away, placing the makeup back on the table. "Okay, I think you're ready."

Fuck. Had Neve missed her chance? Had Diane been expecting her to share her feelings? Had she wanted Neve to say she wanted to see her again? *Did I blow it?*

While Neve sat tongue-tied, once again wishing she could go back in time and make a different choice, Diane took a short, sharp breath and spun around to face her.

"Break a leg tonight," she said, then leaned over and kissed Neve lightly on the cheek before dashing out of the dressing room.

TWELVE

"YOU WERE AMAZING!" KELLIE COOED AS SHE EMBRACED NEVE after the performance. "I really mean that."

"Thanks." Neve's hands were shaking, her feet felt as if they couldn't stop moving, and her entire body was charged. Electric. This showcase had been her first-ever performance unless you counted the elementary-school holiday show where she'd represented the Partridge in a Pear Tree in a performance of "The Twelve Days of Christmas." She had to waddle across the stage in her bird-and-tree costume at the end of every freaking verse, eventually stepping on a drumstick that one of the twelve drumming drummers had dropped, which caused her to hydro-plane three feet across the stage before losing her balance and landing face-first on one of her pears.

That was definitely *not* electric.

But performing Diane's scene had been an amazing experience. She and Inara, though still not on speaking terms, had been in sync. Inara's Francisco was more menacing than ever, and Neve as Ryanne felt a new depth of desperation and hopelessness in her quest for justice. Gone were her caricatures of Mary Astor and Anne Shirley—what had emerged that night was purely Neve Lanier.

They'd received a standing ovation at the end—one of only two during the whole evening—and after the show, campers and counselors alike had sought both actresses out to compliment them on their performances.

It was like nothing Neve had ever experienced, and suddenly ideas of being an actress swirled around in her mind. Was that something she could actually aspire to?

"Please tell me you're joining a theater group when you go back to school next week," Kellie continued, hands still grasping Neve by the shoulders. "It would be an absolute shame to see your talent go to waste."

"Agreed," Inara said. It was the first off-script word she'd directed at Neve since the night of their argument, and Neve felt shamed by their tacit silence. She wanted to hug Inara, to apologize, and to tell her that she'd been a total stubborn asshole, and hey, maybe they could still be friends after GLAM?

"Thank you," she said, and meant it.

Inara opened her mouth to reply, but Kellie had shoved a business card in Neve's hand. "I know I'm in Seattle and you're way down south," she said, "but if you *ever* want to do a virtual coaching or scene study, *please* call me. Promise, promise, promise?"

"Um, sure." Neve was pretty sure she'd never need that card but tucked it into her pocket anyway. "I promise."

Kellie flitted off and Neve turned toward Inara. She wanted to say a million different things, all of which started with *I'm so sorry*, but she'd only managed to smile at her roommate when Diane swept in between them, throwing her arms around Neve.

"You were . . ." She swallowed, fighting back emotion as she squeezed Neve tightly. "Transcendent. Thank you."

"You're welcome." Neve felt her heartbeat quicken as Diane held her.

"Come on," Diane said, taking Neve's hand in her own. "There's a party in the lounge. I bet everyone's going to want to talk to you."

As Neve allowed herself to be led away, she noticed that Inara had disappeared.

GLAMsters trickled upstairs and the lounge finally emptied out, and though Neve was yawning with exhaustion, she didn't want to go back to her room. She clung to her last moments of GLAM with all the strength she could muster.

There hadn't been any booze at the after-party, but Neve felt slightly tipsy, like the time she and Yasmin had busted into her dad's hard-cider collection in the garage refrigerator. Except without the almost instantaneous dehydration. And without Yasmin.

Who? Neve laughed at herself. As reticent as she had been to buy into the GLAMster lifestyle, she had to admit that something inside her had shifted. She was still the slightly jaded, way too snarky seventeen-year-old behind a protective armor of forties-inspired fashion and film noir quotes that she'd been before, but Neve now felt as if she could take on anything. Or anyone. So what if everyone at LCC hated her guts? She only had to survive one more school year, and then they'd all be in the rearview mirror. After two weeks at GLAM, she felt like she had the strength to endure her senior year.

"Is your dad picking you up tomorrow?" Diane said, collapsing onto the love seat beside Neve.

"Yep." She paused, pushing aside the knot of sadness in her stomach that tightened the moment Diane mentioned the morning. "I can't believe GLAM's already over."

"I knoooooow." Diane sighed happily. "Camps go so fast. You just make a new friend and then suddenly you're going home."

Camps. Right. Because Diane had done this before. Every summer, it seemed. She probably had a BFF from every camp she'd ever attended, and Neve felt very small and very silly to have thought her friendship with Diane was more than a relationship of circumstance. She stood up, succumbing to insecurity, desperate to get out of there. "I should go to bed."

"Do you have to?"

Neve shrugged. She didn't really want this night to end but wasn't exactly sure what to do next.

Diane smiled. Charming. Confident. "Come on. I don't have a roommate. You can crash in my room."

"Isn't that against the rules?"

Diane laughed. "What are they going to do, kick us out? Besides, I'm not sleepy." She leaped to her feet and playfully pushed Neve toward the staircase.

Not sleepy?

They silently mounted the stairs, the stillness of the dorm settling in around them as everyone else seemed to have gone to bed. Even though they didn't really care about rule-breaking, Neve and Diane didn't say a word as they tiptoed down the second-floor hallway.

"Everyone loved your scene," Neve said as soon as Diane locked her dorm room door. She sat down on Annabelle's abandoned bed and tucked her legs up beneath her.

"Only because of you." Diane tossed a blanket across the room to Neve, then pulled her comforter around her, snuggling it up beneath her neck as she propped herself against the wall. "You're an excellent actress. I still can't believe you'd never done any theater before."

Neve smiled to herself in the near darkness of the room, lit only by the glow of Diane's charging phone and the moonlight streaming through the slender window. So much of her life had been an act, hiding her true feelings from everyone around her while trying to fit into a world of privilege and money where she definitely didn't belong. Maybe she'd simply internalized the process?

"You had to notice that everyone loved you."

Neve wanted to say yes, to tell Diane that the performance and the applause she'd received had inspired possibly the best feelings she'd ever had in her life, to say that the radiant look on Diane's face when she hugged her afterward made Neve's insides melt, but admitting to either was setting herself up for disappointment.

"Everybody's somebody's fool," Neve said instead, retreating behind her safety wall of movie quotes.

Diane clicked her tongue. "Is that from another movie?"

The Lady from Shanghai," Neve said, embarrassed at being called out.

"Ooooooh my God, stop!" Diane grabbed her pillow and launched it across the room at Neve's head. "Can't you just be real and admit that you're good at something? And that you enjoyed it?"

"I . . ." Neve winced as her voice trailed off. "I guess I can't."

Instead of mocking her, like Yasmin would have done, Diane fell quiet. "I totally understand," she said after a pause. "It's hard to admit you want something in this world. Seems like we're all just waiting for our dreams to be crushed."

She could have taken the words right out of Neve's mouth. "My grandma says that the only person who can control your destiny is you."

"She sounds like a very wise lady."

Neve snorted. She never used to think so, but maybe she'd been wrong. "Just a very rich one."

"Money isn't everything."

"It's a good start."

Diane paused. Even in the dim light of the room, Neve could see that her friend had tensed. "I guess you think my life is pretty perfect," Diane said slowly.

Neve wasn't sure how to respond. "I didn't mean—"

"It's not an accusation. I totally understand how things look from the outside." Diane crossed her legs in front of her. "But I haven't been completely honest with you."

"Okay . . ." *Here's where she tells you she has a boyfriend back home, dumbass.*

"Javier's not just some rando guy from school." Diane exhaled slowly. "He's my stepbrother."

"What?"

"Yeah. We live in the same house. So all those things I put in the scene . . ." She let her voice trail off, leaving time for Neve to cycle through all the horrors Diane had written into her scene—from the sexually explicit comments to a sexy lingerie gift to Diane waking up to find Javier in her bedroom. Neve shuddered.

"Exactly."

"Can't your parents do anything?"

"My mom thinks I'm overreacting." Diane's voice sounded very small. "Misinterpreting. You'd think she'd get it by now. Women don't make this stuff up."

"Fuck."

"It's not that she's an awful mom, don't get me wrong. She really wants this blended family to work. And my stepdad thinks the sun rises and sets on Javier, so he's not listening." She held up a hand as if anticipating Neve's next suggestion. "And living with my dad isn't a possibility. He died when I was ten."

"I'm sorry." It sounded so inadequate. *I'm sorry.* That's what people said when they didn't know what else to do, when they were uncomfortable about the feelings you'd shared and desperately wished they could relieve themselves of the unwanted burden. She didn't want to be that person for Diane, but what could she do? There had to be someone who could help. "What about a teacher at school?"

Diane sighed heavily. "Not unless I want to get Child Protective Services involved, you know? It isn't like Javier's actually done anything violent. Yet."

"Oh." She had no idea how it worked, but Child Protective Services sounded ominous.

"Now *I'm* sorry," Diane said, trying to force some of that old cheerfulness back into her tone. "I've totally ruined our last GLAM night with my stupid bully problems. I didn't mean to bring you down."

"Don't apologize!" Neve said quickly. "I get it. I totally do." She paused, not sure she wanted to rehash her own Yasmin drama after two blissful weeks of barely thinking about it, but maybe if Diane knew about Neve's struggles, it would make her feel better?

"I have my own Javier," Neve began. "I mean, not nearly as bad and not sexual or anything, but I have my own bully situation." She didn't want to compare her mean-girl bullshit with the sexual harassment Diane had been facing.

"But still really bad?"

Now it was Neve's turn to sigh. As much as she didn't want to admit it, *pretty bad* summed up her last few months succinctly. "I sent a text to my best friend over spring break. Something I thought was totally private and confidential. And then she shared it with the whole school."

"WHAT?"

"I know." Neve recalled that first day back at school. She'd arrived totally clueless that her world was about to implode, though by the time she made it from the front entrance to her locker, she knew something was horribly wrong. Everyone was pointing and whispering. She found Marisol waiting at her locker, flanked by Luna and a scowling Yasmin.

And then everything went to shit.

"But why would she do that? She's your friend."

"*Was* my friend," Neve corrected her. "My *best* friend. And she threw me under the bus so she could get close to a boy she didn't even know." Neve pictured those hazel eyes and wondered if Yasmin had ever gone out with him or if her betrayal had all been for nothing.

"Maybe it was a mistake?" Diane suggested. "Or an accident?" Always wanting to see the good in everyone.

"I wish I could believe that," Neve said as spite and bitterness crept back into her heart. "But Yasmin initiated the conversation that led to my text."

"You're sure it was deliberate?"

So sure. "The party I mentioned at Confessional? That was the guy Yasmin wanted to meet and then I totally fucked that up for her by getting into a fight with the hostess. But Yasmin acted as if she wasn't mad and that our friendship was totally fine. Then she started texting me all the time about what bitches those girls were, which eventually provoked the comment from me that went viral."

"So she set you up?"

Neve nodded. "And then the day after I sent the notorious text, Yasmin was playing with my phone. Taking photos of me. I found out later that she was actually deleting the rest of the texts from that conversation, erasing proof of her own participation."

"That's awful. I mean, truly evil. And for some guy? What the hell is wrong with this girl?"

"So many, many things," Neve said, laughing slightly. The unburdening was already making her feel better. She couldn't believe that she'd ever cared for Yasmin Attar. "Now no one at school will talk to me. It's like I'm in quarantine."

"Shit."

"I can handle it." She didn't want Diane to think she was completely pathetic. "Just one more school year, and then I can go off to college."

"I wish I could help you."

It was the first time anyone had said that to Neve, and it meant a lot. "Thanks. Me too. And I wish I could do something about Javier."

Diane looked up at the ceiling, head tilted to the side. Neve could see her smile illuminated by a shaft of moonlight, highlighting her face in shades of bluish gray. "That would be kind of funny. Like, if I took care of Yasmin and you got rid of Javier."

Got rid of. "What do you mean?"

"If they were both gone, our lives would be *so* much better."

"No joke."

Diane dropped her voice to a mere whisper, so low that Neve could hardly make out her words. "I could kill Yasmin."

"What?"

Diane's eyes flicked up to Neve's face. "What did you think I said?"

Neve stiffened, feeling like the mood in the room had suddenly shifted from speculation to something more serious. "I thought you said, *'I could kill Yasmin.'*"

"Ding! Ding! Ding!" She put one finger on her nose and pointed the other at Neve. "We have a winner."

Neve pushed herself to a sitting position. "Diane, I don't like where this is—"

"Calm down!" She laughed as she launched another pillow at Neve's head. "I'm just pretending! Taking control of our destiny, like your grandma said."

The heaviness in the room immediately lifted. "Fine," Neve said, tossing the pillow back as she played along. "And I'd totally murder Javier for you."

"That's the spirit." Diane laughed. "And no one would suspect us because neither of us had an actual connection to our victim."

Neve laughed. "That sounds exactly like *Strangers on a Train*."

"What's that?"

"Old Hitchcock noir, based on a book. Two strangers meet on a train, and one proposes that they swap murders because no one would suspect either of them."

Diane laughed. "Great minds think alike."

"But in our case," Neve added, "we're not strangers."

"Right, of course." Diane grinned her goofy smile. "But love *is* a good motivation for murder."

"Love?" Neve said with a nervous laugh. *Is she saying what I think she's saying?*

"Friendship love," Diane said slowly, and Neve felt her heart sink.

"Right," she said, hoping the ache inside her didn't come through her voice. Diane was letting her down easy. Which was kind, though totally pathetic.

"Best friends," Diane added. "And that's what best friends do. They take care of each other." She lay down on her bed with the comforter wrapped around her. "And who knows where it leads?"

"Where what leads?" Neve felt that spark of hope reignite.

"Friendship love." Diane let out an audible sigh. "You never know what best friends might turn into."

"Ah." Neve yawned, not even sure what time it was. She felt all warm and fuzzy. It wasn't a declaration of love, but it was something more. Friendship. Hope. A future.

Most importantly, Neve didn't feel alone anymore. She had a best friend.

She had Diane.

THIRTEEN

NEVE WASN'T SURE WHEN SHE DOZED OFF, BUT WHEN SHE FINALLY woke up the next morning, it took her several minutes to realize that she wasn't in her room. The decor was the same—wooden twin beds, matching desks, single wardrobe, and vertical blinds—but her perspective was all off. For starters, she was sleeping on the wrong side of the room, a thin blanket draped over her instead of the black Target comforter she'd brought from home; plus, even in the bleary-eyed haze of early morning, she recognized that Inara's plaid accessories weren't draped over every visible surface.

She sat up, rolling her head to release the tension in her neck, and pushed the pink blanket aside. She was still wearing her clothes from last night. Right. She'd crashed in Diane's room, which left only one mystery: Where was Diane?

Neve pushed herself to the edge of the mattress, testing her bare feet against the frigid wooden floor, and stared at Diane's bed. It had been stripped. The wardrobe door stood open, exposing the emptiness within, and Diane's chic Coach rollie bag with matching purse and laptop case was gone.

The only things left in the room other than Neve were the pink blanket and a piece of paper on Annabelle's old nightstand with the letters *BFF* printed in Diane's neat, upright handwriting with a phone number written underneath.

Neve smiled. Diane had probably left super early due to the long drive home and didn't want to wake her. She gathered the blanket under her nose and inhaled deeply, noting the coconut scent of Diane's shampoo, and smiled. *You never know what best friends might turn into.* With more excitement than Neve thought she'd feel on move-out day, she threw the blanket over her shoulder, tucked Diane's phone number into her pocket with Kellie's business card, then grabbed her shoes and hurried upstairs to her own room.

Inara was already up when Neve quietly unlocked the door, tossing her plaid clothes unceremoniously into her bag without any attempt at organization. Her bedding and toiletries were already packed.

"Hey," she said, without looking at Neve. At least the gulf of silence between them had been bridged. "Sleepover?"

Neve dropped the pink blanket onto her mattress. "Yeah."

Inara glanced over her shoulder, eyes narrowing in accusation. "Diane?"

Why was Diane such a barrier between them? "Yeah."

"Ah."

There was a pause, thick and weird, before Inara turned and faced her. For a moment, Neve thought she was going to say something, but Inara pulled her phone from her pocket instead and hurriedly typed something. Neve assumed that the wall was back up until her phone buzzed with a text from an unknown number.

Inara. Reach out if you need anything. I'll always reply.

Neve froze in shock. Not because Inara somehow had her number but because *you* and *I'll* were the first personal pronouns Inara had ever used outside of their theater scene, and Neve wasn't sure if it was an indication of her roommate's emotion at leaving GLAM camp for the last time, or whether she couldn't figure out a way to impart that information without them. Neve was tempted to ask, just to lighten the mood, but before she could even form the words, Inara grabbed the double handle of her duffel bag, whipped it over her shoulder, and disappeared into the hallway.

Neve's dad was standing by the minivan, parked in almost the exact same spot he'd been when he dropped her off, wearing his favorite tweed cap, with the same tense, forced smile on his face.

Neve must have been smiling as well as she muscled her bag across the pavement because she noticed some of the tension drain from his body as she approached. It was a dramatic change. His shoulders unfurled from their protective hunch, the wrinkles and lines of anxiety smoothed away. He looked taller, younger, less stressed than she'd seen him in years, since even before her troubles began, and she realized in that moment that whatever other benefits she'd derived from her time at GLAM, the stress it had relieved in her dad was worth every penny Grandma K had spent.

"Sorry it's just me this time, Neevy. Deirdre didn't want to sit through another drive."

He wrapped his arms around her, and Neve could feel his hands trembling. "It's so good to see you."

Subtext: *It's so good to see you looking happy.* Not that Neve begrudged him the sentiment: She was feeling the same about him. "Missed you too, Dad."

Neve exhaled slowly and enjoyed the embrace. It felt nice, not forced, not painful like she was going to have to lie and say that she was *fine* afterward. She *was* fine, and they both knew it.

"Did you have fun?" he asked, finally releasing her. The late-morning sun was behind him, obscuring his face in shadow, but Neve was pretty sure she saw tears glint in the corners of his eyes. "Because your mom has sent me about five thousand texts asking."

"So few?"

"You know your mom."

I sure do. "You can tell her that I had a really good time." She paused, grinning from ear to ear. "And I'm not even bullshitting."

FALL

FOURTEEN

"SURE YOU'RE OKAY?" NEVE'S DAD SAT HUNCHED OVER THE steering wheel, squinting through the bright sunshine at the gleaming entrance to La Costa Canyon High School. He wasn't wearing his usual cap this morning, and Neve noticed how thin and wispy his blond hair had become at the top of his head. "We could always talk to your mom about homeschooling."

Homeschooling? No way. Neve took a deep breath, her eyes fixed on the looming glass facade. "I'm fine, Dad."

"I don't want it to be like it was last spring."

"It won't be."

"Are you sure?"

No. How could anyone be sure of anything in an American high school? It was prison rules in there—the strongest live, the weakest flee, and everyone else picks a side. But those rules had already chewed Neve up and spat her out once. She wasn't about to let it happen again.

Neve was a different person now. Different than before GLAM, different than before spring break. Hell, different than she'd been since they moved to Carlsbad. She felt stronger, more capable. Like she could take on Yasmin and Marisol and the whole whisper network of LCC if she needed to.

Diane's text that morning had really bolstered Neve's confidence. Just a simple *Today will be better! Talk soon!* but it reminded Neve that she wasn't alone. Wasn't isolated. She could endure whatever abuse LCC doled out because she'd be able to bitch about it later with Diane. She had someone who understood her, someone who had her back, and it made facing the first day of senior year much less terrifying.

"I'm sure," Neve said, exhaling slowly. And she meant it. "Today everything changes."

Neve was able to hang on to that swagger as she marched up to the main building and yanked the door open. But the second she set foot inside LCC, the bravado faltered.

Something was off. Wrong. Neve had gotten used to the whispering behind her back, the rude, biting comments that were intentionally voiced a little too loudly so that she'd be sure to hear herself being referred to as *that jealous I Love Lucy bitch* or some other not-so-creative insult. That was her normal.

What wasn't normal was the crying.

Students were openly weeping in the hallways. Hugging one another. Consoling one another. The normal frenzy of first-day-of-school gossip and catch-up and general excitement was utterly absent, replaced by sadness and mourning.

What the hell happened now?

Insults and jeers she expected, but the crying? That was creepy as fuck. Neve wanted to spin around, race out to the parking lot, and hope that her dad was still waiting there, car idling for a quick getaway.

But she couldn't. If Diane could spend every day and night with a stepbrother who literally made her life a #MeToo story, Neve could face the demons of her high school. She squared her shoulders, focused her eyes straight ahead, and kept walking.

She rounded a corner and froze. Marisol and Luna stood in the hallway, the former doubled over as she wept loudly, theatrically. Luna rubbed her friend's back as she tried to soothe her.

"I'm so sorry, Mari," Luna said. "I'm going to miss her, too."

"It's . . . It's not *fair!*" Marisol wailed.

"I know."

"And why haven't they done anything?" Marisol straightened up, wiping mascara-filled tears from her cheeks. "What if one of us is next?"

Her. One of us. Next. Neve's brain chewed on those words as she realized that she didn't see Yasmin anywhere. She was about to ask what had happened when Luna finally noticed her.

"You!" she shouted, pointing an accusatory finger at Neve, who wasn't entirely sure how she was supposed to react.

"Yeah?"

Marisol turned. As she recognized Neve, her eyes grew wide, nostrils flared like a bull readying to charge. "Oh my God."

Neve's heart rate was accelerating with every passing second, pumping blood through her veins so quickly, the dizzying rush threatened her balance. She tried to say something, to ask what the fuck was going on, but all she could manage was a guttural hiccup as her vocal cords refused to vibrate.

"I bet you're happy," Marisol continued.

"She's not even crying," Luna added. "Probably laughed when she heard."

"Heard what?" Neve managed, her voice hoarse.

Marisol narrowed her eyes. "Like you don't know."

"I . . ."

"I told them it was probably you," Marisol said smugly, taking a step toward her.

Luna tried to hold her back as if Neve was dangerous. "Mari, no!"

But Marisol shook her off. She stormed up to Neve, her face so close Neve could see the pulsating veins in her neck. "You're not going to get away with it."

"What's going on?" Neve said. She was sweating now, the back of her neck damp and clammy. Some indescribable fear made her add: "Where's Yasmin?"

"How dare you say her name!" Marisol cried, tears falling anew. "You . . . you *murderer!*" Then she hurried back to Luna, who cradled her friend with open arms. But Neve didn't care about Marisol's hysterics. She was fixated on her words.

Did she say murderer?

Cold panic washed over Neve, like the winter tide lapping at North Ponto Beach. She shook herself, assuming she must have heard wrong. Why would anyone call Neve a murderer?

"What are you talking about?" Neve felt her phone vibrating in her bag but ignored it.

Marisol halted weeping abruptly and wheeled around on her, fists clenched against her body. "Like you don't know," she repeated.

"I don't!"

"Liar." Marisol turned to leave, but Neve grabbed her by the arm.

"Tell me what the fuck is going on!"

Marisol's eyes grew wide, and she flinched away from Neve in a panic.

"Don't touch her!" Luna shrieked. Actually shrieked in fear as if Neve was going to kill her best friend. "Leave her alone."

Neve spun around, staring at the faces of the students who had packed into the corridor during her exchange with Marisol and Luna. The eyes she saw held fear, sadness, questions no one dared ask. "What's going on?" Everyone just stared. "Someone please tell me what the fuck—"

"Neve Lanier?" The voice was sharp and biting, slicing through the weighty silence of the crowded school corridor like a knife through warm butter. "Are you Neve Lanier?"

Neve looked up to find Ms. Eagen, the registrar, clomping toward her. Ms. Eagen was one of those twentysomethings who thought that if she dressed like a teen and wore impossibly bright lipstick shades, people might mistake her for one of the high school students, and today's getup of open-toed ankle boots, denim skirt with a ruffled hem, and skintight raglan tee sporting a rainbow iron-on intentionally meant to look as if it had been applied in 1985 was no exception. Neve and Yasmin used to make fun of Ms. Eagen's outfits mercilessly during lunch or between classes when the registrar was usually out and about, fraternizing with students, so normally Neve would have smirked at her arrival. But not today.

"Are you Neve Lanier?" she repeated, stopping in front of Neve while making direct eye contact. The question was a joke—she and everyone else in that school knew exactly who Neve was—but instead of the usual snarky comeback, all Neve could do was nod. Because in addition to the silly outfit and way-too-pink lips, there was an unfamiliar look in Ms. Eagen's eyes: fear.

Ms. Eagen gestured for Neve to follow and she fell into step behind the registrar, moving swiftly back toward the office. "There's been an . . . an incident."

Neve wasn't going to accept anything that vague. "An incident?"

"Yes." Ms. Eagen sighed as she reached the office door, then glanced over her shoulder. "Yasmin Attar has been murdered."

FIFTEEN

THE WALLS OF THE SCHOOL OFFICE WERE IN MOTION. AN earthquake, the Big One, rocking the building to its foundation. Or a freak *Wizard of Oz*–esque tornado that had actually picked up the entire high school and was now spinning it through the air like a leaf on the breeze. Those were the only explanations for the sudden and complete loss of equilibrium Neve felt as Ms. Eagen stood before her, arms wrapped around her rainbow T-shirt as a protective shield, and informed her that Yasmin was dead.

Neve staggered, unable to maintain her balance. She knew it wasn't actually an earthquake or tornado causing her vertigo, just the mother of all panic attacks. She squeezed her eyes shut, reaching one hand out toward what she thought was the nearest wall and clamping the other across her mouth as she tried to keep the vomit, which was rocketing up the back of her throat, from spewing all over Ms. Eagen's suede booties.

Yasmin was dead.

Yes, Neve hated her. Yes, she'd fantasized about Yasmin's death a million times. But those were revenge fantasies, nothing more. Yasmin had been her friend, her best friend, and even though they hadn't spoken in months, Neve was overwhelmed by loss and grief.

She thought of Mr. and Mrs. Attar and the horror they must be going through. Yasmin was their only child, their princess, the sun around which their lives orbited. They doted on her, adored her. And to have their daughter ripped so abruptly from their lives must have left them heartbroken. Especially since . . .

Murdered.

Did her parents have to identify the body? Or worse, did they find her? Neve couldn't even imagine how agonizing that must have been. She wanted to call them, hug them, even though she knew her presence wouldn't have been welcome. Not after her fight with Yasmin, and certainly not after what Neve's dad had done after.

Murdered.

Neve's hands shook. She couldn't get past that word. Dead was one thing, but murdered? No wonder Marisol and Luna had looked so scared in the midst of their mourning. They were terrified that Yasmin's murderer might come after them next.

Neve froze. The white-hot panic that had overwhelmed her at the news of Yasmin's death turned to a bone-chilling cold as Marisol's words flooded her mind.

You murderer.

Holy shit. They think I did it.

"Steady," a female voice said as Neve swayed. Her tone was authoritative rather than kind. Definitely not Ms. Eagen's nervous squeak. It was someone more controlled, more accustomed to dealing with stressful situations. "You're okay."

She felt two hands grab her outstretched arm, and she leaned into them, allowing the stranger to keep her balanced. When she opened her eyes, Neve saw a woman with a tightly coiled bun and a bulky black uniform standing before her where Ms. Eagen had been. A female police officer.

"Ms. Lanier?" Principal Sanders's voice now. Over the officer's shoulder, Neve saw that the principal's office door stood wide open. "Is she okay?"

"She's in shock," the officer said. The strength in her voice and body was both comforting and alarming. "Can you walk?"

Neve nodded, free hand still clamped over her mouth. She didn't trust herself to speak with vomit churning in her belly.

"Why don't we talk somewhere private?" the officer continued, guiding Neve toward Principal Sanders's office. "We've called your father to come down while we ask you some questions."

Right, of course. They'd need him there before they asked her anything substantive. Like whether or not she'd murdered her ex–best friend.

New voices emerged from the quad outside the school office, where a small crowd of students had gathered, whispering as they watched Neve and the police officer.

"Are they arresting her?"

"Who?"

"Neve Lanier!"

"That's enough," Principal Sanders said, ushering Neve and the police officer inside her office. She turned to Ms. Eagen before she shut the door. "Please hold my calls."

This wasn't Neve's first time in Sanders's lair: She'd been summoned last semester, in the wake of Yasmin's betrayal. Principal Sanders had made it very clear that while she didn't condone the texted innuendo in regard to another LCC student, technically Neve hadn't done anything wrong. Her words weren't threatening. She hadn't violated any laws. But she also couldn't expect any protection from the administration unless she felt her personal safety was at risk. Basically, she was on her own.

Which had been fine. Neve had neither hoped for nor desired Principal Sanders's interference, which she figured would only make the situation on the ground that much worse for her, and at the time had only wanted to get the hell out of her office as quickly as possible, before the whole school knew she'd been there. But that interview came back to her in exquisite detail as she felt the heavy oak door click into place behind her, and the need to escape boiled up within her afresh.

Neve sat down in one of two stiff-backed faux leather chairs that stood perfectly parallel to each other in front of Principal Sanders's desk. The female officer didn't take the seat beside Neve, reserving it, theoretically, for Neve's dad, and instead sat in one of the old metal cafeteria chairs that lined a wall of the tight office. She didn't say a word, deferring to Principal Sanders, but Neve felt the officer's eyes on her, watching.

"We will wait until your father arrives to ask you any questions, Neve," Principal Sanders began, slowly lowering herself into the black executive chair behind her sleek glass-topped desk. "But I want you to know that I have filled Officer Hernández in on your, er, conflict with Yasmin Attar last year."

Normally, Neve would have snort-laughed at the idea of Yasmin's betrayal being described as a *conflict*, but she was still too much in shock to have normal reactions to anything. She was fighting to remain upright in her chair, resisting a deep, primal urge to lie down on the floor and go to sleep.

"Did you hear me?" Principal Sanders said.

"She's still in shock," Officer Hernández said. Again, authoritative but quiet. Neve kind of liked her style.

Principal Sanders let out a guttural *hrmm*. "In my experience, high school students are very rarely shocked by anything."

"Perhaps," Officer Hernández said softly. "But this is murder."

Neve flinched at the word, as if she'd been stabbed. *Yasmin was murdered.* It still seemed fantastical. Impossible. Maybe there'd been some mistake?

In her bag, Neve felt her phone vibrate again, but she made no move to answer it. Probably her dad. He'd be here soon enough.

Sanders twittered about her desk, organizing papers, logging into her desktop computer, and generally moving with the kind of nervous energy indicative of a person who abhors a vacuum. A stark contrast to Officer Hernández, who was perfectly at ease. She sat very still, knees apart, elbows resting on her thighs. Her head was tipped forward as if she were staring intently at the floor, but Neve noticed that her eyes, large and brown and painfully observant, routinely flicked up toward Neve's face.

What was she looking for? If she truly believed that Neve was in shock, that should at least count toward her innocence: Despite her recent acting success, Neve would have to give an Oscar-worthy performance to fake the kind of panic and grief she'd felt when she heard the news about Yasmin.

She felt tears welling up in her eyes as she sat in that uncomfortable chair, staring at Principal Sanders's desk. Yasmin was dead. Her friend was dead. Though she was still furious with her, Neve couldn't ignore the hole she felt in her heart as the realization of her loss sank in. She hated Yasmin, but she'd loved her, too. They'd shared so much during their junior year—laughter, tears, goofiness, dreams—and though it had ultimately been Neve's undoing, Yasmin had known her better than anyone else alive. And now she was gone.

The tears spilled down Neve's cheeks, but she didn't even wipe them away, letting them drip off her chin onto her black pleated skirt as she stared straight ahead, past Principal Sanders's disapproving pout, out the large picture window that opened onto the main parking lot. Long rows of solar panels soaked up the late-summer sunshine while simultaneously shielding the student body's luxury cars from those same harmful rays. Yasmin used to park her Tesla there, and she'd wait for Neve under the awning every morning, leaning back against her car as Neve trudged up the sidewalk from the bus stop. They'd enter school together. A team. And now Neve would never see her face again.

The radio affixed to Officer Hernández's shoulder crackled to life, and Neve jumped in her chair, then quickly wiped her cheeks with the sleeve of her sweater. Had Officer Hernández seen her weeping?

"This is Hernández," she said into the mouthpiece of her radio.

"Mr. Lanier has arrived," a male voice replied, his words somewhat garbled by the receiver.

"Copy." She looked up at Neve. "My partner, Officer Lee, is bringing your father in now."

Neve felt her stomach tighten. Her poor dad. In the week since he'd retrieved her from GLAM camp, she'd seen him happier, more relaxed, and less anxious than he'd been in years. It was as if Neve had finally found the secret formula to restoring her dad to the way he used to be. If Neve was happy, he was happy. And Yasmin's name never came up anymore. Now this. Would it remind him of the night he drove to the Attar house in a blind rage and threatened Yasmin's parents? Tempers had flared, the police had been called, and though the Attars didn't press charges, there had been a strict warning from the police: Neve and her dad were not to have any contact with Yasmin or her parents.

Watching his daughter questioned by the police in regard to Yasmin's murder might set his mental health recovery back months or even years.

The office door swung open, flooding the silent room with a cacophony of ringing phones and angry voices.

"What's going on?" Neve's dad's voice was breathless as he hurried inside. "Why are you holding my daughter?"

Officer Hernández rose slowly to her feet. "Mr. Lanier? My name is Officer Hernández." She gestured to the male cop who had filled the doorway behind Neve's dad. "And this is my partner, Officer Lee. Your daughter isn't being charged with anything. We just want to ask her some questions about her friend and needed to have you present before we began."

"Principal Sanders?" Ms. Eagen appeared behind Officer Lee in the doorway, waving down her boss. "We have calls from parents and the local news, and I don't know what to—"

"No comment!" Principal Sanders snapped, cutting her off. Did the entire city know about Yasmin's murder?

"But—"

Officer Lee didn't let her finish her question, closing the door in Ms. Eagen's face.

"Please take a seat, Mr. Lanier," Principal Sanders said, gesturing to the chair beside Neve.

Neve half expected her dad to meekly comply, but instead, he stood squarely behind Neve with a protective hand on her shoulder. "What is this in regard to?" It had been a long time since her dad, a former IT executive, had used so forceful a tone, and it jolted her out of whatever shock still lingered.

"The death of one of our students," Principal Sanders replied. Her eyes darted to the phone on her desk, and Neve noticed that every single line seemed to have a flashing light next to it.

"And why would this concern my daughter?"

Principal Sanders sighed. "Because Neve and Yasmin had a somewhat complicated history."

Her dad gasped. "Yasmin's dead?" Neve felt his grip on her shoulder tighten.

"Yes." Officer Hernández stood up and walked behind Principal Sanders's desk to get a good look at Neve and her dad. "I know you and your daughter have a history with the Attar family, so perhaps I should explain why we're asking for Neve's cooperation."

The reference to her dad's confrontation with Yasmin seemed to steel his resolve, and instead of caving, he turned even more combative. "No need." He reached down and took Neve's hand. "Because you're not getting it. My daughter hasn't seen Yasmin Attar in months, so if you want to accuse Neve of murder, you'll have to arrest her."

Then he pulled Neve none too gently from her chair and whisked her out of the office.

Neve and her dad drove in silence, which was fine. Neve needed to think.

Yasmin was dead. And it must have happened recently, because it seemed as if everyone was just finding out. Marisol and Luna looked as if they'd heard the news mere moments before Neve arrived, and judging by the flurry of phone calls at the school office, the information had started to trickle out to parents as well.

Had it happened that morning? The night before? Had Yasmin been out and not come home? Or had someone broken into the house and . . .

Neve swallowed, picturing every detail of Yasmin's room, from the floral comforter to the princess vanity she'd had since she was eight to the framed inspirational quotes she hung on the wall.

YOU ARE AMAZING!

FOLLOW YOUR DREAMS, THEY KNOW THE WAY.

YESTERDAY. NOW. TOMORROW.

She'd spent so many hours in that room it had practically been a second home, and to imagine Yasmin's body there, dead . . . Neve shivered, suddenly cold.

How could this have happened?

The Attars had an alarm system they put on every night, so it couldn't have been an intruder. Maybe a mugging? That seemed out of character for sleepy, suburban Carlsbad. Or maybe Marisol and Luna were right— there was a killer on the loose.

Only one thing was sure: Yasmin's death was definitely being investigated as a murder. Officer Hernández had used that word. There was no way it had been a mistake.

Her phone buzzed again, the third time in the last half hour, and this time she knew it wasn't her dad. His phone was right there, tucked into the cup holder. Had he told her mom what was going on? Or worse, Grandma K? The last thing she needed right now was a lecture.

Curious, Neve slipped her phone out of her bag and swiped open her text messages. As expected, there were two from her dad, the first asking if she was okay, and a second more frantic text asking what was going on. But the third and most recent came from a number she didn't recognize, and the message sent a chill straight to her heart.

Your turn, BFF.

SIXTEEN

BFF.

That's what Diane had scribbled on the note she left for Neve in her GLAM dorm room, only this text didn't come from Diane's cell. Why would she be texting Neve from an unknown number at nine o'clock when she'd used her regular number at six? And what the hell did *your turn* mean?

If I took care of Yasmin and you got rid of Javier.

Neve's temples throbbed as she recalled the conversation from the last night of GLAM. She couldn't have. It was just a fantasy, a joke. Neither of them was actually thinking about murder. There had to be another explanation.

Neve's hands shook as she typed a response.

Who is this?

What do you mean my turn?

The reply came back immediately.

You know.

Then a pause before another text.

I did my part. Now it's your turn.

All of Neve's revenge daydreams about Yasmin flashed before her, from her ex-bestie contracting a disfiguring disease like a mutant strain of leprosy that left her mangled and gross, to an epic case of mono, to pointing a gun at Yasmin and making her confess everything she'd done and beg for forgiveness. Those daydreams were her subconscious way of working through trauma and crisis, which was perfectly normal.

As long as you didn't act upon them.

This was *actual* murder. Yasmin was *actually* dead. Mr. and Mrs. Attar were *ACTUALLY* going to have to bury their only child.

"I'm sorry about your friend," her dad said at last. His voice was soft and subdued, but it sounded like a trumpet blast through the muddled fog that was Neve's mind. She jumped, her mind so far away that it took her a moment to remember where she was.

"You okay?" Her dad darted a look at her sidelong.

No. "Yeah."

"Really?"

She swallowed, trying to control herself enough to make the next lie sound more believable than the last. "In shock still, I think."

"Okay." He cleared his throat. Her dad was about to launch into an official parental monologue, which was the last thing Neve wanted to deal with as her brain swirled around the mysterious texts. "I know how you felt about Yasmin, but losing her like this is still traumatic. And trauma makes the brain react in strange ways. Laughing when you feel only sadness. Sitting calmly when you actually feel like your insides are trying to jump out through your skin. Rage that . . . that seems to come out of nowhere."

Now it was Neve's turn to cast a furtive glance at her dad. He drove with his eyes locked on the road, hands firmly at ten and two, but his shoulders were raised halfway to his ears and he bent forward at the waist as he drove, both of which were signs of escalating anxiety.

Was he trying to convince Neve that her reactions had been justified, or himself?

"I didn't kill Yasmin." Neve wasn't exactly sure what the appropriate reply was when your father thought maybe you killed someone. She wanted to take out her phone and show her dad the texts from the mysterious number but realized that would probably make the situation worse, not better.

"Of course you didn't." It was a matter-of-fact statement, not a comforting one, and once again, Neve realized he was making it more for his benefit than hers. Shit. If her own father didn't believe her, how would anyone else? She was so boned.

Neve ground her teeth as her dad pulled his electric car into the garage, more pissed off than scared about her current situation. She couldn't even look at him while he plugged the car in, just grabbed her bag and bolted for her room.

Had Diane really texted her and claimed responsibility for Yasmin's murder, or was Neve's brain so addled with shock and mourning that she was reading into an otherwise innocent conversation? She pulled out her phone and read through the texts again.

Your turn, BFF.

You know.

I did my part. Now it's your turn.

It was the *BFF* that made Neve assume the texts came from Diane, but again, why would she be using a different phone number than the one she usually texted from?

Maybe because the texts weren't from Diane at all.

But who else would want to fuck with her? Who else knew about Yasmin's death?

The answer was pretty obvious: Marisol and Luna.

She sat down on the edge of her bed and stared at the messages, formulating a response. The texts gave no specifics, just innuendo. Like they were trying to get her to incriminate herself. Neve typed quickly, fingers steadied by her rage.

Ha, good one. Marisol? Luna? Or is it both of you?

I'm pretty sure there's a law against accusing someone of murder.

She waited, eyes fixed to the screen until a response came back.

You know what you said.

Neve rolled her eyes. This reeked of entrapment. Did Marisol and Luna really think she was stupid enough to admit to a murder she didn't commit? She was practically laughing as she responded.

If you have information about Yasmin's death, I suggest you contact the police.

That should shut them up. They had no evidence, nothing more than conjecture. But instead of falling silent in their defeat, the phone buzzed long and loud as an incoming call from the unknown number lit up Neve's screen.

"What do you want?" she said, hoping there was no shake to her voice.

"Hey you!" the voice on the other line was upbeat and perky, and though it was a voice Neve recognized, it didn't belong to Marisol or Luna.

"Diane?"

"Duh. Who did you think it was?"

Neve's calm abandoned her. "What the fuck did you do?"

Diane snorted. "What we talked about. What you *asked* me to do."

"I never asked you to do anything." *This can't be happening. This can't be happening.*

"Uh-huh," Diane said, a hint of giggle in her voice. Neve could picture her nose wrinkling up as she laughed, as if she was making a joke about camp or a cute girl or something. "Sure you did."

Neve rose to her feet, her knees shaking so badly she thought she might fall backward onto her bed again. "Diane, tell me what you did."

"Okay!" She paused, and when she spoke again, the bubbly, outgoing Diane had vanished and a steely, cold bitch had taken her place. "But not on the phone, get it? We meet in person."

Meet up alone with a murderer. Not exactly high on Neve's to-do list.

"I'm not going to do anything to you," Diane said. As always, she could read Neve's mind. "I need you."

Need me to kill your stepbrother. "No way."

"Yes, way." Even though it wasn't a video call, Neve could see Diane's lips curling into a broad smile. "You're going to fulfill your side of this bargain. Or else."

"You're insane."

"Labels." Diane sighed. "Pick a quiet place. Public, if you want. Like a beach."

Neve bit her bottom lip. She thought she knew this person, trusted her, and now it was as if Diane had been replaced by an impostor. Like in *The Maltese Falcon* when Sam Spade discovered his innocent client Ruth

Wonderly was really the not-so-innocent Brigid O'Shaughnessy. This was not her Diane.

"If you don't pick a place, I'll show up at your house," Diane said, interpreting Neve's silence as defiance. "Might be nice to meet your parents and your sister."

Neve stiffened. That was a threat, unmistakably. If Diane *had* murdered Yasmin, what would stop her from hurting someone else? Someone Neve cared more about?

"There's a stretch of beach north of Pelican Point," Neve said, grasping at the first place that came to mind. "Near the parking lot."

"One hour," Diane said. Then, without waiting for Neve to answer, she ended the call.

SEVENTEEN

YASMIN WASN'T ANSWERING HER PHONE. NEVE KNEW IT WAS *an intentional snub after the thirty-seventh or so attempt, but she hit the call button again with a shaky finger and waited all six rings before the call went to voicemail.*

She didn't leave a message, because she'd already left four. As soon as she'd gotten home from school she'd tried calling Yasmin, unwilling to do so on the public bus ride home, especially since there were two sophomores a few rows behind her still whispering about Neve's epic callout that morning at school.

Neve had been completely blindsided to find Marisol, Luna, and Yasmin waiting for her at her locker. They confronted her about a screengrab of a text Neve had sent to Yasmin. Marisol spreads faster than the plague *had apparently gone viral, thanks to Yasmin, and when Neve pulled out her phone to show Marisol how the real conversation had gone down, she found that the rest of the conversation had been deleted. It was her word against Yasmin's.*

No contest.

The rest of the day had been a complete nightmare. Between classes, people shouted comments like "Slut shamer!" *and* "Girl traitor!" *at her in the hallway, and when she opened her locker at lunch, she found half a dozen death threats had been shoved inside. Yasmin avoided her. She skipped the one class they had together and the rest of the day she spent attached to Marisol and Luna. The third musketeer. Neve wasn't even sure how she made it through the day other than that she was focused on one thing: talking to Yasmin after school to find out why she would do this.*

Call number thirty-nine, and Neve had no expectation that it would go any differently than the rest, so she was completely caught off guard when Yasmin actually picked up the phone.

"What?" *Yasmin barked, as if she was the one who was the victim.*

"Yasmin?" *Neve began, her voice cracking.* "Why . . . I don't understand what happened."

"I shared your wretched text. Not much to understand." *Her voice sounded hollow, like she was answering from a cavernous space.*

"But why would you do that?"

"I'm a girl ally," *Yasmin said.* "Not a girl traitor."

Neve had to laugh. "You said like a million things worse about Marisol and Luna."

Yasmin paused. "Says you."

"Why are you doing this?" *Neve repeated. She felt the sob well up in her chest and could not repress it.*

Yasmin sighed, heavy and labored, as if Neve asking for justification of her betrayal was too much of a burden. "Look, it wasn't personal, okay? I felt like I needed to level up."

"How is that not personal?!" Neve screamed into the phone. If Yasmin had been in the room, she might have slapped her.

On the other end of the phone, Neve heard someone knocking on a door. "Yasmin, you okay in there?" A guy's voice.

Then suddenly, Neve knew exactly why she'd been thrown under the bus. "The guy from the party. Hazel Eyes."

"I'll be right out!" Yasmin replied, her voice light and cheerful. Then she dropped her voice and practically hissed into the phone. "Yeah, that's right. We're friends now and who knows from there. Sorry, Neve. You lost."

Then she ended the call.

Neve sighed as she parked her dad's Chevy Bolt in the public lot above a lonely stretch of state beach. Her last communication with Yasmin was still painful to relive, only now instead of impotent rage, Neve felt an overwhelming sadness.

There were several cars parked nearby, including a couple of camper vans that were commonplace up and down the San Diego coast, but Neve had managed to find an isolated spot near the north end of the lot where a pathway led down to the sand. This way she had full sight lines in every direction, plus it would ensure that foot traffic would pass by her car while she was having her meet and greet with Diane.

She gazed out over the Pacific Ocean, stretching north and south in a long, straight line of blue and gray, the shallow patch of beach smoothed by the encroaching waves and broken only by the occasional, and currently abandoned, lifeguard stand. Strings of whitecaps rolled inland, the foaming waves breaking in both directions, fanning in beautiful symmetry before washing up over the sun-bleached sand. This had been one of Yasmin's favorite places to hang out, especially at sunset, and suddenly Neve felt like an asshole for suggesting it as a meeting place.

"Get out of the car."

Neve nearly screamed at the sound of Diane's voice. So much for open sight lines. Diane had seemingly materialized out of nowhere at the car window—Neve hadn't seen her BMW pull in nor had she heard the crunch of approaching footsteps on the gravel. But there Diane stood, just on the other side of the glass, glaring down at Neve.

She looked the same, superficially at least. Same silky blond hair, fashionable clothes, perfect makeup. And yet Neve felt as if she were staring at a stranger. GLAM Diane's airy-fairy brightness and positivity had vanished, replaced by combative arms folded across her chest and a sharp chin thrust forward in challenge. The ever-present hint of a smile that had lived around her mouth last week had completely vanished. The corners were tight now, lips pressed together, and her wide eyes were narrowed, reflecting only cold, harsh determination.

Neve felt like Edward G. Robinson in *Scarlet Street* when he finds out that Joan Bennett has been playing him all along. Only that ended with him stabbing her to death with an ice pick.

Why didn't I bring an ice pick?

"Get out," Diane repeated.

Much to Neve's horror, she did exactly what she was told, slowly opening the door as Diane stepped aside. She climbed out and awaited further instructions. The actions were meek, submissive, and felt foreign to Neve, who practically lived her life with a giant DON'T TELL ME WHAT TO DO banner flying above her. But she felt broken in Diane's presence. Weak and hopeless.

The same way she'd felt on that last phone call with Yasmin.

"Where's your phone?" Diane barked.

Neve glanced through the car window at her phone sitting in the cup holder.

"Good." Then without even asking, she unfolded her arms and began patting down Neve's body. Arms, legs—her fingers slipped into the pockets of her jacket and even combed through Neve's hair, actions that might have given Neve a thrill a week ago but now filled her with revulsion.

"What are you doing?"

"Looking for bugs," she said simply. "Recording devices."

"Okay." Diane was giving her more credit than she deserved. She probably should have thought to bring something like that to record this conversation. That and the ice pick. But she was an idiot.

Diane continued her search, even checking the soles of Neve's Mary Janes to make sure she didn't have anything taped to the bottom. Satisfied at last, she stood up and flicked her head toward the beach path. "Let's go for a walk."

The beach wasn't crowded at this hour on a weekday, but there were a few people here and there: joggers, dog walkers. There were even some toddlery-looking kids with their grandma, poking around in the rocks with sticks. All perfectly normal if your brand of normal was taking a beach stroll with a murderer.

Diane is a murderer. Neve let that idea seep in for a hot second. Could she really believe it? She'd trusted Diane. Cared for her. Was it possible she'd killed Yasmin? Neve wasn't completely convinced it had happened.

Everybody is somebody's fool.

They passed the first lifeguard stand, and Diane paused to look around, assessing their location. They were pretty much alone: The kids and their grandma were the nearest humans, and even if they'd theoretically been close enough to pick up pieces of conversation, the roar of the incoming waves would have drowned out Neve's and Diane's voices. If Diane wanted to have a private tête-à-tête, this was as good a place as any.

"Why are we here?" Neve started, hanging on to the last shred of hope that this was all some elaborate joke.

Diane's eyes were still sweeping the beach and the dunes behind them. "We need to discuss our plan."

"Our plan?"

"The one we made the last night at GLAM." Diane paused, but Neve refused to say a word. After a moment, Diane sighed, resigned to spelling it out. "The one where I take care of your problem and you take care of mine."

"I don't know what you're talking about."

Diane arched an eyebrow. "Oh really?" She reached into the pocket of her jeans and pulled out her phone. As soon as she swiped on the screen, an audio recording began to play, and despite the roar of the waves, Neve could clearly discern her own voice coming through the tinny speaker.

"I could kill Yasmin. And I'd totally murder Javier for you."

Neve's stomach sank as if she were falling through the sand into an endless pit. Her words from the last night of camp, taken out of context and edited together, sounded like one hell of a confession. "You recorded that?"

Diane rolled her eyes. "Duh."

"Why?"

"Because I didn't think you were in love with me enough to kill for me."

She knew Neve had been falling for her. Ugh.

"And because most people don't like to commit murder. They need a little push."

"Do *you* like committing murder?"

And though Neve supposed she meant the comment facetiously, the tiny, secretive smile that crept onto Diane's face caused a steely chill to spread from the tips of Neve's fingers up her arms to her chest. She shivered, the coldness seeping through her skin and into her bones as if one of the big waves had washed over her, dousing her in the frigid northern Pacific.

"Why are you being so puritanical?" Diane said at last with a heavy, beleaguered sigh. Like she was the most put-upon girl in the entire universe. "I took care of Yasmin. Gone. Dead. Surprisingly simple."

"What did you do to her?" Neve asked sharply. She wasn't sure she wanted to know, but she *needed* to know.

Diane waved off the question. "She hardly felt a thing. Don't even think she woke up."

Diane had gotten into her house? How?

"Now you need to return the favor." Diane barreled forward, all business. "Like you promised to do on this recording."

This can't be happening. "You set me up." Just like Yasmin. She'd been playing Neve. That whole time at GLAM. Their friendship, their bond, all lies. And when she felt that she didn't have Neve hooked as deeply as she wanted, she'd resorted to blackmail.

"Here's how this is going to work," Diane said, sounding impatient. She was glancing around again, fidgety. "You're going to kill Javier for me."

"No way."

Diane ignored her. "This week. Otherwise I'm going to take this"—she jiggled her phone in Neve's face—"to the police."

Neve's eyes drifted to the phone. She could grab it. Toss it into the ocean. The evidence would be gone with the retreating waves.

"Don't even think about it." Diane smiled, tight and grim. "I've got it backed up in, like, ten different places."

Fine. She should have known Diane would be a step or two ahead of her. She had been all along. "I'm not going to do what you want."

"Then I hope you like prison."

Neve thought of Officer Hernández, her sharp eyes and her practical mindedness. She might believe Neve's story. Diane had that recording, but there wouldn't be any crime scene evidence that Neve committed murder. DNA. Fingerprints. Neve had watched enough *Law & Order* reruns with her parents to know that the recording would merely be circumstantial.

Besides, as the shock of her situation was wearing off, anger was filling the void. She wasn't going to be bullied or manipulated by this crazy person. She wasn't a puppet, and despite whatever Diane believed, she wasn't weak.

"Fine," she said, calling Diane's bluff. "Good luck with that." She trudged through the sand toward her dad's black car, her mind fixed on Officer Hernández. She was going to head to the Carlsbad police station right freaking now and tell her everything.

But Diane wasn't done. "You think that's the only evidence I have?"

Evidence. As if. "Don't care," Neve shouted over her shoulder. She wasn't going to let Diane control her. Well, not anymore.

"Would you care if I told you this evidence relates to your dad?"

It was the second time that day Diane had mentioned her family. Neither had been a direct threat, but bringing them up had felt pointed. Ominous. Neve might have been able to face her own fate with defiance, but not her dad's. She swung back around, arms crossed protectively over her chest. "What about him?"

Once again, Diane turned to her phone. After a few short swipes and taps, she turned it around. The image on the screen froze Neve's heart.

It was Yasmin, asleep in her bed. Neve recognized the floral comforter and lace-edged shams. But then Diane swiped to the next photo, and Neve realized that Yasmin wasn't sleeping.

It was a photo of a hand. No, not just *a* hand. It was Yasmin's hand, draped across her floral duvet cover. The distinctive ring on her middle finger—calligraphic letters of Yasmin's name written in Farsi—was impossible to mistake, as was the deep blue nail polish. Yoga-ta Get This Blue! was Yasmin's favorite shade, and it really popped in Diane's photo, accentuated by the trickles of red liquid that snaked down her forearm across her wrist, over the ring, and then dripped artistically from the blue tip of her middle finger.

Neve didn't register right away that it was blood. Yasmin's blood. This was literally a photo of the life draining out of her former friend.

"Knife to the heart," Diane said softly. Almost a whisper. "She never even opened her eyes."

But Neve was hardly listening. At that moment, she didn't care how her old friend had died. Her eyes were fixed on something gripped in Yasmin's hand. It looked like a scrap of fabric.

"Is that . . . green tweed?"

"Yep."

Neve felt all the warmth drain from her face, replaced by a creeping, prickling chill. She knew that fabric, had seen it every day for the past three years since her dad was released from the hospital and started wearing a hat to cover his newly thinning hair. It was the same fabric as his Trinity cap.

Which he wasn't wearing this morning.

"It was torn from the hat her attacker wore," Diane said cheekily. "Or at least that's what the police will conclude if they ever find it."

"How . . ." Neve tensed. "You were in my house?"

"Your parents aren't great about locking that sliding door."

The thought of Diane rummaging through their stuff while the family was out made Neve's skin crawl, but she refused to let Diane see that she was getting to her.

"Even if you're telling the truth and that *actually* came from my dad's hat, the police will be able to tell that it was planted." Would they? She had no idea, but it was a good bluff.

Diane laughed. "Oh, please, *you* don't even believe that."

Neve grimaced. Her emotional transparency had failed her again.

"I don't care what Kellie said—you're not a very good actress."

"Fuck you."

"That hat will be crawling with your dad's hair, easily tying him to the crime scene. Plus, I understand your dad has a history with the Attars. A motive. Something the police know all about."

No one was supposed to know about her dad's threats against Yasmin, since the police never filed charges. "How did you know that?"

Diane ignored the question. "You may not give a fuck about your own future, but I seriously doubt you'd like to see your precious, fragile daddy doing hard time at San Quentin."

Rage boiled inside Neve. She balled her hands into tight fists, aching to take a swing at Diane's smug face, and clenched her jaw so ferociously she thought her teeth might shatter from the force. She'd spent much of her high school years obsessively watching old noir movies where people are moved to incredible acts of violence through the rage of betrayals, and though she'd always appreciated those scenes for their starkness and theatrics, she'd never really understood the emotion behind them.

Until now. She hated her former friend, more than she'd ever hated Yasmin. Neve had never thought herself capable of murder, but as her vision narrowed on Diane, still holding the photo of Yasmin's hand for her to see, she could imagine standing over Diane's lifeless body on the ground, posed like Yasmin's, while Neve still held the bloody knife in her hands.

"You fucking bitch." It was all Neve could manage.

"I've been called worse."

I'm sure.

"Javier takes batting practice every day after school on the Holy Name baseball field. Usually alone, just him and the pitching machine."

Of course she'd already scoped out the best way to do it.

"And don't even think about going to the cops, or you know who'll get an anonymous tip about the whereabouts of your dad's hat."

Damn it. Diane really had thought of everything.

She stepped closer, her cold, calculating eyes fixed on Neve's. "One week." She felt Diane's humid breath on her cheek. "I'll be watching."

EIGHTEEN

NEVE DROVE HOME ON AUTOPILOT. SHE COULD HAVE BEEN navigating a blizzard, weaving through a Mardi Gras parade, or fleeing a freaking alien invasion and she wouldn't have noticed. All she could see, all she could think about, was Diane.

Who was batshit fucking insane.

This person that Neve trusted, cared for, thought she knew on an extremely intimate level was actually such an outright sociopath that she murdered a complete stranger just to manipulate Neve into offing her stepbrother. Neve had somehow ended up in her own noir plot, where Diane was a seductress like Barbara Stanwyck in *Double Indemnity* with her blond wig and alluring anklet, seducing an unsuspecting insurance salesman into murdering her husband. That's what Neve had been reduced to—a hapless Fred MacMurray who killed for money and a woman and didn't get either.

Pretty, isn't it?

Except this wasn't a movie, so there was no script to read from. Neve was still in possession of her own free will, which left one very important question:

What the fuck am I going to do?

Realistically, she had two choices: kill Javier or not. By going the non-murder route, she'd be risking not only her own freedom but her dad's. She probably could have handled jail, an arrest, a trial, but her dad? Diane was right—he was fragile, and one or way or another, prison time would be the end of him.

But the other option entailed killing someone. Not pranking him, not exacting revenge—literally ending some guy's life.

Which was exactly what Diane had done. In fact, she'd bragged about how easy it had been to plunge a knife into Yasmin while she was sleeping. Had Yasmin felt anything? Seen it coming? Had she opened her eyes the moment the blade pierced her skin or had she gone to sleep that night and never woken up?

Neve pictured Yasmin's blood-drenched body on her bed and wondered who had found her. Yasmin's mom, probably. What had Mrs. Attar felt in that moment? The horror, the panic, the shrieks. As much as Neve hated Yasmin, she couldn't imagine inflicting that kind of pain on her or her family.

Of course, Diane didn't know Yasmin or the Attar family. Had that made it easier? Would killing Javier be emotionally painless simply because she had no connection to him? She thought about *Strangers on a Train*, which reminded her of this horrible situation. The playboy villain had been so cavalier when he strangled that tennis player's wife. Was that because he was a psychopath or because her life or death meant nothing to him outside of his own gains?

In the movie, the main character didn't uphold his end of the bargain, but in the book, which Neve had devoured in a day, the guy absolutely went through with it, though guilt eventually consumed him. Still, a normal person had been able to kill a stranger. Could she do the same?

"What the actual fuck?" she said out loud as she pulled into her driveway. She was contemplating murder. That was *not* okay.

The house was quiet when Neve opened the door that led from the garage to the laundry room, hoping to find her dad waiting for her at the dining room table with that stupid Trinity cap—intact and unmarred—firmly fixed on his head, but the room was empty. Based on the stillness, Neve was pretty sure he'd gone to sleep soon after they'd arrived home and hadn't gotten out of bed yet, hadn't even noticed that she had taken the car. She walked over to the sliding glass door and noted that it was unlocked.

"God damn it!" she screamed as she flipped the latch. She was angry—at herself, at Diane, and at her dad not only for his lax parenting but also because she really, *really* needed to talk to him.

Are you sure about that?

Neve slumped against the glass door. It was true. How, exactly, would he be able to help her? He'd tell her to go to the police, consequences be damned, and tell them the truth. Which was the right thing to do. The smart thing to do. Neve totally recognized that.

Then she pictured her father being arrested, taken away in handcuffs.

The mug shots, the trial. Her dad wearing an orange jumpsuit, trying to survive in prison. Was that really the "smart" thing to do?

One week. I'll be watching.

Neve slunk back to her room, feeling defeated. Yasmin had been a selfish, backstabbing bitch, and based on Diane's stories of Javier's assault and harassment, he was also a terrible human being. Yet neither of them deserved to die. She couldn't save Yasmin, but she could make sure that Javier didn't suffer the same fate. She needed time to figure out how to beat Diane—trick her into a confession or something—and until then she was going to have to play along.

Which meant she was going to batting practice.

Neve parked in the student lot at Holy Name Academy the next afternoon. The lot, perched on the side of a hill between the athletic fields and the main campus, was mostly empty by the time she arrived, which was a good thing. Neve didn't want anyone to see what she was doing.

That morning, Neve wasn't even sure if she could get to La Jolla. She had converted to distance learning for the foreseeable future, a plan suggested by Principal Sanders, and had sat around all day doing not much other than obsessing about how to convince her dad she needed the car. She'd constructed a whole elaborate story about a therapist and a last-minute appointment and needing to go alone. Taking her dad's car in the afternoon meant he'd have to make alternate arrangements for picking Deirdre up from school, so Neve wanted to make sure the whole scenario sounded really important and plausible, but her dad had merely smiled, sent two quick texts, and told Neve she could have the car for as long as she needed it.

So much for backstory.

Much like when she'd met Diane at the beach, Neve had chosen a spot away from what few cars remained in the student parking lot but that still afforded her a good view of the athletic fields. Below her, the football team was breaking up practice, players dragging their gear up the path beside the bleachers that led to the main campus buildings, while coaches and assistants packed up equipment in a series of storage lockers housed beneath the stadium seating.

The adjacent baseball field was less populated; at first Neve thought maybe Diane's intel had been wrong and Javier didn't take batting practice that late in the day, but as she stared at the field, she noticed that there was something perched on the pitcher's mound. A big red box on wheels. The pitching machine, just like Diane promised. Moments later, a solitary figure emerged from the dugout, bat in hand, and approached the box before striding back to home plate.

Javier.

Confirming that no one was paying attention to her, Neve slipped a pair of binoculars out of her bag. They were Deirdre's pride and joy, the astronomical pair she'd gotten for Christmas last year, and she'd have an unholy fit if she discovered them missing, but it was a risk Neve felt like she had to take. She needed to make this look good.

Because though she couldn't see anyone else around, she was one hundred percent sure that Diane was watching.

So "looking good" was the key here. Diane said she wasn't a good actress, but Neve was about to prove her wrong by playing the role of a murderer stalking her prey. But just acting the part.

Because she sure as fuck wasn't going to actually kill this guy today.

Was she?

No, of course not.

Although she'd be lying if she said the thought hadn't crossed her mind. Maybe it was Diane's influence or her own noir-influenced macabre curiosity, but ever since she'd turned up Holy Name Road, she'd been examining the campus with a critical eye, planning the theoretical crime.

Earlier in the day, she'd thought about fiddling with the pitching machine so maybe it threw an errant ball at his head, but that would require actual mechanical or engineering knowledge—which she didn't possess—plus some luck in hoping that Javier's reflexes would be too slow for him to get out of the way. Once she saw the campus, perched on an isolated hillside and surrounded by majestic Torrey pines, she thought that maybe she could lure Javier into the trees, where no one would find the body for a while, then stab or strangle him. Though looking down at the tall, muscular figure currently hitting balls sky-high to left center, she decided that she wouldn't be able to overpower him. Not without help.

Which led to her current observation. Above the football bleachers, between the athletic field and the main school building, was a narrow road. An access pathway, probably for maintenance vehicles, that snaked back around the lower part of campus. The path was closed off from the student parking lot by a simple chain bearing a sign that read NO UNAUTHORIZED ACCESS. The football players crossed this access road in small groups before they disappeared into a side door of the large school building nearby. The gym. They were probably headed to the locker room.

And if they were going that way, so would Javier.

It would be pretty easy, depending on how long it took for the football team to clear the area. Once Javier was alone, she'd wait for him to head to the gym. Timing it perfectly, and with an electric car like her dad's Bolt that accelerated quickly and silently, she could blow through the chain barrier and mow him down as he stepped out from behind the bleachers. He'd never even see her coming. It was a perfect plan.

A line from *Strangers on a Train* popped into her brain: *"My theory is that everyone is a potential murderer."*

Maybe Bruno Antony was right.

She shook her head, raising the binoculars to her eyes. She wasn't here to actually *plan* Javier's death, only to make it look like she was. Until she could figure something else out.

But with just six days left until Diane's deadline, she was running out of time.

Neve adjusted the lenses on Deirdre's prized possession until the figure in the batting cage was crisp and clean. Javier's back was to her as he bent down to rub some dirt on the handle of his bat, his baggy athletic shorts and tank top more appropriate for a basketball court than a baseball field. He was tall, a fact she could discern even though he was bent at the waist, and muscular in that way that varsity athletes usually were. Neve had never understood how someone could put so much time and energy into something as capricious as the human body, even in a society where looks outweighed personality and intelligence when it came to how others assessed your worth. Jocks were the worst when it came to body vanity, and while she gazed at Javier through the binoculars, she could tell that he was one of those gym rats who probably measured his body fat on a daily, if not hourly, basis.

She was already predisposed to dislike Javier, based on Diane's depiction of him in her scene, and the muscle-bound, empty-headed jock standing alone in the batting cage only cemented the opinion she had already formed: one more soulless, heartless dickwad who didn't care about anyone but himself.

"Asshole."

Instantly, Javier straightened up and looked around the abandoned field, searching for something. There was no way in hell that he could have heard her—not only was she too far away, but the windows on her car were rolled up—but something had spooked him. Did Javier have any idea that his stepsister wanted him dead? Was he already on guard against anything unusual?

He turned around, facing the parking lot for the first time, and Neve gasped.

It wasn't that she was surprised Javier was handsome—jocks were usually good-looking, it came with the territory, so the chiseled chin, high cheekbones, and aquiline nose were expected—but because that handsome face and, more memorably, those soulful eyes, were familiar.

It was Hazel Eyes.

NINETEEN

THOUGH SHE'D ONLY SEEN HIM TWICE, NEVE WOULD HAVE recognized those eyes anywhere. They haunted her nightmares. Large and light and full of sadness, Javier's hazel eyes had been the cause of all her misery, the reason Yasmin had put her plan in action to elevate her social standing by destroying Neve's. Neve didn't even know this guy, yet she hated him.

Doubly so. Because he was also a sexual predator. Wow, Yasmin really knew how to pick them.

She yanked the binoculars away from her face. Was it a coincidence that

Yasmin's Hazel Eyes and Diane's stepbrother were one and the same? Diane couldn't have known about Neve's connection to Javier . . . could she?

Neve inhaled slowly, trying to process this new twist in her already crazed life, when a tap at the window sent her pulse racing again. She screamed involuntarily, half expecting to see Diane glaring at her through the window. But though she knew the person standing outside her car, it wasn't Diane.

"Charlotte?" Neve started the auxiliary power and rolled down the window.

"I thought that was you," Charlotte said, her face expressionless.

"What are you doing here?" Neve blurted out in confusion, realizing as soon as the words left her mouth that they would have been more appropriate if directed at Neve herself.

Charlotte glanced over her shoulder at the Spanish Revival facade of Holy Name Academy, then slowly turned back to Neve, eyebrows raised. "I go to school here."

"Right."

"And you?"

"Me?"

"Why are you here? Don't you live in Carlsbad?"

Neve felt the blush race up from her chest as she realized that she needed a reason to be twenty miles from home, sitting in a car by herself, stalking a strange guy at batting practice. "I'm . . . uh . . . waiting for a friend."

Charlotte tilted her head to the side. "Diane."

"Right."

Charlotte's eyes shifted down to the baseball field. "And watching her brother play baseball."

Shit.

Neve bit her lower lip, searching for some kind of lie that made sense as Charlotte continued to study her closely. She had no idea how she was going to explain this in a way that wasn't going to bite her in the ass later and realized with a twinge of anxiety that this was how people ended up as serial killers—one murder led to two led to ten. Was Neve the next Ted Bundy?

"Look, we didn't get to know each other at GLAM and that's totally my fault because, well, just *because*," Charlotte said, speaking more effusively than Neve had ever witnessed from her. "I realize that you have no reason at all to trust me but I really, really, *really* need to talk to you about—"

Neve's phone rang, interrupting Charlotte's words. She glanced down and saw the unknown number of Diane's secondary phone. Shit.

Was Diane watching her? Did she know she was talking to Charlotte? Was she about to drag another innocent person into this shitshow? "I gotta go."

"Wait!" Charlotte cried as Neve shifted the car into reverse. Charlotte reached out toward the car as if she could grab the side-view mirror and keep Neve from escaping.

But Neve ignored her. Whatever Charlotte wanted to say, it wasn't worth risking the girl's life for. She threw the car into drive and stomped on the accelerator so fiercely the electric car spun out on the asphalt before regaining traction and racing down the hill toward the main road.

"Who the hell were you talking to?" Diane's voice ripped through the car speakers the instant Neve accepted the call. If Neve didn't know better, she'd have thought Diane was jealous.

"Huh?"

"In the parking lot."

So she *had* been watching. Neve wondered where Diane had been hiding. In the school building? In another car in the parking lot? The creepy-crawly feeling returned, racing up Neve's arms and down her back. Diane's eyes were like a million spiders swarming her body.

"I wasn't making friends."

"I'm supposed to believe that some stranger walked up and started talking to you?" Diane snorted. "Not likely."

Diane had been close enough to see that Neve was talking to someone but not close enough to recognize it was Charlotte. Maybe she was on the other side of the baseball field?

"Do I need to remind you what's at stake for your dear old dad?" Diane continued. "Do I need to call Officer Hernández with an anonymous tip about—"

"No!"

"Who were you talking to?"

"It was Charlotte, okay? From GLAM. She recognized me."

Diane paused. "Charlotte Trainor?"

"Yeah. And I couldn't exactly mow Javier down with her standing there, okay?" Charlotte's unexpected appearance was fortuitous after all. It gave Neve an excellent excuse for not joining the murder club. Yet. "You're going to have to be patient."

"Oooo!" Diane squealed with delight. "Is that your plan? Run him down with your car?"

Neve felt sick to her stomach as Diane giggled. It was a glimpse of the old Diane—lighthearted and fun. She even elongated the vowels on *plan* and *car* like she used to. Except for the murdery context, it was like they were gossiping back at camp again.

"Good choice," Diane said, then sighed happily. "You're a natural at this, you know that?"

"I am *not* a natural murderer."

Diane ignored her. "But you'll have to do a full bleach clean of the car after."

"Um, okay." The way Diane talked, it was as if she'd done this before.

"But that's up to you. Not gonna tell you how to do your job."

"Great, thanks."

"Remember," Diane said, ignoring Neve's sarcasm. Her voice all business again. "You've got six days."

Then the phone went silent.

TWENTY

NEVE WAS BACK AT HOLY NAME THE NEXT AFTERNOON. SHE needed to be there, needed Diane to see her again, noticing her effort. But she absolutely, positively *wasn't* going to mow Javier down with her car. No way.

Except she hadn't exactly come up with a viable solution, and the only alternate plan she'd considered was basically another version of Diane's request. Kill someone.

Only in this plan, Diane would be the victim.

It made sense. If Diane died, her photographic and recorded "evidence" died with her. And if Neve *had* to murder someone, it might as well be Diane. She would be doing the world a favor by stopping a murderer from killing again.

Not that Neve would.

Unless she had to.

And so she was back at Holy Name. Hoping for new inspiration that didn't involve her earning a teardrop tattoo.

She'd waited until later in the afternoon this time, when more of the students had left campus for the day. Including Charlotte.

It was a cloudy afternoon, the sun's rays diffused through fluffy white-and-gray clouds that drifted onshore before a stiff wind, shadowing the athletic fields at Holy Name and giving the whole campus a rather gloomy, isolated atmosphere.

The football team had cleared the field by the time Neve parked in the near-abandoned student lot, with a few stragglers moseying up the hill toward the gym. The coaches and equipment managers had already hauled the team gear beneath the bleachers and cleared out, and as Neve cut the Bolt's battery, the last of the football team disappeared into the locker room.

Everything was still and quiet. Eerily so. The only movement was the occasional sway of the trees and the solitary figure on the baseball diamond.

Javier.

Like yesterday, he was taking batting practice from the pitching machine, but instead of the sleeveless shirt, he wore a zip-up athletic jacket and jogger's leggings, coving every inch of skin. Pitch after pitch, swing after swing. Sometimes he'd let a pitch or two hit the backstop while he fidgeted with his grip or adjusted his gloves, but for the most part, he was swinging at everything, launching liners and fly balls out of the infield with ease.

Neve wasn't even sure how long she watched Javier—his rhythmic routine was hypnotic—and time slipped by as she sat in the car until suddenly, he stopped and the world seemed to boot back up. The pitching machine must have been out of balls, which signaled the end of his practice, and Neve sat straighter in the driver's seat as she watched him jog around the field in the waning light, picking up his spray of white baseballs. He amassed an armful before he raced back to the machine at a full sprint. Rinse, repeat. Every single thing he did on the field was part of the workout. Typical jock.

Javier's cleanup effort took forever. Neve rapped impatiently on the steering wheel with her fingers, trying to hurry him up. Though why she was anxious for him to be done, she had no idea. It wasn't like she was actually waiting for him. She could leave at any time.

But she didn't.

My theory is that everyone is a potential murderer.

Finally, satisfied that he'd retrieved every last ball, Javier shouldered his bat with one hand and grabbed the front of the batting machine with the other. Tipping it back on two wheels, he dragged it off the field toward the storage lockers beneath the bleachers. Neve waited, holding her breath, while he disappeared from her view. Her heart was pounding when he reemerged, slowly trudging up the hill toward the gym.

This is it.

Um, would *have been it.*

If she'd actually been there to murder someone, this was the moment when she would have started the car, silent with its electric engine, and eased out of the parking spot. Javier was so deep in thought—head bent forward, staring at the asphalt—that he'd never even see her coming. She'd creep toward the chain barrier with her lights off, wait for him to step onto the path, then floor the pedal, snapping the chain like a twig as she barreled down on her victim before he'd even had a chance to—

Neve's morbid daydream was interrupted by a flash of movement at the far end of the gym. Way down where the access road disappeared around the side of the building, she caught a blur of black and a muted flash of light. She caught her breath for the second time. Careening around the gym, headed directly toward Javier, was a car.

It was as if Neve's murderous plan had leaped out of her head and into reality. The black car was stealthily silent, lights off, accelerating. Javier didn't see it, still wrapped up in his own thoughts as he slowly meandered onto the path, turning toward the side door of the gym so his back was to the approaching vehicle. It was going to plow right into him.

For a split second, Neve thought about doing nothing. If that car hit Javier, then her problems would be over. It was tempting. But she knew deep down she'd never be able to absolve herself of the guilt if she sat idly by and let some guy get hit by a car, even if she did secretly loathe him, and even if it did benefit her in some way. She'd still be responsible. She couldn't let that happen.

Neve smashed her palm into the middle of the steering wheel, blaring the horn. She pumped it three or four times, hoping the erratic sound might snap Javier back into the moment. At first, it didn't work. The car was almost on top of him. Neve held down the horn this time, and that did the trick. Javier's head popped up as he glanced toward the parking lot. Then he must have sensed the movement of the speeding car or heard the crunch of tires against gravel because he spun around to face it.

Whether it was his athletic training or excellent natural reflexes, Javier registered the danger and leaped back toward the bleachers in one fluid motion. Neve saw his arms flail, his legs soar through the air, and in the twilight, she wasn't sure if he'd been hit or not.

The car didn't slow down as it careened past him, snapping through the chain barrier as if it were made of string before speeding through the parking lot. All Neve could see as it disappeared down the hill was a hooded figure in sunglasses behind the wheel.

Even so, she was pretty sure the driver was Diane.

TWENTY-ONE

NEVE JUMPED OUT OF HER CAR AND RACED ACROSS THE parking lot toward Javier. He lay in a heap on the asphalt, still and unmoving. Neve wasn't sure if he was breathing.

"Oh my God!" she cried as she collapsed to her knees by his side. Should she turn him over or not touch him? If he was seriously injured, moving him might make it worse. But what if he needed CPR? Shit, did she even *know* CPR?

Neve laid a hand on Javier's arm, unsure what she should do. At her touch, she felt his body stir and he let out a low groan.

"Are you okay?" she asked breathlessly, embarrassed by her question. Of course he wasn't okay. He'd just been maybe almost hit by a car.

Javier rolled onto his back. Bits of gravel were embedded in his left cheek and the palms of both hands were scraped and raw, but otherwise, he wasn't bleeding or missing any limbs, and he didn't appear to be in excruciating pain. "What the hell happened?"

Your sister tried to kill you. "I—I don't know," Neve stuttered. How was she going to explain this? "I was, uh, in the parking lot. In my car. Waiting for a friend." *Right, because this lie worked so well with Charlotte yesterday.* "And I saw a car come around the building."

Javier pushed himself up on his elbows. "The horn. That was you?"

"Yeah."

With another groan, Javier crunched himself into a sitting position. He wiped his palms on his leggings, wincing as the raw skin brushed against the fabric. He was lucky he'd been wearing long sleeves and leggings because otherwise his arms and legs would have looked like raw hamburger. "That asshole didn't even stop."

"Didn't even slow down."

"Damn." He paused, still staring off into the trees beyond the parking lot. "She could have killed me."

"She?" Had he seen the driver or did he suspect who'd try to kill him?

"Uh, yeah." He looked down, brushing dirt from his clothes. "I thought I saw a girl driving."

"Oh." Totally plausible, but Neve sensed he was lying.

Javier shook his head and sighed. Letting out an uncomfortable laugh, he faced Neve for the first time. Those hazel eyes bored into her own, and though they had been the cause of Neve's undoing, Neve instantly felt her stomach tighten.

She'd experienced the pull of those stupid hazel eyes before, and

Yasmin had fallen dangerously in love because of them. Neve loathed the idea that something as complicated as the connection between two human brains could ignite at first sight without either person having intimate knowledge of the other, but now, as she sat with Javier on the asphalt, she felt a strange tug deep in her lower intestines, like her internal organs were getting all mixed up. It was a familiar feeling—uncomfortably so. She'd felt the same thing when she first spoke to Diane at GLAM.

God, I am so fucked up.

Neve pushed the attraction aside. Yes, Javier was handsome, but he was also rich and popular and oh yes, a freaking sexual harasser and stalker. So her feelings needed to piss right off.

"Do I know you?" he asked.

Neve started. Did he actually remember her from Marisol's party?

He tilted his head to the side. "You look really familiar."

"I don't think so," she said, trying to meet his gaze. His eyes were more world-weary than freaked-out by his sideswipe with death.

"Oh, okay," he said, sounding unconvinced. "Either way, I owe you my life."

Neve dropped her eyes to the ground, embarrassed. Five minutes ago, she'd been planning his murder and now he was thanking her for saving his life. "No, you don't."

"I *do*," he insisted. "I never even heard that car coming." He looked at her again, head inclined, and Neve was pretty sure he was still trying to recall why her face was familiar.

"I'm Javier, by the way. I'd offer to shake your hand, but . . ." He held his palms up to face her, exposing the angry red scrapes bubbling up with beads of coagulating blood. "Don't want to gross you out."

Neve laughed. She had to appreciate his ability to find humor in the situation. "We'll pretend we shook on it."

"Deal."

With a degree of athleticism that should have felt like he was showing off, but somehow didn't, Javier rolled back onto his shoulders, then vaulted forward to his feet, landing with perfect balance. He offered his arm to Neve. She stiffened, remembering the scene Diane had written where the Francisco character offered Ryanne his hand to help her up and then twisted her arm around her back and tried to kiss her. She couldn't let herself get lost in his affable manner and swoony eyes. This guy was dangerous, like his sister.

"I should have been helping you up," she said, forcing a laugh as she ignored his offer and pushed herself to her feet.

"I'll lie back down if you want." He smiled for the first time. It was lopsidedly charming and magnetic. Like a serial killer.

Neve backed away. "I should probably go."

"Weren't you waiting for someone?"

DAMN IT! She was the worst liar in the world, which wasn't such a horrible characteristic to have unless you were caught stalking the guy you were supposed to murder and then yeah, being able to keep your lies straight might be a tad helpful. "Riiiight. I meant, I should go check and see where my friend is." She hurried toward her car. Time to get the hell out of there before she said something really stupid.

"Wait up!" She heard the gravel crunch as he jogged up behind her, and Neve fought the urge to break into a full sprint. But instead of grabbing her, he stopped several feet away. Respectful. Nonthreatening. And against her better judgment, Neve turned to face him. "You didn't even tell me your name."

"Neve," she blurted out. Why was she talking to him?

"Hey, Neve," he said, maintaining a healthy distance between them.

"This might seem like a creepy serial killer thing to do, but could I, like, take you to lunch tomorrow?"

"Um . . ." Holy shit, was he asking her on a date?

"Not a date or anything," he said quickly. Neve hated how transparent her face was, reflecting every thought that popped into her head. "Just a thank-you for saving my life."

She should have said no for a variety of reasons, one of which was that she definitely didn't want to get too close to this guy who factored so heavily into the current drama of her life. Then again, she was trying to stall Diane, buy some time until she could figure out what to do, and she could use lunch with Javier to further that goal. She'd tell Diane that she was getting to know him in order to find the best way to make his impending death look like an accident.

But if the whole point of this *Strangers on a Train* murder plot was that neither Neve nor Diane had a connection to their victims, wouldn't going out with Javier destroy that logic?

Which was only something she needed to worry about if she was actually planning on killing him.

Which she wasn't.

Maybe this was her out?

"Okay, sure."

And when they agreed on a time and place, she actually smiled and meant it.

TWENTY-TWO

NEVE'S MIND RACED AS SHE DROVE HOME FROM HOLY NAME, her thoughts moving almost as quickly as her pulse.

Diane had just attempted to kill her stepbrother, and if Neve hadn't been there to warn him, she would have succeeded. Neve let that reality sink in for a moment.

What the hell was Diane playing at? She'd spent a ridiculous amount of time and energy setting Neve up: recording her murder "confession," stealing her dad's cap, not to mention KILLING AN INNOCENT

PERSON. Why take any of those risks? Why manipulate Neve into killing Javier when she was obviously willing to do it herself?

There had to be a reason, something Neve was missing. Diane might have been a sociopath, but she wasn't an idiot.

Neve thought of yesterday's phone conversation when she'd slipped and told Diane what she'd been theoretically planning—to use her car and run Javier down after batting practice when the school was practically deserted. Was it a coincidence that the very next day, a car bore down on Javier in the exact same way?

Neve tensed, her foot easing up on the accelerator even though she was still on the freeway. What had Javier said? *I never even heard that car coming.* She pictured the car rushing past her, small and black. And silent.

Silent because it was an electric car. A black one, exactly like what Neve was driving now.

She gasped. It wasn't a coincidence that Diane was driving a black electric car. She'd have put money on the fact that it was, in fact, a Chevy Bolt and that the Holy Name Academy's grounds were literally riddled with security cameras that would have picked up not only the hit-and-run, but probably Neve sitting in the parking lot both the day of the accident and the day before.

Diane wasn't merely attempting to blackmail Neve into killing Javier: She was trying to frame her—or worse, her dad—for his murder.

For some reason, this epiphany had an oddly relaxing effect. Her grip on the wheel loosened, her jaw unclenched, and the knotted muscles in her shoulders began to unwind. If Diane was planning to kill Javier anyway, there was absolutely no reason for Neve to do her dirty work. Not that she'd been planning to, but she'd been unable to prevent her mind from plotting a murder, and even if she'd never truly have gone through with it, merely *thinking* about taking a human life had been disturbing.

Bruno's line from *Strangers on a Train* felt all the more poignant.

Of course, that still left another problem: saving Javier's life. She'd done it once, but could she guarantee she'd be there the next time Diane made an attempt? Short of transferring to Holy Name, Neve wasn't sure how she could protect him. She wasn't exactly a trained bodyguard, nor was she a femme fatale with a heart of gold who could use her looks and overt sexuality to keep Javier safe, like Bacall lighting Bogie a cigarette before she cut him loose in *The Big Sleep*. Those characters only existed in fiction.

She certainly had landed in her own film noir, that was for sure. But maybe the tropes she so dearly loved could help her? She might not have had Lana Turner's looks—so useful in *The Postman Always Rings Twice*—or Ella Raines's tenacity in *Phantom Lady*, but maybe Neve could plot her way out of this without sacrificing her father's freedom or Javier's life?

She sighed as she pulled the Bolt into the driveway. This wasn't a movie. This was real life. There was no Hitchcock or blacklisted Trumbo to help her out of the corner she'd painted herself into. To keep everyone alive, Neve was going to need professional help.

She'd have to talk to Officer Hernández.

Unfortunately, the resolution to go to the police lasted all of fifteen seconds, the time it took for Neve to get out of the car and walk into her house. Sitting in the living room, chatting happily with her dad while Deirdre played video games, was Diane.

She must have driven straight to Neve's house after she sped away from Holy Name, arriving a few minutes before Neve made it back, though Neve hadn't noticed either another black Bolt or Diane's white BMW parked out front. Not that it mattered. There was only one reason for her to be there, and it made Neve hate her even more. Diane was sending a message: *I can get to your family.*

"Neve!" Diane cried as Neve stood rooted in place at the front door, overcome by a mix of shock, fear, and rage. "You're home!"

Diane raced across the living room, expertly sidestepping an unused controller, and tackle-hugged Neve. It was the old Diane, the one from GLAM, all smiles and openness and positivity and rainbows fucking radiating out of her pores. A complete one-eighty from the Diane she'd seen at the beach yesterday, the Diane who had attempted to murder Javier an hour ago.

"Hey, Neevy," her dad said, pushing himself slowly to his feet. His body looked tired, feeble, an elderly man unsure of his balance who moved with careful purpose to avoid a fall. "Look who's here."

Diane pulled out of her hug and looked Neve dead in the eyes. The smile and body language appeared warm and friendly, but the sharpness in her blue eyes was anything but, and Neve felt a shudder ripple through her. "I heard about Yasmin and wanted to surprise you and see how you're doing."

"Surprise!" Deirdre said, still glued to her video game.

"Anything new on her murder?" Diane asked, turning to Neve's dad.

"We've been advised . . ." Neve's dad began, then faltered and averted his eyes. "I mean, we don't know anything more than what we were told yesterday."

We've been advised? Neve suddenly realized that her parents had spoken to someone outside of the family about the situation. A lawyer, probably. Did her parents think she was going to be arrested for Yasmin's murder?

The punching and shooting sound effects from the TV speakers punctuated Neve's tension, and she winced at a particularly furious barrage.

Neve's dad saw her reaction and picked up the remote control, totally misinterpreting what Neve wanted. "Come on, Erdried. Let's give your sister some privacy."

Deirdre didn't put down the game controller. "Isn't that why she has her own room?"

"Deirdre . . ."

"But I'm about to break into the bunker," she whined. "Do you know how hard this is?"

"Now." Her dad pushed a button on the remote, turning the flat screen black. "Come help me make dinner."

Deirdre groaned in disappointment. "Fine. But I'm playing again after. Don't care what Mom says."

"Nice seeing you again, Mr. Lanier!" Diane called after him. "I liked that nifty hat you were wearing last time I saw you."

Bitch.

Neve's dad rubbed his head absently, his wispy hair sticking up on end. "Yeah, um, thanks." Then he spoke under his breath as he passed into the kitchen. "No idea where that thing is. . . ."

Neve watched her dad go, still rubbing his head as if doing so might jog his memory, and her resolve strengthened. She had to protect her family from this psychopath at all costs.

The instant Neve's dad disappeared into the kitchen, Diane exhaled violently, as if she'd been holding her breath throughout the entire exchange, allowing her head to flop forward, a balloon figure deflating. When she started breathing again, the happy-friend routine was gone, and cool, calculating Diane Russell had returned.

She smiled as she meandered around the living room, examining the various family photos that adorned the walls and tabletops. Her body snaked as she walked, a sinuous undulation of hips and torso that a week ago would have left Neve panting with desire but was now only nauseating.

"Nice family," Diane said at last, shattering the silence with a threat that set Neve's teeth on edge.

"Stay away from them."

"As long as you cooperate, I'll have no reason to pay you a visit at home ever again."

Cooperate, my ass. Neve moved her hand toward her skirt pocket, where she'd shoved her phone as she climbed out of the car. If she could just get the video camera recording, maybe she'd catch audio of Diane incriminating herself. "Cooperate?" she asked innocently, hoping to prolong the conversation while she grappled with her phone.

"You know what I mean."

Neve dipped her hands into the pocket, hoping the move looked casual, unpremeditated, innocent. "I *am* cooperating." Her fingers fumbled blindly with the phone until they located the side button that opened her camera app, which was all well and good, but how the hell was she going to get video feed recording without being able to see anything?

"Hands where I can see them," Diane barked, eyes narrowed. "Now."

All Neve could do was randomly tap the screen of her phone before she pulled her hand free.

"I saw you today," Neve began, hoping her phone was actually recording. "Driving the car that almost mowed Javier down."

"You probably saw someone who looked like me," Diane said, cagey as always. "And what's this about Javier?"

Neve stuck to her guns. "You could have killed him."

"What?" Diane sucked in an audible breath. "Someone tried to kill Javier? Is he okay?" Her voice was sickly sweet, but she rolled her eyes as the words came out of her mouth.

Does she think she's being recorded?

"Don't worry," Neve said, her voice as deadpan as her face. "I was able to warn him."

"Oh." Her blue eyes bored holes into Neve's skull. "That's wonderful."

"Yeah, it is." *Ugh, now what?*

"Did you talk to him?"

Neve paused, then nodded, wondering why Diane wanted to know. "We're having lunch tomorrow."

The smile vanished. "Lunch?" Diane sounded shocked, alert, maybe even a little jealous. Definitely off-balance. Neve being seen in public with Javier was definitely throwing off her murder plan.

"He wanted to thank me for saving his life."

"You can't have lunch with Javier," Diane said, back to her old smiling self. "Didn't you listen to anything I told you about him? Javier is a predator. I'm worried about your safety, Neve."

Neve snorted. *As if.* She needed to get back on the topic of Yasmin's death just in case she was actually recording this conversation. Diane might slip and say something incriminating.

"You want to give me some tips on having lunch with someone you want to murder?" Neve asked. "Since you've obviously done this before."

A half smile crinkled the corner of Diane's mouth. "Unless you think going to lunch with me is murder, I don't know what you're talking about."

Fuck.

Diane stepped toward the door, glancing back over her shoulder as she reached the entryway. "You can tell me all about your experience with Javier next time I come over."

Next time. The thought of finding Diane in her house again made her skin crawl.

"See you then!" Diane gave a sickeningly girlish wave before she slipped out the door, leaving Neve in the family room, palms sweaty, heart racing. She waited a full minute before she slowly walked to the front door and bolted it, to make sure Diane wasn't going to barge back inside. Confident she was safe from her psycho ex-friend, she gently pulled the phone from her pocket with trembling hands.

It had been a long shot that she'd actually be able to start the video recorder, and as she swiped the screen to life, she felt her stomach drop.

The camera was on, but all she'd managed to catch was a dark, blank photo of the inside of her pocket.

TWENTY-THREE

NEVE SAT IN HER CAR, PARKED ON THE STREET AROUND THE
corner from the beachy, surf-themed diner, and stared at the clock on the
dashboard. She was supposed to meet Javier five minutes ago, but despite
arriving early, Neve hadn't been able to get out of the car.

She was rattled. Finding Diane in her house yesterday had reminded
her of the stakes for her family, the threat that Diane posed to their safety.
Neve had been too spooked to call Officer Hernández, and she'd even
briefly revisited the idea of doing what Diane wanted in order to protect
her family.

But as Neve drove to the diner, a new idea had popped into her head. *What if Javier could help?*

The idea seemed repugnant at first. This guy was a sexual predator—did Neve even want his help? But having octopus hands was a lot less horrible than being a murderer, and if she had to metaphorically get in bed with one to stop the other, so be it.

Once she got past her initial distaste, Neve's idea posed a second problem. Her murder-swapping tale was outlandish at best, and she doubted whether Javier would believe the word of a stranger over that of his alluringly hot stepsister. Diane had charmed her way through GLAM camp and even into Neve's own home, shooting the shit in the living room with her dad like they were old friends. Sociopath or not, Diane was charismatic. Why would anyone believe surly, friendless Neve over her?

Because he knows her.

Javier lived with Diane every day, and there was no way she'd be able to keep up her perky sunshine routine twenty-four/seven. Maybe Javier had seen Diane's darker side? Maybe even been the target of it? Hell, maybe Diane's stories of sexual harassment and stalking had been as truthful as her sunny GLAM disposition? She'd lied about everything else, why not lie about Javier?

If so, if Javier wasn't a douchebag, if he was just one of Diane's victims like so many others, he might believe every word of the story Neve was about to drop on him.

Or he'd think she was a nut-job conspiracy theorist, tell his friends and family about the lunatic he met for lunch, and then if anything *did* happen to him, Neve would be the prime suspect. Again.

With a sigh that encompassed her entire soul, Neve got out of the car. None of these options were good ones, but at the moment, Javier represented her only hope.

"Hey!" Javier's face lit up as Neve approached his table. He'd nabbed a spot out front, in the shade, she noted with approval. Her pale skin hated the Southern California sun.

"Hey, yourself," she said, forcing a smile and hoping she didn't look as miserable as she felt.

Javier tilted his head to the side. "Are you okay?" Once again, Neve's lack of a poker face had failed her.

"Sorry, my brain was elsewhere."

He slowly regained his smile. "I know that feeling. It almost got me killed, remember?"

"Heh."

"I mean, not that I'm planning to kill you or anything. That's totally not what I meant."

Oh, the irony. "That's good to know."

She sat with her hands folded in her lap, eyes resting anywhere but on Javier's face. The full awkwardness of the situation weighed her down, and she wondered if the other diner patrons were looking at this hot, affable guy and trying to figure out why the hell he'd be having lunch with the weirdo chick with the pin-curled hair and black pinafore dress.

"Are you at La Jolla High?" Javier asked, breaking the silence. It was a casual question, but for some reason, it made Neve jump in her chair.

"No," she said, trying to regain her composure. "La Costa Canyon."

His brows shot up. "Oh yeah? Maybe that's why I thought you looked familiar. My best friend's girl goes there."

Shit. How could she have been so stupid to think he wouldn't remember her?

"So you like baseball?" she blurted out, changing the subject. Nuance was not her forte.

Javier laughed. "You could say that. Do you play any sports?"

Now it was Neve's turn to laugh. The idea that her extremely uncoordinated self was good at anything even remotely athletic was hilarious.

"Music?" he pressed. "Band. Maybe theater? You look like a theater type."

Neve tilted her head. He appeared keenly interested in her extracurriculars. "What does that mean?"

"Oh, you know. Black dress. Stylized hair. Very dramatic." He was smiling. Teasing her. "You look like the kind of girl who goes to theater camp over the summer."

Again, the words were so casual and yet bringing up summer camp put Neve on edge. "I've done a little acting," she said carefully.

"Ah," he said, turning back to the menu. "So has my stepsister."

Neve stiffened at the mention of Diane. Even though she wanted Diane to come up in conversation so she could try and figure out if Javier had any clue about his stepsister's plot, she wasn't ready for the emotional body blow that a reference to her would bring.

"Stepsister?" she stumbled, grasping at conversational straws. Shit, she sounded like an idiot. "D-do you have other siblings?" *You're horrible at this.*

He blinked, but looked otherwise unfazed by her awkward question. "No. Parents divorced when I was in middle school. Mom's back east with her new girlfriend. Near Boston. And my dad and stepmom don't have kids together."

"Ah." Diane had been telling the truth about moving from Boston, at least.

"You grew up in San Diego?"

"No, thank God," Neve said without thinking. She hadn't been prepared for the conversation to turn back to her.

Javier snorted. "What do you have against San Diego? It's beautiful here."

This isn't about me. "Boston's not?"

He shrugged. "Freezing in the winter. Humid as fuck in the summer. Allergies all spring. But, you know, *the leaves.*"

"I've heard that leaves change color and fall off of trees," Neve said with a wry half smile, "but I always assumed that was a fairy tale."

"We New Englanders make that shit up to lure unsuspecting Californians into spending their vacation dollars in our states."

"You bastards."

Neve tried to ignore the weird fluttering feeling in her stomach, the same sensation she used to get while hanging out with Diane. What was wrong with her? This wasn't a date. They weren't best friends. She wasn't there to learn about his family life, only to figure out if she could trust him enough to help her. But maybe if she steered the conversation back toward his family, she could bring up Diane again and gauge his reaction?

"So, um, how did you end up out here?"

"The usual," he said with a sigh. "My dad got a job offer he couldn't refuse. He does pharmaceutical research on gastrointestinal viruses, which is about as sexy as it sounds. But there are very few places doing that kind of research. So here we are."

"Oh."

Neve was trying to find a way to bring up Diane again, but Javier had other plans. "I know I said it before, but I want to thank you for saving my life yesterday."

"Oh, I didn't really do anything." Taking credit for saving his life when she'd been plotting to kill him, even theoretically, felt super ick.

"Of course you did! That car wasn't going to stop."

I know.

"And the driver must have seen me."

She did.

"You didn't happen to get a good look at her, did you?" he asked. "The car passed right by you."

Neve was struck by the juxtaposition of Javier's tone of voice and the look on his face. The tone was casual, easygoing, like he was just asking a perfectly normal question. But his eyes were sharp like a predator stalking its prey. It was a look she'd seen recently. From Diane.

Saving her from the necessity of replying was the waitress who appeared at their table. She looked harried, more so than the half-full restaurant should have warranted. Her movements were quick and flippant, like someone unable to hide their irritation with the world, and though her eyes were fixed on the order pad she whipped out of her apron, they looked ready to roll at a moment's annoyance. "And what can I get for you kids . . . ?"

The last word died on her tongue as she looked up at Javier for the first time.

Neve watched in amazement as the most shocking transformation overcame her: chin and nose instantly relaxed as her lips, lined with lipstick that had long since been chewed away from the center, curved into a smile. She quickly tucked her pen behind her ear and used her free hand to smooth back the flyaway hair from her sagging ponytail, and seemingly without knowing it, she straightened up and pinned her shoulders back, thrusting her small chest forward. It was like watching a peacock prepare for a mating ritual.

"What can I get for you, honey?" she said to Javier, dripping with sweetness. The word *kids* was utterly forgotten.

Javier was flustered. "Oh, um, I didn't really have a chance to—"

She leaned in. "Would you like me to recommend something?" The innuendo was *not* subtle.

"I'm not sure that's what he had in mind," Neve grumbled under her breath.

"Hm?" The waitress's eyes never left Javier's face.

Sure, they weren't on a real date, but the waitress didn't know that. "I'll have the tuna melt on sourdough," Neve said, her voice sharp. "Cheddar cheese. With fries."

"Same," Javier said quickly, pushing his menu toward the waitress with a weak smile. "And a Diet Coke."

"Anything to drink for you?" the waitress asked Neve without looking at her.

"Iced mocha," she said.

"Okay." The waitress smiled at Javier. "I'll be back with your order as soon as I can."

I bet you will.

"Iced mocha?" Javier said, tilting his head to the side. "How can you handle all the sugar?"

Neve tilted her head to match. "It's the only sweet part about me." The waitress had lit Neve's snark spark, and now it was in full effect.

"Simmer down." The words were casual, but Javier looked sheepish as he spoke. "I was just teasing."

The waitress flew by their table, delivering food to another customer, and winked at Javier. Neve scowled. "Does that happen a lot?"

"What?"

"Chicks throwing themselves at you."

He shrugged again, his go-to move when he was uncomfortable. "I'm an asshole if I say yes."

"So that's a yes."

"I have a bad track record with girls."

Perfect. She wanted to bring this conversation back around to Diane. "Yeah?"

"Recently this girl was throwing herself at me. Like all over me every time I saw her. I wasn't interested and tried to be polite, but she only got more and more aggressive."

This sounded exactly the way Diane described her situation with Javier. Neve had taken it for granted as truth a few weeks ago, but now, knowing Diane the way she did, it actually made sense that *she* had pursued *him,* and her plot to get rid of Javier was less an act of self-preservation and more one of vengeance.

"Couldn't you walk away?" Neve prodded, knowing this answer already.

Expectedly, Javier shook his head. "I wish. I had to see her almost every day."

Yep, Diane. "I'm sorry."

"Maybe you knew her from school?" he said.

Neve blinked. "From LCC?"

"Yeah, she went to school there."

"Went?" His use of the past tense was almost as disturbing as the realization that he wasn't talking about Diane.

Javier nodded, his knowing hazel eyes locked on to hers. "She died four days ago."

TWENTY-FOUR

THE WAITRESS ARRIVED WITH TWO PLATES OF TUNA MELTS and fries while Neve was still grappling with a response to Javier's question. "Here you go, honey. Is there anything else I can do for you? Anything at all?" Neve was actually thankful for the waitress's infatuation with Javier, as it distracted from her own confusion.

Javier was talking about Yasmin.

Of course Yasmin hadn't wasted any time in making her play for Javier. Ingratiating herself with Marisol and Luna, being accepted into their circle. Neve was still so freaking bitter that she was actually pleased that Javier had repeatedly rejected Yasmin.

God, you're an asshole.

The girl was dead. Neve had to let it go.

Fingers on the back of her hand yanked her into the present. Javier had reached across the table and nudged her gently.

"What?" she said, instantly on guard, though from what she wasn't sure. There had been something off about this entire lunch. She'd shown up hoping to interrogate Javier about Diane, to see if maybe he'd be able to help Neve out of this predicament, but the entire time she'd felt as if Javier was controlling the conversation and where it went, and she had no idea why.

"Are you okay?" he asked. For the first time that afternoon, he looked genuinely concerned.

"Yeah," she said. "Fine."

"So you knew her, then?"

"Who?"

"Yasmin Attar. The girl who died." The sharpness had returned to Javier's eyes.

The girl who was murdered.

"I thought maybe you two had been friends."

"Oh. No," Neve lied.

Did Javier, like everyone at LCC, think that she had killed Yasmin? If so, maybe he was trying to trap her into confessing, or at the very least, giving up information that might lead Officer Hernández to arrest her. It had been three days since her meeting with the police in Principal Sanders's office. Three days without a call from the police, three days without questions. So the police hadn't identified the tweed fabric in

Yasmin's hand and they certainly hadn't connected it to Neve or her dad, which was why neither of them had been arrested. Was Javier part of some friends-based plan to change all that?

Suddenly, his open but watchful manner made perfect sense. He was trying to manipulate her just like everyone else.

Neve and Javier were adversaries, each with their own agenda. Javier certainly wasn't going to believe that Diane killed Yasmin if he was already convinced of Neve's guilt. It was looking more and more like Neve would have to throw herself on the mercy of Officer Hernández.

"Okay," Javier said slowly, retracting his hand. "I guess I was wrong. Her friends Marisol and Luna are pretty popular at your school."

"They might be," Neve said, forcing a smirk. "But I'm not. So we don't exactly run in the same circles."

He pulled his head back. "Oh."

"Sorry she's dead," Neve added, sounding anything but. At least that wasn't a total lie.

He shrugged. "I didn't actually like her, but yeah. She didn't deserve that."

"I guess not."

Javier stared at her for a moment, his eyes shifting through emotions so fast she thought maybe she'd broken his brain. She saw disbelief, anger, and even a brief flash of sadness, the last of which made her feel like more of an asshole than she usually did.

"I probably sound like a douche," he said at last, leaning back in his chair. "Complaining about her when she's dead and all."

"I get it."

"Do you?"

You have no idea.

"I'm just tired of dealing with all the . . . attention, I think," he said after she didn't reply.

"Attention from who?"

He pushed his plate aside, appetite lost. "There's another girl who acts like that with me. She's . . . she's my stepsister."

Neve worked to keep her breathing steady. She wasn't even trying to steer the conversation anymore and here they were. "That sucks."

"Worse than Yasmin. Things with her have been really . . . weird."

"Tell me."

And much to Neve's surprise, he did. She sat quietly, picking at her tuna melt while he talked. Javier's version of events was a helluva lot different than Diane's. Instead of him perpetrating the sexual advances, it was Diane. Almost as soon as his dad met her mom, she'd been fixated on him. At first, it was just a weird touch on the arm, a seemingly innocuous comment that dripped with sexual innuendo.

"It was easy to kind of brush it off at first," he said, running his fingers through his hair. "We didn't live in the same house yet, so I only saw her at school. I told myself I was imagining things."

Neve's eyes trailed toward the waitress, still hovering nearby. "I doubt that."

"This is going to sound like bullshit, but honestly, I'm not that guy," he said, exasperated. Neve put down her tuna melt and focused on Javier. He might have been there to play her, but at the moment, he was telling the truth. His emotions were real, the flush on his neck unmistakable. He was angry and embarrassed about his situation with Diane, and for the first time, Neve thought maybe she was getting the real version of events.

"Like, I know what you see," he continued. "I'm big. I'm a jock. Yeah, I'm popular at Holy Name. But I know what it's like to feel invisible."

Something in Javier's tone tugged at Neve's heart, and once again, she felt her guard drop.

"Baseball made me visible." He said the words slowly and with purpose. "Popular in a way I'd never been before. But I'd give it all up if it meant Diane Russell would forget I ever existed."

Neve flinched at her name. "That's your stepsister?" she said, trying to cover up her mistake.

He nodded.

"Did you tell your dad about Diane?"

"I did," he said through clenched teeth. "He told me to try and keep my distance until I graduate this spring."

"Kind of hard to keep your distance when you live in the same house."

"Tell me about it." Javier's shoulders lowered, his tension ebbing. "I make sure that I'm never home alone with her. Last time we were . . ." He shook his head as his voice trailed off. As if he was remembering something particularly disturbing. "Let me put it this way: I keep a nanny cam in my bedroom now."

"Wow."

"You don't believe me," Javier said, misinterpreting her comment. "No one does."

"No, I do," she said, despite herself. Knowing Diane as she did, it was hard not to believe that Javier was telling the truth.

"You look like you're ready for the check." The waitress had appeared as if by magic, placing the slip of paper between them on the table. Neve's eyes flicked to it as she walked away and was unsurprised to find a phone number scribbled at the top.

Javier immediately put two twenties down on the bill. "My treat, remember? Payback."

Neve felt herself blush at Javier's very date-like behavior after what was very much not a date. "You don't have to."

"I want to."

She stood up, desperate to be free of that table. The whole lunch had been a weird roller coaster, a tennis match where the advantage kept shifting back and forth between the players. Neve still had no idea what Javier had wanted when he asked her to lunch. Was it really just to say thank you for saving his life? Or had he recognized her as Yasmin's old friend and thought she might have had something to do with her death? Or had he already connected her with Diane?

All of these scenarios made sense and yet none of them did. And as Javier silently followed her onto the street, she grappled with the urge to spin around and ask him point-blank what his game was.

But she didn't because somewhere nearby, Diane was watching.

TWENTY-FIVE

NEVE WAS DEPRESSED AS SHE WALKED BACK TO THE CAR after a hasty good-bye to Javier. Her plan to enlist him as an ally against Diane had failed, and she was very quickly running out of options on how to get out of this mess.

She needed to think.

Neve sat in the car and stared out the window. She'd been stupid to believe she could outsmart Diane, who'd been one step ahead at every turn. Literally from the beginning. Had every single thing Diane had done or said since the moment she arrived at GLAM been part of her plan to entrap Neve? Her personality, her attention, her roommate's illness . . .

Her roommate's illness. Annabelle.

Her illness had been sudden. Vomiting and diarrhea so intense she'd ended up in the ER. What was it Javier said his dad specialized in? Gastrointestinal viruses.

What if Annabelle's illness hadn't been random at all? What if she'd been drugged or intentionally infected with something? And if that was the case, maybe there would be medical proof that would point the finger at Diane.

It was surprisingly easy to find Javier's dad and his San Diego company online. Neve knew his last name, his specialty, and his current and former cities of residence, which was enough for Google to spit out Dr. Richard Flores, infectious disease specialist. He'd been on staff at Tufts Medical Center in the Division of Geographic Medicine and Infectious Diseases, specializing in cryptosporidiosis and other diarrheal diseases, tropical and parasitic diseases, and noroviruses.

Norovirus was a word Neve had heard recently: Inara announced that Annabelle had been tested for it when she was admitted to the hospital.

Not a coincidence.

The description of Dr. Flores's new position at a pharmaceutical company in La Jolla was slightly vague, Neve found when she looked at the company's website. Something about genetically mutating nonlethal virus cells in order to more effectively treat common seasonal outbreaks, which sounded a lot like how pandemics started, and Neve was horrified to think that kind of research was being done so close to her home.

Apparently, norovirus was a super-nasty form of the stomach flu that was transmitted through direct contact with infected vomit or fecal matter, which was super fucking gross. Especially when she learned that either could become airborne and infect large groups.

Infectious airborne diarrhea was the stuff of nightmares.

Neve put down her phone. It all made sense and yet it was all completely circumstantial. In order to go to the cops, she needed a direct connection to Diane, and Annabelle's mystery illness was the surest way to make one. *If* her tests showed norovirus. But how was Neve going to find that out?

She felt a tug of shame as she realized the answer.

Inara.

Text if you need anything. I'll always reply.

Inara been suspicious of Diane all along, though Neve had never understood why. But now . . . What if Inara knew something? Or at least suspected?

There was only one way to find out. Scrolling back through her texts, she breathed a sigh of relief as she saw Inara's message from the last day of camp. Thank God she hadn't deleted it.

Fingers trembling, Neve began to compose a message but got immediately stuck after a simple *Hey, it's Neve!* Because what the hell was she supposed to say? *Do you know anything about Diane Russell? I think she might be a homicidal sociopath. . . .* You don't open with that.

Okay, maybe she'd just mention Diane. See if Inara jumped in with anything. That seemed like a much better idea.

Hey, it's Neve! From GLAM. I have some questions about Diane Russell. Can we talk?

The message was innocuous. It could be in reference to whether or not Diane was a murderous psycho *or* simply asking if Inara had heard from her since GLAM. Right? Right.

Neve stared at the screen, willing the dots to appear, indicating that

Inara had read the text and was composing a response, but as the moments crept by, nothing appeared. No response.

She probably hates your guts.

Neve deserved that for sure, but then why would Inara have specifically reached out that last day of camp? No, Neve had to assume that Inara was busy and would get back to her soon.

She hoped.

Neve checked her phone forty-seven bazillion times during the drive home, snatching it from the cup holder at every red light, but sadly, she still didn't have a reply from Inara. Her plan was to lock herself in her room, wait another half hour, then call. Unfortunately, Neve walked through the door at the exact moment her mom was exiting the laundry room with a loaded basket.

"Good timing!" her mom said cheerfully. "I could use some help with these linens. You know how much I hate folding a fitted sheet."

More like the worst timing. "Actually," Neve started, her eyes shifting down the hall toward her room, "I need to make a call for—"

"Neevy." Her mom's smile went from easy to forced in a heartbeat. "That wasn't a request."

Neve reluctantly followed her mom into the family room. "You sound like Grandma K."

"I do not!" her mom snapped, dropping the laundry basket on the coffee table with a violent thud.

Neve smiled. If there was one thing in the world that could reliably get under Siobhan Lanier's skin, it was any suggestion that she was like her mom.

Because she was exactly like her mom.

"Whatever."

Her mom huffed, a short inhale and exhale that sounded like a bull preparing to charge a matador as she bent over to rifle through the clean laundry, and when she straightened up she was all smiles again. Which was like the most Grandma K thing she possibly could have done, especially considering what was going on. Three days ago, Neve had been hauled into the principal's office to answer police questions in regard to the murder of her former best friend. Their parents had consulted a lawyer, Neve gathered from her dad's comment in front of Diane, but not once had Neve's mom brought up the subject with her. Not to ask if she was okay, not to ask if she needed to talk, and certainly not to ask if she was guilty of murder. Neither had Grandma K, who, Neve guessed, had been fully briefed on the situation. Everyone ignored it, pretending that life was fine and normal. Same thing her mom had done while her dad was institutionalized. Just ignored it was happening, as if her mom's force of will could hold the family together.

Siobhan Lanier was strong, but not *that* strong.

"Soooo . . ." her mom began, holding up a sheet by two corners and inviting Neve to grab the others. "How was your date?"

Neve winced. Of all the things her mom could ask her about, her non-date with the guy she was supposed to murder should not have been the opener. "He's just a friend."

"Are you sure?"

"Yep."

Her mom rolled her eyes, a move she probably thought relatable to her teenaged daughter. "Fine, fine." She paused, stepping toward Neve to bring their corners together, and then her face lit up as she hit upon another avenue of conversation. "Your dad said he met your friend Diane. From GLAM."

Shit.

"And that she's absolutely lovely."

Lovely and psychotic.

"I'm so glad you made a friend at camp!" her mom continued, oblivious to her daughter's growing discomfort. The surreality of the conversation was out of control. "You know, I met your godmother, Eliana, at GLAM. Aiko and Aunt Connie as well. We've all been friends ever since, and I can't tell you how many times I've been able to lean on them over the years when I've needed to." She brought another set of sheet corners toward Neve. "I'm so glad you have a friend like that."

"Diane is *not* a friend like that!" Neve blurted out. She hadn't meant to, but as her mom droned on about the BFFs she'd made when she was sixteen, an overwhelming sense of sadness grew in Neve. She wanted that, wanted to have exactly what her mom was describing. Friends who would be there when she needed them, who would laugh at her jokes or offer advice or be a shoulder to cry on or whatever the hell it was that best friends did, and she'd wanted it so badly that twice in rapid succession she'd been willing to see that potential in utterly unworthy people. What the hell was wrong with her that all she did was attract sociopaths? Couldn't she have one normal, awesome friend in her life?

A look of alarm flashed across her mom's face, eyes wide, lips parted. She wasn't sure if her mom was worried about Neve's sanity or her dad's. "What do you mean?"

"I meant," Neve began, attempting to backpedal, "she's not like Eliana or Aunt Connie or . . ."

Neve's voice was choked off by emotion. She was thinking about those three women—Eliana, her godmother, who lived in Washington, DC, but made sure to visit them whenever she was in California for work. Aiko and her wife, Brooklyn, who always made room for the Lanier family to stay with them in their two-bedroom Upper West Side apartment in New York. Aunt Connie (the aunt part being honorary), who, despite having six children of her own and running an organic clothing company, always made time for coffee dates with Neve's mom and never forgot a birthday card for either of the Lanier kids. Siobhan Kerwin (now Lanier) was the kind of person who made friends with good, wonderful people and then was able to maintain those friendships for the long haul, through bad and good. Through Aunt Connie's cancer and Aiko's coming out. Through the death of Eliana's husband and Aiko's wedding.

The only thing Neve had been able to maintain over the years was her snark.

"Oh, Neevy." Her mom's arms were around her neck, the sheet dropped to the floor, forgotten. "I'm so sorry. Diane told your dad what a good friend you'd been to her at camp. That you'd told her you'd always be there for her if she needed anything."

Needed anything murdered.

Her mom stroked her hair. "I know you can be that friend to someone. You have so much kindness in you."

Kindness. Neve hadn't been kind in her text about Marisol. She hadn't been kind to Inara. Maybe that's why she was friendless—because she was a horrible person.

"I don't, though, Mom," she said, pushing her away. "I'm not kind at all. You don't even know what I am." Then without stopping to explain, Neve ran to her bedroom and locked the door.

TWENTY-SIX

NEVE LAY ON HER BED, STARING UP AT THE CEILING FAN LAZILY rotating above her. The tears had dried, but her eyes were raw and puffy, and a migraine-like pounding had set in at the back of her skull.

She'd saved most of the ugly crying for when she was alone in her room, barely containing the rage tears until she'd closed her bedroom door. Only then had she really let loose.

It wasn't so much that she didn't want to cry in front of her mom as she didn't want to explain the violent emotion that accompanied the tears, an embarrassing mix of shame, anger, and hopelessness. Her mom might not have believed that Neve's breakdown was merely a result of Yasmin's death, and there was no way Neve was looping her mom into this Diane murder business. She didn't need a phone call from Grandma K about *that*.

But Neve did need to loop someone in, and the longer she lay on her bed, staring blankly at the ceiling, the more she realized that she needed to get the professionals involved and that meant Officer Hernández. Since Inara hadn't responded to Neve's text, she was utterly isolated and she could not deal with this problem anymore on her own. Peeling her aching eyes away from the fan blades, Neve sat up and reached for her phone.

She found the non-emergency number for the Carlsbad Police Department and hit call quickly before she could second-guess herself. She spent several minutes on hold and endured a short conversation with a receptionist before she was transferred to the right extension and heard the strong, confident voice that both impressed and intimidated her.

"This is Office Hernández."

"Th-this is Neve Lanier," she stuttered.

There was a pause before Officer Hernández spoke again. "How can I help you, Neve?"

I wish I knew. "I wanted to talk to you about . . ." Shit, about what? A possible murder? A murder plot? A real murderer plus a would-be murderer that happened to be Neve herself?

"About what?"

"About Yasmin Attar."

"Do you have information about Yasmin's death?"

"Yes." *Sort of.*

Pause. "You and one of your parents should come down to the station to make an official statement. I don't want you saying anything over the phone that might incriminate you in a murder investigation."

The police station? Yeah, no. Neve had to assume that Diane was watching her house, waiting for her to do something stupid like go to the police. And while she could easily have snuck out of the house through the backyard, over the fence to the Zhang family's property, pop out one street away, and then call for an Uber, there was no way Neve could explain to her parents why they couldn't simply get in their car and drive to the police station like normal people.

"Neve, did you hear me?"

"I can't come into the station."

"Why not?"

Neve ignored the question. Her answer would only confuse things. "And the information I have isn't about me. I didn't kill Yasmin."

She heard a rustling on the other end of the line, as if Officer Hernández was searching for a piece of paper. "Once again, I strongly urge you to come down to the station, accompanied by your mother or father." She paused again, and when she spoke, the words came slowly. "Unless you'd rather we come to your house?"

Why couldn't they do this over the phone? Neve just had to get the whole story out.

"I know who killed Yasmin." Neve spoke quickly, not even daring to take a breath, as she didn't want to give Officer Hernández the opportunity to interrupt. "A girl named Diane Russell in La Jolla. She has a picture on her phone of Yasmin's . . ." She had to force herself to keep talking even though on the inside she was recoiling in horror as she thought of those photos and the blood that dripped down Yasmin's lifeless hand. "Of Yasmin's body. She broke into Yasmin's house Monday night and stabbed her in her bed."

There. She'd done it. They'd have to investigate Diane now. Find the photos. Some forensic evidence. The real killer would be arrested, Neve's dad would be safe, and this nightmare would be over.

"That is a very serious accusation," Officer Hernández said, hesitating between each word as if choosing them carefully.

"I know."

"In the state of California," Officer Hernández continued, picking up speed as she went, "false accusations are a misdemeanor crime, punishable by up to six months in jail."

Wait, what? *"False* accusations?"

"And if said accusations resulted in an arrest or trial, you could be charged with criminal conspiracy."

Which sounded less horrible than being charged with murder, but Neve was hoping to avoid criminal charges altogether since she was completely innocent. "I'm telling the truth!"

Officer Hernández paused and Neve felt as if a noose was tightening around her neck when the policewoman spoke again.

"The details of Yasmin Attar's death have not been made public."

All the more reason to believe Neve's story. "Exactly. But Diane was *there.*"

"Someone was there."

Neve froze. Shit. Not only was Officer Hernández not buying her story about Diane, but she assumed that the reason Neve knew anything about the crime scene was because she had been there. When she murdered Yasmin.

"Officer Hernández, I'm not making false accusations and I did not kill anyone. Diane and I were at summer camp together, where I told her all about Yasmin and how she tried to ruin my life. And then I got a text from an anonymous number right after Yasmin died telling me it was, and I quote, *my turn* and then Diane called me and said she'd killed Yasmin and that I had to murder someone in return to make it right and—"

Neve paused, choking back a sob for the second time that hour. She was really tired of crying.

"And I don't know what to do now."

Officer Hernández sighed. Did that mean she was actually going to listen? "What did you say this person's name was?"

"Diane Russell."

"And she *told* you how she killed Yasmin?"

Bragged about it, more like. "She said she stabbed Yasmin in her bed."

"And did Yasmin know this person?"

"I don't think so."

"Ah."

Ah. What did that mean? Good ah? Bad ah?

"Well, I'm sorry to disappoint you, Neve, but your friend from camp is lying to you."

"What?"

"There were no signs of forced entry at the Attar house."

"But . . ."

"The Attars' alarm system wasn't triggered. Yasmin let her killer or killers into the house. Possibly because she knew them."

"But . . ." Fuck. Yasmin didn't know Diane. How did she get into the Attars' house?

"Moreover," the police officer said pointedly. "The Attars have a Ring door camera, but no one was seen entering or exiting the house that night. Whoever was inside with Yasmin came through the back and probably knew both the house *and* its inhabitants very, *very* well."

The accusatory edge to her voice was unmistakable.

"I didn't do it!"

"I'm sorry, Neve, but until you're willing to come down to the station and make a statement"—Officer Hernández sighed—"this conversation is over."

TWENTY-SEVEN

NEVE DROPPED THE PHONE ONTO THE BED, DEFEATED. THIS was utterly hopeless. No one believed her; no one took her seriously. And unlike her mom, who had plenty of friends she could talk to if she was in need of advice, Neve had no one she could call.

As if the universe was throwing her a bone, the phone buzzed beside her with an incoming call.

It was Inara.

"Hey!" Neve said, embarrassed to hear so much relief in her own voice. "How are you?"

Inara dispensed with pleasantries and got right to the point. "What happened?"

Neve choked back a sob of happiness and tried to make her brain function. "I . . . I don't even know where to start."

"Start with the beginning."

Right. Start with Annabelle and then ease her way into the murder plot. "I know you talked to Annabelle after she was admitted to the hospital, and I was wondering if you'd talked to her since."

"About the virus?" Inara was always one to cut to the chase.

"Yeah." Neve took a deep breath. "And if Diane was involved with that. Somehow."

Inara was silent and Neve bit her lip. Was her roommate debating whether or not to share information? Or wondering why the hell Neve thought Diane Russell might have something to do with Annabelle's barfing?

"Meet up in Oceanside?" Inara said at last. "Tonight?"

Thank freaking God. She'd have to wait until after dinner, before she could sneak out through the Zhangs' yard and into an Uber, but it would be worth it to see Inara tonight. "I can be there by eight."

"Cool." Inara rattled off her address, which Neve quickly typed into her phone's GPS. "Talk then."

Neve ended the call feeling more hopeful than she had in days.

Inara's house was in an older development, blocks and blocks of ranch-style houses on palm-tree-lined streets that reminded Neve of Grandma K's house in Carlsbad. The front lawn had been replaced by sensible drought-resistant ice plants and lantana, and the terra-cotta tile roof complemented the Spanish style of the home. Two large pickup trucks were parked side by side in the driveway, a matching pair of Silverados in black and white. Basically, it was every non-McMansion in San Diego County, and somehow the familiarity of it calmed Neve's jittery nerves as she stepped out of her Uber and approached the front door.

She knocked tentatively instead of ringing the bell, which felt too intrusive for that hour of the night. Like if no one answered her knock, she could just slink away. But thankfully, within seconds Neve felt the thundering of footsteps as someone raced through the house.

A boy around Deirdre's age yanked open the front door with such force he momentarily lost his balance, sliding backward in sock-clad feet on the tile floor as he righted himself against the door handle.

"Victor or Inara?" he asked unceremoniously, his mouth puckered in disapproval.

"Um, Inara."

He let out a sigh of either annoyance or relief, Neve wasn't sure which, then promptly closed the door in her face. From inside, she heard him scream his sister's name at the top of his lungs, and then the padded footsteps retreated.

Neve contemplated sending a text that she'd arrived, but before she could even retrieve her phone, the door swung silently open again.

Inara looked exactly as she had two weeks ago when they'd last seen each other. Her long brown hair was swept up in a loose bun, her jean shorts and boots and T-shirt were all familiar items, and she was dripping with mismatched plaids. Once again, the familiarity was comforting.

"This way," Inara said in her usual brusque manner, nodding toward the back of the house before turning away.

Neve followed, closing the door behind her as she hurried after Inara's quick strides. A kitchen-slash-dining-slash-family-room opened up beyond a short hallway, where Inara's little brother sat playing the same first-person-shooter video game that was Deirdre's brain poison of choice on a seventy-five-inch wall-mounted TV, and Neve wondered if the two kids had ever played this game together through the anonymity of the internet.

Inara's room was at the end of a long hallway, in almost the exact same location as Neve's room in the similarly laid-out home. It was small but surprisingly tidy, considering the chaos that Inara's side of their dorm room had devolved into by the end of GLAM. Her desk was neatly arranged, laptop closed and charging. Bookshelves held only books instead of Neve's mishmash of books and clothes and knickknacks, and through a partially open closet door, Neve saw that Inara's plaid wardrobe was hung neatly on wooden hangers, arranged by color palette.

"Diane Russell," Inara began, saying her name as if she were a known criminal and Inara was wondering with amusement what laws she'd broken now. She plopped down on her desk chair and gestured for Neve to take a seat on the plaid beanbag in the corner, then leaned forward, resting her elbows on her knees, looking a little bit like Officer Hernández in Principal Sanders's office. "Wanna explain what's going on?"

"She's blackmailing me." Neve hadn't meant to be so blunt, but there was something about Inara's personality that demanded the fastest route to the truth.

Inara didn't even blink. "Not surprised."

"What?" Neve's eyes widened. "You knew Diane before GLAM?" She'd never said anything, not even when Neve had asked her point-blank.

"No," Inara said, her face still unreadable.

"But you told me she was dangerous." If Inara had known that Diane was a psychopath, Neve might have appreciated a heads-up.

Would you have listened?

"Didn't know for sure," Inara said, her voice calm. "Only suspected."

"Why?"

Inara took a steadying breath. "Gina the Ex was at Brown Ledge last summer."

The camp Diane attended where she complained about too many outdoorsy activities and not having a car. It was after Neve blurted out Brown Ledge at lunch that first day that Inara became focused on Diane.

"Wow."

"And told a wild story involving a camper named Diane."

Neve shook her head. "The summer camp community is an incestuous little bunch."

"No joke." Inara laughed dryly.

Her recitation of the events at Brown Ledge took a little bit of concentration to follow, as Inara maintained her pronounless narration, but the gist of her story was pretty simple—and painfully familiar.

Last summer, Diane had befriended a girl named Pamela. An outsider. Someone with baggage from her private school in a Boston suburb, which, conveniently, Diane also attended.

Pamela had been the victim of some pretty extreme bullying, and her parents had sent her to Brown Ledge hoping to boost her self-esteem. Diane had latched onto her from day one, and they'd been inseparable for the full two weeks. Midway through camp, Diane's roommate had to go home with a sudden bout of the flu, and Pamela had requested, and was granted, a transfer to be Diane's new roomie.

Now it was Inara's turn to raise an eyebrow. "Familiar, right?"

"Painfully." She couldn't believe Diane had done the exact same things at a different summer camp last year.

After camp was over, Gina the Ex hadn't thought about either girl until she received a troubling email from the Brown Ledge administration about a month later. Pamela had taken her own life two weeks into the new school year.

"Pamela left a note that said *Didn't want to hurt Mitchell* on a torn piece of paper," Inara explained. "Mitchell was some guy Pamela had a crush on and who had narrowly missed getting killed in a hit-and-run earlier that week."

Neve caught her breath. "Hit-and-run?"

"Yeah." Inara arched her right eyebrow. "Why?"

Neve sat back in the chair, mind whirling. She didn't know the details of Pamela's situation, but the facts were so familiar. Too familiar. Had Diane tried to frame Pamela for almost killing some guy she had a crush on? Then tried to use that as leverage to get Pamela to kill Javier?

And was Pamela's death really a suicide or did Diane have a hand in that as well?

"This wasn't the first time," Neve mused out loud. *Or the last.*

Inara cleared her throat, reminding Neve that she wasn't alone. "What the fuck is going on?"

Neve took a deep breath, wondering if she was finally putting her trust in the right person.

Time to find out.

"Diane Russell is a murderer," she said simply. "And I'm the only one who can stop her."

TWENTY-EIGHT

IT FELT GOOD TO UNBURDEN HERSELF. AND IT HELPED THAT Inara didn't look at her like she was a fringe conspiracy theorist, even though that's exactly how she sounded. A girl who stalked other girls at elite summer camps to blackmail them into killing her stepbrother? Neve had heard more believable plots in one of Grandma K's favorite soap operas. But that pattern was repeating itself too closely to be coincidental, and the more Neve talked, the more confident she felt in her theory.

Inara simply nodded while Neve laid out the facts, only raising an eyebrow when Neve detailed her lunch with Javier.

"Does this guy have a clue what Diane's about?" she asked.

"I don't know." Neve was still trying to reconcile his shifting moods during lunch. "He thinks she's off, but I don't think he knows *how* off."

Inara nodded thoughtfully. "And yet dude still went on the date."

"What date?" Neve asked more quickly than she'd intended. She immediately pictured Javier and Yasmin at a romantic restaurant.

"Neve plus Javier at diner," Inara said through a half smile, "equals date."

"No way." Her lunch with Javier had been many things—a thank-you, reconnaissance, a mental tennis match—but a date wasn't one of them.

"Sure about that?"

Though Neve had absolutely no experience in the world of high school dating, she was relatively sure the way Javier looked at her hadn't been romantic. "Positive."

"Okaaaaaay," Inara said with a smirk. Smiles were rare with her, but now Neve had had two in one night. Well, at least she knew that Inara didn't hate her.

"It doesn't matter," Neve said, steering the topic away from Javier. She didn't like the way his hazel eyes lingered in her mind. "I can't exactly go out with the guy I'm supposed to murder."

Inara shrugged. "Wouldn't be the first time."

"Fuuuuck." Neve groaned, slumping back into the beanbag chair. "How is this helping?"

"Sorry. Back to business." Inara leaned forward, resting her elbows on her thighs. "If Diane's repeating a pattern, or at least trying to, then there should be some evidence that ties the two crimes together. Annabelle, right?"

"I think so." Neve wasn't a scientist and only understood about half of what she'd read in regard to Dr. Flores's research, but the norovirus connection couldn't be a fluke. "You said she was tested for norovirus in the hospital."

Inara nodded.

"And Javier's dad specializes in using mutated forms of the virus in order to treat other diseases."

"Mutated viruses?" Inara said, losing her cool for an instant. "Sounds like some X-Men shit right there. Don't people understand how pandemics begin?"

Neve laughed despite the seriousness of the situation. "That's exactly what I said!"

"Too convenient to be a coincidence," Inara said, echoing Neve's assessment, "but called Annabelle this afternoon. Said the norovirus test was inconclusive."

"Shit." She was so close to having proof of Diane's guilt, but at every turn, she seemed to be one step ahead.

"Doesn't mean the theory is wrong," Inara said. "Mutated virus might not look like the real thing under a microscope. And Annabelle was sick for two weeks. That virus was stronger than a regular stomach bug."

It all tracked, but Neve still felt defeated. "Okay, but we still have no evidence."

"There must be something. Blood. Handwriting samples. Hair follicles."

Neve snorted. "Watch *CSI* much?"

"Binge it with Dad and the brothers all the time!" Inara laughed. Neve had no idea Inara was so close to her brothers and her dad, though her lack of knowledge on that front was entirely her fault. She should have spent more time getting to know her roommate at GLAM rather than getting completely sucked in by Diane. Ugh, if only she could get a do-over.

"Physical evidence sounds like a good idea," Neve said, regret stinging her conscience, "but it's not like we can fly to Boston and search some girl's house for strands of Diane's hair."

"Pamela's death. And the car accident that almost killed the crush. Might be something there."

Sounded like a long shot. "Where do we start?"

Inara spun in her chair and opened up the laptop on her desk. "Emailing Gina the Ex."

"Oh wow." Neve thought of Inara's Confessional about how she was still in love with her ex and immediately wondered if that was *this* ex and if so, how embarrassing or painful it might be to email her out of the blue and ask questions about a suicide that happened a year ago. "I hope that's not too weird."

"Nope."

"Oh good." Neve averted her eyes, relatively sure Inara was lying. Even though she couldn't see the screen from where she sat, it felt intrusive to watch Inara contact an ex-girlfriend on her behalf.

"Question," Inara said as she typed.

"Shoot."

"What's with the forties thing?"

Neve snorted. Normally, she would have deflected the inquiry; in this case, she'd have probably asked a similar *What's with the plaid thing* question in return, but Inara had literally introduced herself to Neve with the words *Don't ask about the plaid*. So, much to her own surprise, Neve answered.

"My dad introduced me to Hitchcock when I was ten," she said, smiling at the memory of watching *Shadow of a Doubt* with him on the couch in their old house. "I just got hooked on the style and the time period."

And the way my dad was back then.

"Gotta favorite?"

"The Maltese Falcon," Neve said without hesitating. "The movie that started it all."

Inara nodded. "But the women. All kind of sexist stereotypes, right?"

"Not necessarily," Neve replied. She'd done a lot of soul-searching on this point. "Film noir was a reaction to changing social norms as men returned from World War Two to find that the women they left behind were newly empowered and not that excited about being resubjugated. The moodiness of the genre reflects a social unrest spurred by feminism."

"Makes sense." Though Inara didn't sound convinced.

"Also," Neve said, feeling a little preachy. "Some of the earliest coded references to lesbianism can be found in classic noir. Even the femme fatale herself is rooted in gender fluidity."

Inara was quiet for a moment, eyes still fixed on the laptop screen even though she had finished typing, and Neve worried that maybe bringing up queer representation had offended her. But when Inara finally spoke, she didn't sound a bit angry.

"It's perfectly normal."

Neve wasn't sure what she was talking about. "Lesbians?"

Inara laughed. "Yes. But also being attracted to both Diane *and* Javier."

Neve's stomach clenched. She had been sure that no one suspected. How did Inara figure it out? Did she have some kind of queer radar? "What do you mean?"

"Pamela and Diane had a not entirely platonic relationship," Inara said with a simple shrug. "Assuming it was the same this summer."

"I . . ." Neve was going to deny that she was attracted to either of them, but lying to Inara while she was trying to help felt oogie. She'd spent so long hiding her real feelings and all they'd done was get her into trouble. She'd absolutely been attracted to Diane. How could she not? A few times she thought that maybe it was mutual, but Diane had held back, and Neve hadn't pursued.

The urge to deny was deeply rooted, but for the first time ever, Neve felt empowered enough to tell the truth. Maybe, just maybe, being open would help.

"I know it's okay that I'm bisexual."

Inara smiled at her. "Good."

And just like that, Neve was out.

It was dark by the time her Uber pulled off the highway in Carlsbad, and even though Neve had the driver drop her in front of the Zhangs' house because she was afraid Diane might still be staking out hers, she felt significantly calmer. She had an ally now, someone she felt she could actually trust, not only with the secret of Diane's blackmail plot, but with the secret of Neve's sexuality. One she'd never explicitly shared with anyone, though both Yasmin and Diane suspected. And took advantage of it.

Diane and Javier. Yes, she was, or *had been,* in Diane's case, attracted to both of them. And even though the lunch with Javier had been weird and uncomfortable, Neve couldn't stop thinking about it. About *him.*

Neve tugged on the sliding glass door, which was still unlocked, since apparently she was the only person in the family concerned with locking doors, and slipped into the dining room unnoticed. Even though it was well past her bedtime, Deirdre had re-entrenched herself in the same video game Neve had seen Inara's brother playing, and the image was so jarringly similar that she actually paused and watched her for a minute.

Neve had a lot more in common with Inara than she did with Diane, and she felt another pang of regret that she hadn't gotten to know her roommate better during their two weeks' worth of cohabitation. They might have had a lot to talk about. Even without pronouns.

She backed away from the family room, smiling for a reason she couldn't quite understand, then turned and had to clamp a hand over her mouth to stop from shrieking out loud.

Peering through the frosted window in the front door was the silhouette of a girl with long hair.

"Hey." The voice through the closed door was familiar. "Neve?"

Swallowing her panic, Neve cracked the door. "Charlotte?" Neve blinked. "How did you know where I live? And why are you here so late?"

Charlotte glanced over her shoulder. "Can I come in?"

The last thing Neve needed right now was Charlotte asking questions about why Neve had been stalking Javier. "Can it wait? I've got a—"

"Thanks," Charlotte said, then slipped by Neve into the house.

She let out an audible sigh when Neve closed the door, and it was only as she visibly relaxed that Neve noticed Charlotte had been tense.

"Is everything okay?" Neve asked.

Charlotte nodded, her long hair waving in front of her face. "Yeah, sorry. Just nervous. I don't go out at night, like, ever. My parents are hella strict, but they're out of town for the long weekend, so here I am."

"So you're here because . . ."

"I was going to wait and talk to you at the memorial service for Yasmin

Attar tomorrow night," Charlotte said, "but then I worried you might not go."

Neve's jaw flapped open. She wasn't sure which piece of information was more of a shock—that Charlotte had heard all about Yasmin's memorial service or that Neve hadn't. "You knew Yasmin?"

"No," Charlotte said. "But a lot of people at Holy Name did because she hung around with Brian Leaf's girlfriend."

"Oh." Marisol.

"With all the rumors flying around, I thought, *Neve wouldn't be caught dead there*, but then—"

"What rumors?"

Charlotte blinked, processing Neve's question. "Um, you haven't heard?"

This did not sound good. "I haven't been at school this week."

"Oh!" Charlotte swallowed and began to speak more quickly. "Well, I'm not going to be the one to share gossip like that, especially since I don't think it's true at all. But then again, you were pretty tight with Diane."

"Diane?" Neve remembered how uncomfortable Charlotte had been with Diane's attention the first few days at GLAM, how her personality seemed to change the moment Diane shifted her friend-ttention to Neve. Did Charlotte know more about who Diane truly was than she was letting on?

She went to school with Diane and Javier, had probably seen their interactions firsthand. Hadn't Charlotte even mentioned at breakfast one morning that she'd seen Diane and Javier together behind the gym? Diane had explained that Javier had assaulted her behind the gym that day, but what if Charlotte had witnessed the opposite—*Diane* making an aggressive move on Javier?

"Yeah." Charlotte's eyes grew wide. "That girl is not right."

"She's dangerous," Neve said, getting excited. Maybe Charlotte could help her. "I know everything she told us at GLAM about Javier and the way he treated her was a lie."

"You know!" Charlotte let out a long breath, visibly relieved. "I'm so glad. I thought maybe you and Diane were . . . I mean, she did flirt with you a lot."

Well, at least *that* wasn't all in Neve's head.

"And I was worried that you wouldn't believe me when I told you about their relationship."

Neve laughed, dry and bitter. "With what I know of her now, I can absolutely believe that she stalked and harassed her stepbrother."

Charlotte didn't immediately respond. She angled her head, looking at Neve sidelong. "Who told you that?"

"Javier."

"What?"

"Yeah, at lunch today he told me the truth about how she pursued him and—"

"You went on a date with Javier Flores?" Charlotte said sharply.

Once again, the idea that her lunch with Javier had been a date made Neve blush, the heat rushing up to her cheeks before she could suppress it. "I—I guess."

Neve had thought it was an innocent enough response, but it seemed to light a fire under Charlotte. "I see," she said, turning for the door. "I have to go."

"Wait, what?"

But before Neve could stop her, Charlotte had sprinted down the walkway.

TWENTY-NINE

"NEEVY? IS SOMEONE AT THE DOOR?" HER MOM'S VOICE RANG out from down the hall. Neve stared at Charlotte's back as she raced across the street, into her car, and screeched away from the curb.

"Neevy?"

Closing the door, Neve leaned against it, weighing her options. Responding to her mother was an invitation for yet another heartfelt conversation about friendship and GLAM and whatever else her mom had on her agenda, but Neve wasn't sure she could endure two of those in one day without crawling out of her skin. She needed to be alone.

Without responding, she headed down the hall to her room, tossed her messenger bag on her desk, and immediately started a playlist from her phone. Music was the universal don't-bother-me teen-to-parent signal, and she prayed that her mom both recognized and respected it.

Because Neve needed to think.

She was at a loss to explain Charlotte Trainor. She'd been so desperate to talk to Neve that she'd showed up at her house well after ten o'clock, but then bolted without actually telling Neve anything. She only confirmed what Neve already knew, which, while encouraging, didn't bring anything new to the table.

Javier had been a promising lead, but he turned out to be just as suspicious of Neve as she was of his stepsister, which left her nowhere. Officer Hernández had offered some modicum of safety, but she didn't believe a word of Neve's story. Now the only glimmer of hope in this entire murderous debacle was Inara.

She smiled as she thought of her roommate, who had jumped in to help without question. That was a friend.

Neve needed to remember what real friendship felt like. For the future.

Without getting off her bed, she stretched an arm across to her phone, which sat on the seat of her desk chair. She managed to grip the cushion of the chair with her fingertips and was able to slowly drag it toward her without setting foot on the carpet. It reminded her of the game she and her dad used to play when she was little, where the carpet in their old two-bedroom condo was molten lava, and they had to move around the living room by hopping from sofa to chair to ottoman without setting foot on the ground.

Neve smiled at the memory. Her dad had been happy then. Sure, they'd lived in a cramped Silicon Valley condo, where Neve and her baby sister shared a room, there was no backyard to run around in or outdoor space of any kind other than a three-foot-wide balcony, and every available square inch of space inside, from the overflowing bookcases to the portable drawer units stuffed with baby toys and art supplies, was utilized for something.

A far cry from the three-bedroom, three-bath, twenty-two-hundred-square-foot ranch-style house where they now lived, with a landscaped front yard, expansive lawn in the rear, and tons of storage in the two-car garage. Where everyone could disappear into their own room and the family members weren't constantly on top of each other. Sure, the space was nice, but it had also separated them all into their own little private hells: Deirdre in front of the family room TV with her endless supply of video games; her mom at her built-in desk nestled between the kitchen and laundry room, which served as her home office; and Neve and her dad closed up in their respective bedrooms, each hiding from their own demons.

Somehow, the cramped, chaotic condo felt like a happier alternative to Grandma K's charity.

Neve shook off the gloomy reminder of Grandma K, whose ever-present moralizing ruled the Lanier family even from afar, and tried to focus on the positive. Grandma K wasn't all bad. She did care about Neve, in her own hyper-controlling way, and she'd actually given Neve a wonderful piece of advice that first day of camp. *There is only one person in this world who controls your destiny, and that is you.* Neve hadn't even realized that she was heeding Grandma K's words. She wasn't going to let Diane control her; she was taking charge.

Her phone buzzed and Neve picked it up, smiling to see a text from Inara.

Call with Gina the Ex tomorrow. More info coming.

Neve yawned as she typed a quick reply of thanks, then lowered her phone to the bed. She might have been shitty at friendship, but Inara was aces at it.

Neve only realized that she'd fallen asleep when the sound of distant pounding woke her up. Not a sudden, jarring thud that caused her to wake in a panic, more like a dull, far-off noise that broke through the thickness of her dreams and reminded her that there was an outside world beyond her bed, down comforter, and cushy memory-foam pillow.

It was morning, as the sunlight filtering through the blinds indicated, and Neve was surprised that she'd managed to sleep all night. She must have been more exhausted than she'd realized. Her limbs felt heavy, like the time she'd taken one of her dad's sleeping pills to see if it would help her post-Yasmin insomnia and she'd slept so hard it was as if her subconscious couldn't wake her brain up. In that moment of lying in her bed, wanting to move but unable to do so, she understood every alien abduction story she'd ever read about on the internet.

The deepness of this sleep and the suddenness of the disturbance that woke her had a similar effect, and she was still trying to process what the dull thuds could be when the distance of the sound evaporated and the dull thuds morphed into sharp raps on her bedroom door.

"Neve?" Her dad's voice. "Neve, are you awake?"

She sat straight up in bed, jolted by the edge in his voice. He sounded scared. "Yeah."

"You need to come out. Right now."

Shit.

Thankful that she'd fallen asleep fully dressed, Neve swung her feet to the floor and bounded across the room to the door, where she found her dad's face, hollow and worn, on the other side. It reminded her of how he looked in Principal Sanders's office on Wednesday, and she knew right away who had been the cause of all that door pounding.

"The police are here," he said softly. "Th-they need to talk to you."

"Scott?" her mom called. "Is she there?"

Ugh. The cops. Were they finally going to question her about Yasmin's death? A direct result of Neve's phone conversation with Officer Hernández, no doubt.

She followed her dad down the hall, mentally bracing herself for the inevitable questions. *Where were you on the night of August twenty-eighth? When was the last time you spoke to Yasmin Attar? How did you know the details of her murder?*

Officers Hernández and Lee stood in the entryway exactly where Charlotte had been the night before, their stances squared off, radios crackling. Neve's mom fidgeted in the kitchen door, still in her pajamas, one arm wrapped protectively around her own waist, the other draped over Deirdre's shoulders. Deirdre gaped wide-eyed at the real-life police officers in her house, as if she couldn't quite take in the awesomeness of what was happening.

"Neve," Officer Hernández said as soon as she spotted them coming down the hall. "I need to ask you some questions." No niceties, no greetings.

"Okay."

"Should my daughter have a lawyer present?" her mom asked, matching Officer Hernández's businesslike tone with one of her own, her demeanor shifting from nervous mom to Mama Bear in a heartbeat.

"If you'd like," Officer Hernández replied, ridiculous in her calmness. "But she isn't being charged with anything yet."

Yet. That word sucked so hard.

"Then what is this about?" Neve's mom asked sharply.

Officer Hernández's eyes shifted to Neve. Cold. Dispassionate.

Observant. "We want to know where Neve has been since yesterday afternoon."

Since yesterday? That was easy. "Here."

"What time did you get home?"

She didn't really want to mention her secret trip to Inara's after dinner last night, and as far as anyone knew, she'd been home since . . . "Three o'clock yesterday afternoon."

"Can anyone corroborate that?" Officer Lee asked dryly. He was less impassive than his partner, and his single raised eyebrow suggested that he didn't believe a word of her alibi.

"Mom saw me come home," Neve said, thankful for her mom's nosiness for possibly the first time ever.

"And after that?"

"We had dinner at seven," her mom said. "Then Neve went to bed early with a headache."

Neve winced, remembering the lie she'd told to facilitate sneaking out of the house to see Inara. She really hoped no one asked to see her Uber account.

"What is this all about?" Neve's dad asked, stepping close behind her. She could feel his body trembling with the effort to remain calm, and she imagined that he was barely containing his anxiety.

"Anyone else?" Officer Lee pressed, ignoring him. "Someone who's not a member of the family? A neighbor maybe?"

"My daughter isn't answering any more questions until we know why you're asking them," her dad said.

"Neve isn't being accused of anything," Officer Hernández repeated. "We've had a complaint and we're following up on it." Her lips smiled, engendering trust, but her eyes were sharp as razors, slicing at lies in search of the truth underneath.

Neve wondered if the Zhangs had seen her sneaking through their backyard. "Complaint about what?"

Officer Lee sighed. He had zero chill. "About someone stalking their house. Parked outside in a black Chevy Bolt, which I believe is the car that you drive?"

"It's my husband's car," Neve's mom said pointedly. "Which Neve borrows on occasion."

"And was one of these 'occasions' last night?" he said, using air quotes to mock Neve's mom. Unlike Officer Hernández, for whom Neve held a begrudging respect, Officer Lee was exactly the kind of douche cop who sent people protesting in the street.

"No," Neve repeated. "I was home all night."

"With no one but your family to confirm that."

Now it was Neve's turn to smile. She reveled in the idea of showing up the smug Officer Lee. "No, actually. My friend stopped by around ten."

Officer Hernández pulled a small notepad from the breast pocket of her uniform. "And this friend's name?"

"Charlotte Trainor."

It was as if Neve had dropped a bomb. Officer Hernández froze, pen hovering over the small spiral pad, her practiced impassivity vanishing as her jaw literally dropped. Officer Lee's head whipped up, eyes as wide as Deirdre's, before he shifted his gaze to his partner. "She's got to be kidding."

Something about his tone made Neve's hands go numb, the tingling radiating up her arms and down her back. "What's wrong?"

Officer Hernández pursed her lips, visibly irritated with her partner's inability to control himself, before she folded up the pad and slipped it back into her pocket.

"Charlotte Trainor is the person who called in the complaint."

THIRTY

"CHARLOTTE CALLED THE POLICE AND SAID THAT I WAS stalking her house?" Neve asked, trying to process the words as they came out of her mouth.

Officer Lee flipped open his own notebook, a twin to the one Officer Hernández held. "The complaint came in to San Diego PD Northwestern Division at eleven twenty-three last night. Caller identified herself as Charlotte Trainor. She reported a black Chevy Bolt parked in front of her house. Ms. Trainor told the officer that she knew the person in the car and identified her as Neve Lanier of Carlsbad."

"That wasn't Charlotte," Neve blurted out. She knew it wasn't. That had to be Diane.

Officer Lee turned his disapproving countenance on her. "In my experience, people don't call in fake stalking claims."

Well, you don't have any experience with Diane Russell.

Neve was about to explain to Officer Lee why he was an idiot when Neve's mom stepped forward, shouldering her way between her daughter and the officer. "If this call was placed with SDPD, then why are you here asking questions?" She pointed to the Carlsbad Police Department patch on the sleeve of his uniform. "Seems like you're out of your jurisdiction."

Neve buttoned her lips together to keep from smiling. All that *Law & Order* they'd watched together when Neve was a kid was totally paying off.

Office Lee wasn't intimidated. "We're investigating this incident in connection with the death of Yasmin Attar."

Neve's mom pursed her lips. "It seems to me as if the only connection between these two things is my daughter, and yet you claim she's not being charged with anything. That sounds like an abuse of power, if you ask me."

Deirdre leaned into Neve. "When did Mom get so badass?"

"Language!" her mom snapped without turning around to face them.

"*Badass* isn't even a swearword!" Deirdre protested.

This time, her mom spun around, hands on her knees, bringing herself down to her youngest's level. "It sure the fuck is and if I hear you using it again, Dad's not taking you to Maddox Malone's birthday party this afternoon. Get it?"

Neve snorted. *With a name like that he'll either be an astronaut or a porn star.*

"Yes," Deirdre said meekly.

"Good." Her mom straightened up. "And for the record, yes, I am a badass."

With Neve's mom momentarily distracted, Officer Hernández took the opportunity to sneak in another question. "Neve," she said, her tone less deprecating than her partner's, "if Charlotte didn't report this, then who did?"

"Don't answer that," her dad said, gripping Neve's shoulder.

But Neve didn't listen. Even though she'd tried to explain the whole situation to Officer Hernández once and been shot down, maybe if she brought Diane up again, it might trigger some kind of investigation?

"Diane Russell," she said. But if she'd been hoping for Officer Hernández to take her seriously, those hopes were immediately dashed.

"Right," she said, snapping her notebook closed. "That again." It seemed like she wanted Neve to open up to her but still thought the Diane story was just a lie Neve clung to, either protecting herself or someone she cared about.

"The Diane who came to visit you?" her dad asked, visibly confused. "But I thought you two were friends."

Officer Lee snorted. "Mr. Lanier, I believe you know all about your daughter's friend history. From that incident at the Attars'?"

"Dustin . . ." Officer Hernández held up her hand, an indication that she didn't want her partner going down that road. But it was too late. Neve watched in horror as all the color drained out of her dad's wan face and the trembling she'd felt moments ago escalated into a full-body tremor.

That was enough for Neve's mom. "Get out. Get out of our house and don't come back without an arrest warrant or you'll be hearing from our lawyer."

Officer Hernández dipped her head in compliance. "Mrs. Lanier." As she turned to leave, the look she gave to Neve was one of annoyance mixed with pity.

"Why won't you listen to me?" Neve pleaded. She felt utterly helpless, and even though she had a plan in the works to expose Diane, she was overwhelmed by the feeling that she'd already lost.

Officer Hernández glanced over her shoulder as she opened the door. "If you had any kind of proof, other than hearsay, perhaps we would."

Proof. *Like a phone number.*

Neve bolted after the officers. "What number did Charlotte's call come from?"

"We've heard enough, Neve," Officer Hernández said without breaking stride.

"Diane texts me from two phones. One's her regular number and one's like a burner phone or something. If the two numbers match—"

"We confirmed that the call came from Charlotte's phone," Officer Lee said, cutting her off as he yanked open the passenger door of the squad car. "This interview is over."

Neve wandered back inside, utterly bewildered. From Charlotte's phone? Really? Why would Charlotte show up at her house late at night acting as if she was being spied upon and then an hour later call the cops and accuse Neve of stalking her? It made absolutely no sense.

"Neve." Her mom stood at the front door, hands planted on her hips. "You need to explain what is going on."

That was, in fact, the last thing she needed to do. "Leave me alone, okay?"

"I will *not*. Police showing up, accusations of stalking and murder. Where were you last night?"

Neve slipped past her and trudged down the hall to her room. "Home, Mom."

"I'm supposed to believe that why?"

Neve reached her door and swung around, facing her mom with steely eyes. "Because I'm your daughter. Just because Grandma K never believed you doesn't mean you need to do the same."

That blow stunned her mom into silence long enough for Neve to storm into her room and lock the door.

Neve's first instinct was to call Charlotte and find out what the fuck was going on, but she didn't have her number. Maybe Inara knew how she could get it? Neve lunged for her phone. It wasn't even nine o'clock yet, but since Inara had been up at six o'clock every morning at GLAM, Neve felt pretty confident that she wasn't waking her.

Got a sec?

As before, Neve's text was immediately answered with an incoming phone call.

"Kind of early to be up," Inara said as a greeting.

"I'm not awake by choice," Neve replied. Then she explained Charlotte's visit the night before and her early-morning interview with Carlsbad's finest. "You don't happen to have Charlotte's number, do you?"

"Sorry. Try Kellie?" Then she laughed, echoing Kellie's final words to Neve after the Activism in Art showcase. "Promise, promise, promise."

Neve was thankful Inara couldn't see her face, because it had turned bright red with shame as she remembered the fight they'd had at GLAM and the olive branch Inara had offered that night.

"Now listen to this." Inara took a slow, agonizing breath. "Gina the Ex said that Pamela and Diane went to school together, and Pamela seemed surprised to see Diane at Brown Ledge. Not really friends at school, but the two got really close at camp. Inseparable, Gina said."

Neve winced. That pretty much described most of her two weeks at GLAM with Diane.

"Gina isn't sure what happened next. The gossip was that Pamela's death was over some guy. Apparently, a witness came forward and said Pamela had tried to run a bicyclist off the road. Not clear if there was actually any evidence, though."

"Let me guess," Neve said. "The almost accident involved the same make and model of car that Pamela drove?"

"Yep."

"Shit." As suspected, Diane was trying to frame her.

"Pamela's death was ruled a suicide, but apparently it took days for that decision to be official."

That sounded odd. "Really?"

"Mm-hm. Gina talked to Pamela's mom, said suicide was bullshit. Said Pamela's crush on this guy Mitchell wasn't unrequited, that the two were dating even though no one at school had ever seen the guy."

"How, um . . ." Neve wasn't sure she wanted to know. "How did she die?"

"Gunshot wound to the head, but Pamela's mom requested a toxicology report, which suggested Pamela had taken a metric shit ton of Norco that day."

Painkillers? Why bother if she was going to use a gun? "Seems kind of sus."

"That's all Gina knew," Inara said. "But going to keep digging. Maybe this Mitchell guy could be a link to Diane?"

"Good idea." She was so thankful that Inara was coolheaded. Someone had to be. "Thanks, Inara. I appreciate this."

"Welcome."

Neve couldn't see her face, but she was pretty sure Inara was smiling.

Neve reached for her laptop as soon as she ended the call. Gina's information was invaluable, and the idea that Pamela's death might not have been suicide was particularly interesting and tragic. What if that had been Diane? The note found with the body was ambiguous: *Didn't want to hurt Mitchell.* On a torn piece of paper. That could have been anything. A page from a diary maybe. Something Diane found in Pamela's room after she'd killed her.

To the police, suicide made sense. They had a note and a witness who said Pamela tried to run her unrequited crush off the road, so all the pieces fit neatly together.

But when Neve backed up a bit, a new story emerged. Javier had rejected Diane, and hell hath no fury like a woman scorned. Diane hatched her plan for revenge, glomming onto a lonely, fragile girl she thought she could control. Had she offered to swap murders like she'd done with Neve? Or just straight-up tried to blackmail Pamela by staging the car accident that almost hit Mitchell, and when it didn't work, Diane had killed Pamela to make sure she didn't talk? That might explain the Norco in Pamela's system.

It was time to dig deeper.

It took Neve all of thirty seconds to find Pamela's Facebook page. It was totally open and unlocked—no approvals for posts and the wall wasn't even closed for comments—which meant everything Pamela had posted since she opened her account was available for anyone and everyone to see. Ka-ching.

The most recent posts had come in since her death, and Pamela's wall was positively clogged with messages of love and hope and condolence, which would have been heartwarming if Neve didn't know the whole story. Pamela had been an outsider at school. Bullied. A pariah. It was a position Neve understood only too well.

How many of these effusive posts were written by hypocritical assholes who had once made Pamela's life a living hell? Quite a few, Neve guessed, and she fought the urge to comment on each and every one of them, asking what they'd personally done to help Pamela while she was alive. Because Neve knew the answer: NADA.

She rage-scrolled through the hypocrisy until she had spanned the period following Pamela's death and was knee-deep in earlier posts. Not that the tone of what she found was much better, but at least these posts only made her sad, not bitter.

Pamela's wall was a classic cry for help. A mix of inspirational kitten memes and those viral cut-and-pastes that started out like *I know no one's reading this so prove me wrong and post one GIF that represents how we met.* Blah, blah, blah. The girl's loneliness and neediness bled through every word of every post. Neve might have been born with an unusually tough disposition, which helped her deal with her own social isolation, but she'd also never sought out the approval of others. Her approach to the high school social structure was less *LOVE ME! LOVE ME, PLEASE!* and more *Take what you get from me, bitches, cuz I ain't changing.* Which didn't always go down so well, especially at LCC, but at least gave Neve the sense of being in control of her own destiny. Pamela was the opposite, practically begging the faceless masses on social media to accept her, include her, and give her life some kind of meaning.

But what Pamela's profile didn't do was offer any insight into her relationship with either Mitchell or Diane. Diane, as she knew, wasn't on social media and no one named Mitchell popped up on Pamela's friend list.

Neve did a sitewide search for his profile, which turned out to be more of a challenge than she'd anticipated. She did eventually find a Mitchell who claimed to be from the same Boston suburb as Pamela, but his page was completely locked down. No access to non-friends. There was one photo, his profile, which was the Boston Red Sox logo, and nothing else that she could see. Not even birthday wishes. Dead end.

Neve switched to Instagram, where, as with Facebook, Pamela's feed was easy to find.

And even sadder, Neve thought, than her Facebook. She scrolled through image after image with one like, two likes. Rarely more than four. Many of her photos were copies of what she'd put on Facebook, the same viral memes and GIFs, mostly about life and love and universality, and Neve's eyes glazed over at post after post after unliked post all spouting the same needy shit. Pamela was so desperately looking for a place to fit in, Neve felt awful for her. At least Neve had been able to roll with the outsider status. Wear it as a badge of honor. Meanwhile, Pamela's social starvation made her a perfect target for Diane.

Neve had scrolled back in time to the middle of last year without finding anything of interest and was about to search for Mitchell's Instagram, when her eyes fixed on something familiar on the page. The screen name of someone who had liked one of Pamela's posts from last spring about attending Brown Ledge.

BostonRyanne.

The role Neve had played in Diane's one-act play from GLAM camp.

THIRTY-ONE

NEVE FELT A FLUTTER OF EXCITEMENT IN HER STOMACH.

Diane had made a mistake.

Finally.

Neve wasn't supposed to know about Pamela, about what had happened at Brown Ledge last summer. It was pure dumb luck that Neve had been paired up with Inara as a roommate, and that Inara's ex happened to have had firsthand experience with Diane. Did Diane know about Inara and Gina? Had that been one of the reasons she'd tried to drive a wedge between Neve and her roommate? Or had she been trying to isolate Neve, making her dependent on Diane for companionship? Probably a little from Column A and a little from Column B.

Considering the argument they'd had, Neve was lucky Inara hadn't just rolled her eyes when she saw Neve's text, abandoning her to her fate. Where would Neve be now if Inara hadn't been looking out for her? In jail probably. Or plotting a murder that would land her in jail.

Shit, what a choice.

Opening Diane's fake Instagram profile for BostonRyanne, she found what was basically a burner account. BostonRyanne had twenty-seven followers but followed only three: Michelle Obama, Ariana Grande, and Beyoncé. Like two hundred million other people. Her posts were entirely stock photos of tropical beaches and scenic mountain vistas with absolutely no personal or identifying information whatsoever. This account was created to maintain anonymity, but why?

To stalk other people's posts.

Was this how Diane knew that Pamela was attending Brown Ledge? And if so, what else had she learned from Instagram?

Neve quickly typed Mitchell's name into the Instagram search box, and his page popped up immediately. But like his Facebook, the account was private, so Neve couldn't find out if Diane had stalked him at all. Who else might Diane have followed online?

With trembling fingers, she typed in Yasmin's handle.

It was telling that Yasmin hadn't actually blocked Neve from viewing her account. If Neve had really been the toxic girl-hater Yasmin had made her out to be, you'd think the first thing she would have done would be to block her ex-bestie on all social media. Only she didn't. And Neve knew why. It wasn't because Yasmin was thoughtless or careless or practically a Luddite when it came to technology. It was because she *wanted* Neve to see all her new photos with all her new friends.

Yasmin was cruel that way.

But Neve hadn't given her the satisfaction. She wasn't interested in watching Yasmin frolic with Marisol and Luna and possibly Hazel Eyes, aka Javier. She didn't care.

Now here she was, confronted with Yasmin's page mere days after her death, and scrolling through those photos was like ripping the scab off an unhealed wound.

Yasmin's feed was definitely "showing my best life," a category of social media that Neve abhorred. It wasn't real. Yasmin's photos were meant to make others think that her life was amazing. Perfect. Worthy of envy. It had been like that before she betrayed Neve, but the volume of posts had gone up since she'd established herself as third wheel on the Marisol-Luna bicycle. And it was all as fake and irritating as Neve had imagined it would be.

Yasmin posted almost nothing but selfies with Marisol and Luna—at the beach, at a party, at school—all peppered with hashtags like #BestLife and #SquadSisters.

Neve wanted to launch her phone across the room. Yasmin had ruined Neve's life in order to achieve this social media fallacy. What exactly was the fucking point? Marisol and Luna were two of the vainest, most boring people Neve had ever encountered, and it wasn't so long ago that Yasmin had agreed with her on both of those points. Now she was pretending that they were all soul mates.

Neve's eyes glazed over as the selfies began to bleed together in their monotony, and she scrolled faster until she abruptly stopped on a photo that contained a familiar face. Javier, posed between Yasmin and Luna. It was the first photo of him Neve had seen in her feed, untagged, taken during the time Neve was at GLAM.

Neve laughed out loud. She couldn't help it. All those Machiavellian machinations to throw herself in his path and the best Yasmin could manage was one photo with Javier? Pathetic. What the hell would Yasmin say if she knew Neve had lunch with him?

Nothing, because she's fucking dead.

Neve froze mid-scroll at the sobering reminder. She could hate Yasmin forever, but that hatred was as pointless as Yasmin's betrayal had been. Yasmin was dead, Neve was not. And unless she wanted someone else to suffer her ex-friend's fate, Neve needed to stop Diane.

She refocused and continued to scroll, slowly this time, and with purpose, going back in time to the first day of GLAM camp. Confessional was the first time she'd mentioned Yasmin by name, so if Diane's pattern was to stalk intended victims on their social media, BostonRyanne would start showing up in Yasmin's around this time. She clicked on a few photos, scanning the likes for the familiar handle. Third photo, halfway down the like list, she found it. BostonRyanne.

First Pamela, then Yasmin. If she could have gotten a look at Mitchell's account, she was pretty sure she'd find the same thing: Diane was stalking her victims.

But why?

Neve forced herself to think rationally. There might have been a dozen reasons why Diane followed Yasmin on Instagram. Yasmin was friends with her stepbrother, for starters. It's even possible they'd met through him, though considering Javier's relationship with his stepsister, it seemed unlikely that he'd want to spend any social time with her outside of school and home. Still, it was a possibility.

If only there was someone else connected to this mess . . .

The answer hit Neve like a runaway freight train.

Charlotte.

How could she have been so stupid? What if she hadn't even been Diane's original target? What if it had been Charlotte?

The pattern fit. They went to school together, and Charlotte looked utterly surprised to see Diane at GLAM. During the early days of camp, Diane had been attached to Charlotte, who always looked miserable when she was in Diane's presence. Charlotte's reaction to her "friend" had confused Neve at the time, but now made perfect sense. Diane had followed Charlotte to GLAM, thinking she'd be an easy target like Pamela, but while Charlotte might have been shy, might have taken a while to warm up to new people, she was perfectly capable of making friends and had done so easily at GLAM.

Charlotte had been suspicious of Diane from the get-go. She'd known Diane was lying about her relationship with Javier and had probably been grateful when Diane shifted her laser focus to Neve. An easier target.

Thankfully, Charlotte had an open Instagram account. Sparse, like Pamela's, but there were posts as recently as yesterday afternoon. All Neve had to do was scroll back a few months and boom, BostonRyanne showed up.

If there was one person on this entire planet who could help Neve point the finger at Diane Russell, it was Charlotte Trainor.

Now she just needed to find Kellie's goddamn business card. What the hell had she done with it?

Neve's mom's type-A personality might have been a pain in her daughter's ass most of the time, but on this one occasion, it proved to be a saving grace. While Neve was prone to shoving things in pockets and drawers and places she might or might not remember, and might or might not be able to locate later, her mom was meticulous in her organization. Laundry was sorted into separate hampers for whites and colors, household bills were clipped together by due date and filed in a folder on her desk, and every single household item—including all of the family's luggage—had a designated drawer, cubby, or cabinet to which it was whisked away after its purpose had been served.

In the case of Neve's wonky-wheeled carry-on, that designated space was a storage cubby in the garage. Hopefully, Kellie's card was still there, tossed into a pocket as Neve carelessly packed that last morning of camp.

Neve crept down the hallway, desperately hoping that her mom wasn't at her desk, which blocked the way from the kitchen to the garage, and poked her head around the edge of the dining room. Her mom was nowhere to be seen. A miracle. She dashed across the dining room and through the long galley kitchen, past her mom's desk and into the laundry room, pausing only briefly to make sure no one had seen her before she twisted the door handle and slipped into the garage.

Her bag was exactly where it was supposed to be: third cubby across on the "luggage row," marked as such in all-bold letters from her mom's prized label maker. It only took thirty seconds of rummaging before she found Kellie's business card in a mesh pocket.

Neve hadn't looked at the card when Kellie had given it to her—she'd been high from her success at the showcase plus dealing with Inara and Diane—but now she was able to give it her full attention.

KELLIE CARPENTER

ACTING COACH, THEATER DIRECTOR, CHOREOGRAPHER

LET ME OPEN YOUR POTENTIAL

And the dot over the *i* in her name was a freaking heart, which made every dark noiry bone in Neve's body ache from the tweeness.

Still, she'd never been so grateful for such an abundance of twee in her entire life, and as Neve retraced her steps to her bedroom, she plotted out what she was going to say. Should she flat-out ask for Charlotte's contact info without giving any context and hope Kellie handed it over? Or should she concoct an elaborate scenario about why she needed to get in touch with Charlotte? Or tell Kellie the truth?

Neve laughed out loud as she closed her bedroom door. The truth. Like anyone would believe it.

Without a clear plan in mind, Neve punched the digits into her phone and hit the call button.

The perkiest voice in the world picked up on the second ring. "This is Kellie. How can I make your day better?"

Give me Charlotte's phone number? "Um, hi, Kellie. This is Neve Lanier. From GLAM." She didn't know why she felt the need to add that since it had been less than two weeks since they'd seen each other, but Neve was never convinced that people remembered her.

"Neve!" Kellie cried, her excitement rippling through the phone speaker. "I'm so happy to hear from you! I was just telling my mentor about you this week, about how thrilling it was to see your talent blossom before my eyes." She sucked in a breath. "Have you tried out for the theater group at school? Or are auditions coming up? We could FaceTime a coaching session for audition monologues if you'd like."

Neve wasn't about to explain that she couldn't audition for theater at school because she hadn't actually been to school except for about thirty minutes on the first day. "Yeah, that would be great."

"YAY!" Kellie cried. "I'm so excited! When can we start? I'm generally free in the afternoons or weekend mornings if you—"

"Actually . . ." Neve felt guilty lying to Kellie. "Actually, I was wondering if you had Charlotte Trainor's phone number?" She paused, wondering if Kellie would jump in with an answer, but when she didn't,

Neve vamped. "I think I ended up with her copy of the script. The one with all her stage manager's notes. I found it in my suitcase when I finally unpacked and thought maybe she'd want it."

"Oh yeah. I bet she'd love to have that back! I have her number." Kellie's voice sounded more cavernous, as if she'd switched to speakerphone. "Let me find it."

"Thank you so much." She was pretty sure a camp counselor shouldn't be sharing contact information for minors, but at that moment, she was thankful that Kellie's sense of security was lax.

"Texting it to you," Kellie said. Neve felt her breath catch as a soft beep indicated that the text had come through. "Now how about next Monday afternoon for a coaching? Say, four o'clock?"

Ugh. "Sure." *If I'm not in jail by then.*

"Awesome! I'm so excited."

"Me too." Neve couldn't even fake excitement. All she wanted to do was call Charlotte.

"Seriously, Neve. You possess one of the most innate talents I've ever seen."

Neve smiled, despite her desperation to get off the call. It wasn't often she got compliments on anything, and since Diane had clearly been lying about what she thought of Neve's acting, it was nice to think that maybe Kellie hadn't been. "Thanks."

"You're welcome. See you next week!"

The second the call ended, Neve tapped in Charlotte's number. She prayed Charlotte, like Kellie, would pick up, but after eight rings, she ended the call. Maybe if she texted, Charlotte would get back to her?

Charlotte, it's Neve.

Sorry to text like this, but I need to talk to you.

Very important.

In regard to our last conversation.

Call me?

Neve leaned back against her pillows, allowing her aching back to unclench and her shoulders to sag as she watched her screen, hoping for a response. Five minutes. Ten minutes. Nothing.

Fuck.

Was Charlotte avoiding Neve? Had Diane gotten to her? Threatened her? Neve needed to find Charlotte ASAP, and thankfully, Neve knew where she was going to be. Unfortunately, it was the one place in the entire world Neve wanted to avoid, but if she was going to protect her father, she needed to find Charlotte right away. And that meant . . .

She grabbed her phone and sent Charlotte one last text.

I'll find you at Yasmin's memorial. Talk then.

THIRTY-TWO

AS NEVE DROVE TOWARD THE COMMUNITY PARK WHERE Yasmin's memorial gathering was taking place, she was thankful that the Attars had picked a large, outdoor space for the service. If they'd used their church, it might have been impossible for Neve to arrive unnoticed, and the shitshow that ensued would have ruined any chance she had at speaking to Charlotte in private. But this park—complete with a skate ramp, aquatic center, two playgrounds, dog run, and a bandstand—was huge, the kind of place where you'd host an eight-year-old's birthday party or a Fourth of July barbecue.

Neve considered turning around as she pulled into a wraparound parking lot that snuggled the thirty-acre park like an asphalt blanket. The last time she'd seen Mr. and Mrs. Attar was when her dad had dragged her to their house to confront Yasmin. She could still hear him screaming at Yasmin's dad in the doorway, his angry threats so menacing that Yasmin's mom had called the police. It had been the ugly exclamation point at the end of Neve and Yasmin's friendship, and though the Attars hadn't filed a restraining order against either Neve or her dad, bad blood had lingered. How would Mr. and Mrs. Attar react if they recognized Neve in the crowd?

Thankfully, Neve had taken some precautions in that regard. Even though her wardrobe was almost entirely black, her vintage clothes and reddish-brown pin-curled hair were easily identifiable, even at a distance. Neve had dug around in her closet until she found an old pair of jeans that still fit and had swiped one of her dad's hooded sweatshirts. She even pulled on the rubber-soled booties she'd bought for GLAM and smiled as she thought of how Grandma K would approve of such utility. Standing in front of the mirror before she left the house, Neve barely recognized herself. Hopefully, no one at the service would either.

Despite her fear of being recognized, Neve felt a sense of calmness as she approached the park. Yasmin and Neve had shared a close friendship for most of their junior year. They ate dinner with each other's families, slept over at each other's houses, shared secrets and plans for the future. She wanted to be at the memorial service, wanted to grieve the loss of her friend, even if that had technically come long before Yasmin's death.

The sun had already sunk behind the foothills that gently sloped between the park and the Pacific Ocean when Neve parked the Bolt and stepped out into the parking lot. The hills blocked the early-evening rays, and much to her surprise, there was a damp chill in the air. Unusual in the late summer heat of Southern California. Still, it gave Neve an excuse to pull the hoodie over her head without looking suspicious.

Neve took a side path from the lot, passing around the back side of the tennis courts to approach the bandstand from the far end. Even from that distance, she could hear the milling crowd noise drifting toward her. Muted but restless, like people shuffling their feet and speaking in whispered tones. Like a lot of people. *A lot* a lot. Neve rounded the fence and stopped dead.

The crowd gathered around the bandstand was huge. Several hundred, Neve guesstimated. How was she going to find Charlotte in a crowd this size? She skirted the edges, eyes desperately searching for Charlotte's long black hair in the pulsating mass of people while praying that no one recognized her. People were chatting in small groups, waiting for something to happen, and Neve was able to move around relatively unnoticed until suddenly, the whole park went quiet.

"Thank you all for coming."

The familiar voice was small and sharp, amplified through speakers Neve couldn't see. She didn't want to look, but she couldn't help herself, and without thinking, she glanced up at Yasmin's dad at the front edge of the stage behind a microphone stand.

Mr. Attar's face was pale and it looked as if he'd dropped some weight. His cheeks were gaunt, with hollow recesses behind his jawbone that made the skeletal frame of his face more angular and pronounced than she remembered. His wife stood by his side, her head bowed. Her black dress and blazer were crisp and sharp, but her body language exuded less of the "corporate attorney confidence" Neve had been accustomed to. Shoulders rolled forward, chest concave, Mrs. Attar looked like a woman who had given up.

"Thank you all so much for coming," Mr. Attar repeated, immediately silencing the low ripple from the crowd. "My Yasmin would have been so happy to see such a large gathering in her honor."

Neve fought back the uncivil thoughts in her head in relation to Yasmin's ego.

"While we don't want to harp on the circumstances of my princess's death," he continued, his voice cracking with emotion, "we would like to encourage the local authorities to immediately question the person responsible for this heinous act of revenge by an angry, bitter soul."

Does he know who killed his daughter? Neve involuntarily took a step forward.

At the microphone, Mr. Attar swallowed heavily, then turned his head away to clear his throat. "Several of Yasmin's true friends have asked to say a few words about the wonder that was her life, and so I'd like to invite them to—"

Before he could finish, his wife nudged him aside, raising her head for the first time as she took possession of the microphone. Her eyes were puffy, and even from the back of the crowd, Neve could see that they were bloodshot and raw. As if Yasmin's mom hadn't stopped crying for the entire week since her daughter's murder.

"I want to say something." Her voice, unlike her face, was strong, booming through the microphone with a force so explosive Neve jumped at its fierceness. Her upper lip curled as she spoke, an ugly, feral sneer like a lioness about to pounce on her prey.

"I don't know why we're pretending," she said, spitting out the last word as if it left a bitter taste on her tongue. "Pretending that we don't know who did this to my beautiful Yasmin. If the police refuse to act on credible information . . ." She let her voice trail off as she turned to the side of the stage and Neve noticed that Officers Lee and Hernández stood casually by the steps.

Why are they *here?*

"Our family came to this country to escape injustice," Mrs. Attar continued, "to live in a place where you can trust the government and the authorities to take care of you. To protect the innocent and punish those who are not. So far, my family, my *daughter*, has seen no justice."

The anger was ebbing now, giving way to a desperate kind of grief. Her voice escalated in pitch, and she had to hold on to the microphone stand with both hands to keep herself upright. Her words were labored and she took frequent breaths.

"If the police stand by and do nothing, then we must take justice into our own hands. We must *act*. Right now. To flush out a criminal." Her husband laid a hand on her arm, but Mrs. Attar shook him off. "I say we go to her house and show that girl and her family what happens to murderers."

Neve's range of vision collapsed. The world swirled around and around until all she could see was Mrs. Attar's mask of rage. *She's talking about me. She's talking about my family.*

That's what Charlotte meant by rumors. The whole fucking town thought Neve had killed Yasmin.

The crowd cheered raucously at Mrs. Attar's call for a posse, and suddenly, finding Charlotte no longer mattered. Neve needed to get home. She needed to protect her family.

Neve's brain told her legs to run for her life, but her feet wouldn't move, her limbs felt heavy and sluggish, and all she could do was stand there and stare in horror as Mrs. Attar egged on the mob surrounding her.

"We all know who I'm talking about," Mrs. Attar continued, gaining strength from the increasingly agitated crowd. "Hiding at home, hiding from justice. I mean—"

But before she could say Neve's name, Officer Hernández stepped forward and covered the microphone with her hand, oozing the quiet strength and authority that Neve simultaneously feared and respected.

Officer Hernández took Mr. and Mrs. Attar aside for a private word, and in the pause the people in the crowd turned to one another to discuss what had happened.

"She's talking about Neve Lanier."

"Who?"

"That chick who does that old-fashioned thing with her hair."

"Neve needs to pay."

"If I ever see her again, I'm gonna punch her in the face."

"I heard Neve's fingerprints were on the murder weapon."

"I heard they found Neve's hair gripped in Yasmin's dead hand."

Panic set it. Her vision blurred, her face burned, and the blood thundered in her ears so loudly she could barely hear Officer Hernández on the microphone, attempting to calm the seething throng. Neve had never witnessed such focused, mob-fueled anger in her life. If someone recognized her . . .

Neve tiptoed backward, slowly, her heart thundering in her chest, expecting at any moment to hear someone cry out her name and find everyone pointing at her. It would turn into Frank Lovejoy and Lloyd Bridges surrounded by an indignant, bloodthirsty mob at the end of *The Sound of Fury*, and it felt like an eternity before she reached the far edge of the barbecue pits. The instant Neve was out of view of the bandstand, she couldn't contain her panic any longer. She turned and broke into a run as she rounded the fence.

But instead of a clear path to her car, Neve hit something hard and tall.

Not something. Someone.

"Neve?"

Even in the waning daylight, Neve could see the fear wash across Javier's face, probably because he realized that the angry cries from the bandstand were about her. He grabbed Neve by the arm and hurried her to the parking lot, pulling her behind a large van parked in one of the accessible spots near the tennis courts. His grip was gentler than she would have anticipated, and Neve wondered whose safety he was worried about: his or hers?

They stood face-to-face, both panting from adrenaline, until Neve broke the soul-crushing silence.

"What are you doing here?"

Which was possibly the stupidest question in the world. Yes, he'd had some uncomfortable moments with Yasmin, but his best friend was dating Yasmin's best friend. *Of course* he'd be at the memorial. Even though he was late, it would have been super weird if he *hadn't* been there.

"I, uh, knew Yasmin, remember?"

"Right." Neve turned away. She didn't want to be reminded of his beautiful hazel eyes. "I forgot you two were friends."

"I was *not* Yasmin's friend." He said it so vehemently, Neve flinched. "And I don't think you were either. So I'm going to ask you the same question."

"What am I doing here?" Neve said. Then she almost laughed at the irony. "What *am* I doing here?" she repeated under her breath.

Javier's eyes narrowed and he angled his head as if examining a particularly abstract piece of art, intent on learning its meaning but totally failing to do so. "Are you okay?"

"No," she said, the laughter coming for real now as hysteria took control. "No, I'm not okay. There are like three hundred people back there talking about marching to my house for some mob justice. Everyone thinks I murdered my ex–best friend and there's a—"

Neve caught herself in time. She was about to say *and there's a sociopath trying to get me to murder someone* before she realized that the "sociopath" was his stepsister and the "someone" was him.

"There's a what?"

"Nothing." Neve took a deep breath. She had nothing to say to Javier. She needed to get out of there. "I need to go."

She tried to squeeze between him and the giant van, but Javier stepped in front of her, blocking her escape route. The panic she'd felt moments before in the riled-up crowd flared anew.

"Let me by," she said, hoping her voice didn't sound as scared as she felt.

"I need to talk to you."

This was neither the time nor the place. "I can't."

"Neve . . ." He grabbed her arm again, stepping close. Neve couldn't tell if the move was menacing or sexy. "Please."

"I didn't do it!" she said, shaking herself free. Tears welled up in her eyes. "Okay? I didn't kill her. Tell your friends that I'm being framed."

Javier reared back, confused. "I . . . I was just going to apologize for being such a dick at lunch."

Neve relaxed a skosh. "Oh."

"I don't think you're a killer."

Neve wiped below her eye with her middle finger, mascara stinging as it bled from her lashes. "Oh."

"But I thought maybe . . ." He paused, swallowing hard as he ran his fingers through his short brown hair. "I thought maybe you knew *why* Yasmin died."

Neve inhaled slowly, careful not to display any emotion. No shock, no surprise, no confusion. Except she was feeling all of them at once.

Did Javier know what Diane was up to? Did he suspect that she'd murdered Yasmin and was trying to blackmail Neve into killing him? If he did, maybe he could help her. They'd go to Officer Hernández together and tell their stories. Neve would bring up Pamela and Mitchell, she could even loop Charlotte in. Surely, their combined accusations against Diane would at least warrant an investigation?

"Why do you care?" she asked.

Javier came closer, reaching out to graze the back of her hand with his fingertips. He was so close now she could smell the laundry detergent scent lingering on his clothes. Tide, like her mom used at home.

"What *do* you know, Neve?"

Nothing. Everything. Javier's attention was confusing and intoxicating, and it reminded Neve of the night she spent in Diane's dorm room where she wasn't quite sure if her excitement was from the girl bonding or the attraction she felt. But Diane had been manipulating her, giving Neve what she thought she wanted in order to get something in return. Javier had no reason to manipulate her. She had nothing he wanted.

"I . . ." She took a deep breath. She'd trusted Inara and that was working out. Maybe she and Javier were on the same side of this war. She looked up into his eyes and remembered why Yasmin had fallen for him in the first place. "There's something I need to tell you."

His eyebrows shot up.

"About why I was at Holy Name the day that car almost hit you."

"It doesn't matter who you were there to see." Those eyes bored into her as if they could lay bare every thought in her head. Even though he was totally off base on this one.

"It does, though."

He paused, thinking. "Okay. If it's that important, I'll try not to—" A muted beep interrupted his thought, followed rapidly by two more. With a sigh, Javier reached into the front pocket of his jeans. His brow furrowed as he stared at his screen.

Neve tensed. "Who is it?"

"My stepsister's looking for me at the bandstand."

Diane is here? Neve should have known. Diane was everywhere. She backed away from Javier, ready to run.

"Are you okay?" Javier asked, stepping toward her.

She could only imagine what he saw. Probably the palest pale-faced Irish girl in the world, since she was pretty sure that all of the color, warmth, and vitality had completely drained out of her body. "Fine," she croaked. Her voice had apparently abandoned her as well.

"You don't look fine." He laid a hand on her arm. "You're trembling."

Fuck. She hated that he was seeing her this vulnerable. Hated even more that the mere mention of Diane sent her into this paroxysm of fear. "I have to go."

"But you were about to tell me something. Something important?"

Nothing was more important than getting the fuck out of that park before Diane saw her having an intimate moment with Javier. She didn't even wait to answer him but bolted around the back side of the van and sprinted to her car.

THIRTY-THREE

NEVE WAS HALFWAY HOME WHEN HER PHONE BUZZED.

She didn't want to look, didn't want to see Diane's latest taunt. It was disturbing enough that Diane was paying respects at the memorial service of the girl she murdered, but then to fuck with Neve, whom she was trying to frame for said murder? That was truly evil.

But even though her brain said not to look, her eyes betrayed her. As soon as she stopped at the next red light, she glanced down at her phone in the cup holder.

Only the text wasn't from Diane's burner phone.

It was from Charlotte's cell.

Got your texts. Can you meet me at 4905 Montaña Road ASAP?

By some miracle, Neve didn't get pulled over for speeding while she raced the Bolt down the I-5 freeway toward San Diego. The GPS had told her it was a thirty-minute drive to the address Charlotte had given, but Neve made it in twenty. She followed the turn-by-turn directions with hands trembling on the steering wheel, not even questioning the app when it took her into a quiet commercial district. But when she pulled into the deserted parking lot of a huge business park, she was completely shocked to hear the app proclaim that she had arrived.

Neve double-checked the address against the one Charlotte had texted, expecting that in her rush to cut and paste it into her Maps app, Neve had accidentally left out a crucial digit, which would have taken her to this weird commercial complex instead of some McMansion on a tree-lined street closer to the coast. No such luck.

The business park was old construction, like, older than her parents kind of old, and had seen better days. The single-story structures were spread out in rows around a tree-lined parking lot off the main road. The buildings were laid out like rows of storage units instead of business establishments. Number 4905 wasn't so much a street address as it was a unit number, a nondescript darkened glass door in a building that held three others exactly like it: 4904, University City Small Appliance Repair, was the kind of outdated business that might well have been a mob front because who the hell got their vacuum cleaners fixed anymore, while 4906 was a catering company. Both offices, like 4905, were dark and empty on a Sunday evening.

Neve got out of the car and cautiously approached the front window. She wasn't sure why she was tiptoeing—there wasn't anyone around to hear her coming. Other than her Bolt and two vans that belonged to the catering company, the business park was silent.

Why had Charlotte brought her here? Neve didn't understand until she was close enough to the window to see the signage above the door: MIRIAM TRAINOR, CPA.

Was this Charlotte's mom's office?

Neve tried the front door, but it was locked, so she cupped her hands around her eyes and pressed her face to the glass. Without the reflected light from the parking lot, Neve could see a little bit more into the space. It was empty.

There were no desks other than a built-in reception counter, and no furniture of any kind. It looked like Miriam Trainor had relocated.

Neve texted Charlotte back, hoping for more direction.

I'm here. Where are you?

While she waited for a response, she looked in the window again. Beyond the reception desk, a hallway disappeared into the darkness. Probably storage and maybe the back entrance. But Neve's eye was immediately drawn to an L-shaped wall that had been built to one side of the space. It had a door, creating what Neve assumed was a private office in the back corner. And there was a light on inside, creeping out from beneath the closed door. A blue light, like the glow from a phone screen.

Charlotte.

She banged on the front door and waited for Charlotte to slip out from behind the partition wall, but the office remained still. Maybe Charlotte had her headphones on. Neve had said she'd be in there in thirty, so Charlotte probably wasn't expecting her so soon. But she felt exposed standing there in the open, the silent darkness pressing in on her. Maybe she could slip in through the back instead of waiting?

Neve hurried around the corner, where an alley separated the office park from the train tracks that ran behind it. Five doors on the rear side of the building were labeled with their unit numbers, and Neve approached the 4905 door, yanking on the handle with the kind of forceful confidence of someone who knew the door was going to be unlocked.

It swung open noiselessly.

"Charlotte?" She waited, but there was no answer. "Charlotte, it's Neve."

In the darkness, Neve crept warily through Miriam Trainor's old office. She pulled her phone from her pocket and switched on the flashlight, which instantly illuminated a swath of the room with focused light.

A single, thin, five-drawer file cabinet lay on its side, a visible dent in one drawer the apparent cause of its abandonment. The tile floor felt gritty beneath her rubber-soled boots, as if the floors hadn't been cleaned in a while, and the room smelled vaguely of wet newspaper and sawdust, a strange combination that tickled the inside of Neve's nose. She pressed forward through the old storage area, past an open bathroom door, and into the main space of the office.

The blue light that Neve had seen under the office door had gone out and the only light in the abandoned office came from Neve's phone. "Hey!" Neve said, approaching the door. "Charlotte?" She wasn't sure why, but she didn't want to open that door.

Flipping her phone around, Neve noticed that Charlotte hadn't replied to her text. So she sent another.

Charlotte, are you okay?

Within seconds, the blue light blipped on inside the office, peeking out from beneath the closed door.

Charlotte's phone was inside that room.

Neve's hand shook as she gripped the knob, and when she pushed the door open, she felt like the dumb girl in a horror movie, the one who goes off alone into the creepy old house and ends up dead before the film's halfway point. She always envisioned herself more as the Final Girl in one of those movies. The survivor. The one who made all the smart decisions and figured out all the clues.

Well, she'd figured out one thing at least. It was Charlotte's phone that had lit up the room. It was right there, gripped in Charlotte's hand, except Neve's brain only registered that fact for a second before her eyes were drawn to Charlotte's face.

It was turned toward the door, her eyes wide and unseeing, her mouth twisted in a silent scream of fear and pain. She lay on her stomach with the handle of a chef's knife sticking out from between her shoulder blades.

Charlotte Trainor was dead.

THIRTY-FOUR

FOR A SPLIT SECOND, NEVE THOUGHT ABOUT WALKING AWAY.
No one knew she'd been to that abandoned office. No one would ever
connect her to it when Charlotte's body was eventually found. And considering how much suspicion was already heaped upon her over Yasmin's
murder, the idea of adding more fuel to the rage-inspired fire she'd witnessed at the memorial service by being discovered beside Dead Body #2
was utterly overwhelming.

But the instinct was a fleeting one, born of panicked self-preservation
and dismissed in an instant. Charlotte had been her friend. She didn't

deserve to lie here, forgotten and alone, because Neve was worried that she would be blamed. Well, blamed by the authorities, as opposed to blaming herself. Because as she pulled her phone from her bag, all Neve could think about was the fact that Charlotte, like Yasmin, was probably dead because of her.

If Charlotte hadn't caught me spying on Javier, she might still be alive.

As Neve waited for the police to arrive after her 911 call, she sat on the industrial carpet outside the private office door, which was still littered with bits of torn file folders, ejected paper clips, and mangled staples that looked as if they had been wrenched away by an angry, aggressive hand. She stared at Charlotte's body, her eyes still open and locked on Neve through the open door.

Neve had wanted to close Charlotte's eyes, check for a pulse, do something to feel as if she could have saved Charlotte's life, but she knew the moment she saw the body that Charlotte was beyond saving, and that even approaching her, let alone touching her body, would probably get Neve into more trouble. So she sat there, impotent and helpless, while her mind raced.

What the fuck am I going to do?

The question was many-pronged.

What the fuck am I going to tell the police when they arrive?

What the fuck am I going to do about Diane?

What the fuck am I going to tell my parents?

Not to mention Javier. Who shouldn't even have been popping into her head at that moment.

Damn it.

Neve took a deep breath, pressing the palms of her hands against her eyelids. She was in way, way, way over her head. Diane had planned this. Had she lured Charlotte to her mom's old office and then killed her? Or killed her someplace else and moved the body here? The police would figure that one out, and it almost didn't matter to Neve. The result was the same: Diane sent those texts from Charlotte's phone so that Neve would be the one to find the body.

Which meant calling 911 instead of walking away was not only the morally correct choice, but also the smart one. This office was probably wired with a camera or some other surveillance device that would have shown, when Charlotte was eventually found, that Neve had been there.

Maybe that had been Diane's intention all along? If Neve didn't call 911 upon finding Charlotte's body, it would look suspicious as fuck if someone could later prove that Neve had been at the murder scene. A killer wouldn't call in their own crime, would they?

Red-and-blue lights flashed through the front windows, lending the darkened interior of the abandoned office an eerie disco-party vibe. Neve sat still, waiting while balls of white flashlight beams scanned the windows. She didn't know if there would be guns drawn or not, and it wasn't really a good idea to startle an armed police officer at a murder scene. She held her breath, wondering if they would try and break down the front door. But the flashlights quickly disappeared around the side of the building.

The next few minutes were a blur. Neve remembered the flashlights landing on her in the darkness, darting back and forth across her face like blinding strobes. Angry cries for her to put her hands up and then not to move, which seemed oxymoronic, but whatever. She did as instructed and remained as still as possible, not saying a word. There were three officers: one focused on her, one attended the body, and one searched the rest of the office for whatever it was police officers searched for at a murder scene.

Voices crackled on police radios; more sirens in the distance. Two officers eventually hauled her to her feet and deposited her in the only other chair in the near-empty space, before handcuffing her. "For your safety and for ours," she heard one of the cops say. Right, except they had guns.

Before long, someone managed to get the lights turned on, and Neve had to squeeze her eyes shut against the blinding pain. The abandoned unit looked even more mundane with the lights on as the detritus of normal everyday office life was offset by the dead body skewered to the floor just feet from her, but Neve wasn't left alone long enough to contemplate the full horror of the scene. A new squad car roared to a stop out front. An officer lifted Neve to her feet and guided her through the now-open front door as Officers Lee and Hernández emerged from the black-and-white.

"She was found at the scene," her escort said. "Just sitting there on the floor in the dark."

"She called it in," Officer Hernández said, staring hard at Neve. What was she looking for? Guilt? Remorse? Understanding?

"We'll take it from here," Officer Lee added, guiding Neve to the backseat of their squad car. The look on his face as he closed the door was much easier to read than his partner's but much more confusing.

Because Officer Lee was looking at her with pity.

No one spoke on the drive to back to Carlsbad.

Neve hadn't expected there to be questioning or small talk, but still, thirty minutes of silence felt weird. Unnatural. It was difficult to explain, but Neve got the distinct impression that Officers Hernández and Lee were on the brink of saying something to her several times during the drive, but ultimately thought better of it.

When they arrived at the station, the conversation was limited to instructions.

"Watch your head."

"This way."

"Wait here."

Then the handcuffs were removed and she was left alone in a small, windowless room.

The waiting sucked. Neve wasn't sure how long she sat staring at the bland gray walls with nothing but her own thoughts about poor Charlotte's last moments and what prison was going to be like and what Grandma K would say when she found out her oldest grandchild had been arrested on suspicion of murder, but it felt like an eternity. She was hungry, her back hurt, and she desperately had to pee.

Maybe it was all a police tactic to force Neve from her comfort zone and then hope to shake a confession out of her. Like when Dana Andrews hit Gene Tierney with the floodlights in *Laura*.

Well, if they wanted a confession, Neve was ready to give one. Just not the one they were expecting. Neve planned to spill her guts. She'd been reluctant to try again after her rejections by Officer Hernández, but if she could just get the police to investigate Diane, her connection to Pamela, the similarities between what happened at Brown Ledge *last* summer and at GLAM *this* summer, and the attempt on Javier's life and Mitchell's hit-and-run . . . Well, of course they were going to see the connection. Perhaps even find the evidence that would link Diane to both murders.

If only she'd been this brave earlier, more insistent with Officer Hernández that morning, maybe Charlotte wouldn't be lying back in that sad, abandoned office staring sightlessly at a cubicle wall while a small army of forensic investigators, cops, and coroners pored over her final resting place like ants swarming out of a flooded hill.

"Ms. Lanier?" A young Latina officer with a long braid snaking down the back of her neck poked her head through the open door. She didn't look much older than Neve, and her voice, though confident, lacked Officer Hernández's authoritative edge.

"Yes?"

"I need to ask you some questions."

"Okay."

The officer slipped into the room, leaving the door ajar. She had Neve's messenger bag in one hand and an iPad in the other. "What time did you arrive at 4905 Montaña Road?"

Neve swallowed. This wasn't Officer Hernández, who looked as if she could sniff out a liar at fifty feet, but she was going to tell the absolute truth anyway. Lies wouldn't help her cause. "I'm not sure exactly." Neve hadn't looked at the time once the GPS deposited her in the business park. "But I got a text from Charlotte around seven o'clock, asking me to meet her."

"You left immediately?"

"Yes."

"And you came from?"

Ugh. This wasn't going to sound good. "The memorial service for Yasmin Attar."

"At the park in Carlsbad," the officer said, nodding her head. The braid didn't move. "Which meant you arrived sometime between seven thirty and seven forty."

Neve shrugged. That sounded about right.

The officer placed Neve's bag on the table. Why were they giving her back her belongings?

"And do you remember any other details about the location when you arrived? Anything that might help the investigation?"

Neve blinked. She was pretty sure there was some kind of law against self-incrimination. "You want me to give you evidence against . . . myself?"

The officer looked genuinely confused as she put the pen down and glanced up at Neve. "No. Against the suspect in custody. They just brought him in." She paused and looked down at her iPad, scrolling up. Then she read something that made her eyes grow wide.

Neve gripped the strap of her messenger bag so fiercely she could feel the leather straps digging into her palm. *Oh God, no.*

She could have asked the nice officer the suspect's name, but Neve already knew it. She needed to see for herself, needed to know for sure if Diane had followed through on her threat. With a swift move that caught the officer off guard, Neve darted around her and dashed down the hallway.

Neve knew what she was going to see before she reached the end of the corridor, before her eyes found two officers bringing a handcuffed figure into the station, supporting his gaunt figure under his arms. She knew, because she'd seen this exact sight in her nightmares for the past week.

The man under arrest for the murders of Charlotte Trainor and Yasmin Attar was her dad.

THIRTY-FIVE

"DAD!"

Neve sprinted across the station. Her father, stretched out and limp like an old T-shirt that had been through the wash too many times and should probably be thrown away because the fabric was threadbare and unsalvageable, looked empty. His face was pinched as if he was in tremendous pain, and it aged him to the point where Neve might not have recognized him if he was walking down the street toward her. It reminded Neve of the way he had looked when her mom drove him to the hospital to check himself in for a psychiatric evaluation that would last two months. All of his strides over the last three years had been for nothing.

An officer stepped in front of her, barring her progress, as they marched her dad over to a well-lit area to take his photograph. His mug shot. "Dad!" she cried again, hoping the sound of her voice might spark some life into his dead eyes. He didn't even look at her.

"Don't smile," an officer said, stepping up to a monitor to check the alignment of the photo.

Don't worry, Neve thought to herself bitterly. She doubted her dad would ever smile again.

"Neve?" Her mom's voice cracked and as Neve swung around, she noticed right away that her mom had been crying. Red eyes and nose, smudged mascara. It was the first time in her entire life that she'd seen her mother cry.

"Mom, what happened?"

"I . . ." Her mom's eyes trailed over Neve's shoulder toward her husband. "I don't . . ." She shook herself, throwing off the unfamiliar confusion and indecision. Neve knew her mother so well. While her dad was giving up the fight and drifting back into the abyss, her mom needed to assert control in order to feel normal again. "Neve Lanier, what in the name of all that is holy are you doing here? Did the police call you in?"

Sort of. "I was in the neighborhood."

Her mom's eyebrow shot up. Glibness would not be tolerated. Just like Grandma K. "Not. Now. With. Your. Snark." Judging by the bulging vein in her left temple, Neve's mom wasn't joking.

"Sorry." Her dad was getting fingerprinted now, at a little table beside the photo stand. His eyes looked deader than ever. "Did they come to the house? Did Deirdre see—"

"Yes," her mom said curtly. "I dropped her off at Aunt Connie's on the way here. She's keeping Deirdre overnight. I packed her a bag."

Typical. Her mom was practical even in the face of a family tragedy. "Are you okay?"

Neve had meant the question benignly, in the sort of I-don't-know-what-else-to-say-and-I'm-feeling-utterly-helpless-but-standing-here-in-silence-will-be-worse-so-I'm-going-to-say-*something* kind of way, but instead of answering in kind, her mom whirled on her, nostrils flared, Irish temper set to erupt.

"Okay? Am I okay? Your father has been arrested, Neve. Do you understand that?"

I'm going to take that as a no on the okay thing. "Yes."

"In front of your sister. They took him away in handcuffs. Do you think she will ever forget that trauma?"

Neve understood that her mom was venting, that her years of putting on a brave face in the wake of her husband's mental health struggles were crumbling down around both of them in an epic explosion of pent-up anger, frustration, and regret, but she had no idea how to help. "I'm sorry."

"You should be!" her mom screamed. Actually screamed in Neve's face, so raw that Neve could feel the hot rush of air against her cheeks. "This is all your fault."

Whoa. "My fault?" She glanced around the police station to see if anyone was paying attention. Her dad had been marched to a back room, and the few officers who remained diplomatically kept their eyes glued to clipboards and paperwork. Still, Neve dropped her voice, nervous about speaking the next words out loud while surrounded by cops. "Do you think *I* killed those girls?"

Her mom winced, slapped in the face by the implication of her own words. She hesitated, unable to immediately deny Neve's accusation, and that was all the answer Neve needed. Her mom thought she was guilty and that somehow her dad was taking the fall.

She backed away, horrified. If her own mother didn't believe in her, who the fuck else would?

"Go home, Neve," her mom said, sighing. "Just go home."

Neve didn't need to be told twice. Hands clenched at her sides, she spun away from her mom and rushed blindly through the door into the darkness of night.

Neve stepped out of the police station, heart pounding so fiercely she could feel its vibrations reverberating through her entire body. She was pissed off and despondent at the same time, and as she stood at the edge of the concrete plaza trying to catch her breath, she realized that she had no freaking idea where the Bolt was. Or how she was going to get home.

The car was probably still down in San Diego or at an impound lot, which left her two options: walk or Uber. But the last thing she wanted at that moment was to be trapped in a moving vehicle with an overly chatty ride-share driver. She'd rather walk all the way home. It wasn't too far, and the route took her on streets that were mostly well lit and lined with businesses. Plus, it would give her some time to think about what she was going to do to help her dad. Because she was the only person who could.

The night air bit her face with a breeze off the ocean, bringing with it a thick, damp layer of fog that made the streets look more like London in winter than California in late summer. Neve was thankful she still wore her dad's hoodie and the only sensible pair of shoes she owned, so if she kept up a decent pace, she'd keep herself relatively warm during the trek home.

She passed several shopping centers with grocery stores and restaurants that were still open. Their overhead parking lot lights flooded the street with a yellowish glow at irregular intervals down Airport Road, and the street was quiet enough that she could hear the roar of waves on the beach a few miles away, a dull white-noise background on an eerie, moonless night.

It wasn't until she turned off the main road to cut through a commercial business park near her subdivision that Neve realized she'd made a mistake in choosing to walk home.

It was darker here, for starters. The streetlamps were farther apart, barely two per block, and without the added illumination from open businesses, the road stretching before her was shrouded in an ominous gloom. The parking lots that would have been full of office employees on a weekday evening were totally empty on a Sunday night. Even the surf had receded into the background, muffled by a marine layer that was thickening by the minute. The silence was so all-encompassing that Neve could hear the muted thuds of her footfalls on the sidewalk, jarring and out of place in the sudden quiet. The silence was tense, dangerous, like the scene in *The Third Man* when Joseph Cotten finds Orson Welles spying on him in the darkened Vienna streets. And *that* had turned out so well.

She quickened her pace, breathing heavily, and had to fight to keep from breaking into a run.

What is wrong with you? Neve was letting her imagination get the better of her. She wasn't in some apocalyptic wasteland, hunted by cannibal gangs of displaced teens. This was freaking Carlsbad. It was literally one of the safest places to live in the entire state of California, for fuck's sake. She was perfectly fine walking home at this hour.

Except two people you know have been murdered.

Neve stopped, forcing herself to calm the hell down. Her heart was racing in her chest, a mix of the unexpected exercise and the uninvited paranoia, and as she stood rooted in place on the sidewalk, attempting to get control of her panic, a new sound caught her attention. The distinct and unmistakable crunch of tires on asphalt.

She spun around to confront the oncoming sound and firmly expected to see a rape van bearing down on her. Instead, she saw a white car, headlights off so that Neve could easily make out the distinctive BMW grille, and before the car even pulled alongside and the driver popped on the interior light, Neve knew who was following her.

Diane rolled down the passenger-side window as she eased the BMW to a halt beside Neve. "Get in."

THIRTY-SIX

NEVE'S FIRST INSTINCT WAS TO RUN.

Her second instinct was to haul Diane from her luxury car and beat her to a senseless pulp on the sidewalk.

Her third instinct was to get in the car and try once more to record a confession on her phone. Maybe she could catch Diane off guard this time?

"Why should I?" she said, turning protectively away. It was a move that she hoped looked perfectly natural, under the circumstances, but was actually one hundred percent tactical. Using her body to shield her bag from Diane's view, she slipped her hand into its depths and gripped her phone.

"Unless you want your dad to rot in jail for the rest of his life," Diane said with a sigh, losing patience, "I suggest you get in the goddamn car."

"Fuck you!" Neve yelled, then stormed away.

The instant she cleared the front of the car, she whipped her phone out of her bag, angling the screen close to her body and hoping Diane wouldn't be able to see the telltale blue glow. Immediately, she heard the crunch of tires again, and the street was flooded with light as Diane switched on her high beams.

Neve unlocked the screen with her thumb and frantically opened the camera function. This time, it was going to work.

"Sooooo dramatic." Diane laughed, her voice jarringly bell-like as she pulled alongside. An evil pixie delighting in the misery she inflicted. "Now get *in*."

Neve stopped walking, took one last look at her phone as she hit record on her video app, then slipped the phone into her pocket before turning to face the car. "Fine."

She refused to look at Diane as she climbed into the BMW and closed the door. She waited for Diane to say something, praying she'd be able to manipulate the conversation toward the murders.

"How's your dad?" Diane began.

Neve wanted to claw the girl's face off. "You managed to get him arrested for murder, just like you threatened," she said, hoping that her phone was picking up every word.

Diane snorted. "I don't know why you're lashing out at me. Your dad needs help, Neve."

"Give it up, Diane." Once again, Neve wondered if Diane suspected what she was up to. "I know you framed him."

"I don't know *what* you're talking about."

"And I know you killed Charlotte because she was your original target." Neve was guessing here, but it was the only thing that made sense. "You followed her to GLAM camp like you followed Pamela to Brown Ledge."

This time, the flinch was undeniable. If only Neve had the video camera pointed at Diane, she would have definitely caught the swift look of worry that crossed her face. Sadly, Neve's recording was audio only, and Diane wasn't about to give her any kind of verbal admission. "Who?"

"I am *not* killing Javier. You've already got my dad arrested—it's not like you can make my life any worse."

She waited for Diane to say something, anything, but as the silence stretched, she kept going. "You can't force me to do your dirty work. You want Javier dead? Do it yourself."

"He's my stepbrother." The response was noncommittal and reinforced Neve's idea that Diane suspected she was being recorded. Damn it, they were almost to Neve's house and she was getting nowhere with this conversation.

"What the hell do you want from me, Diane?"

"I want you to fulfill your promise," Diane said simply. For the first time since Neve got in the car, Diane's voice had a sharp edge to it.

The reminder of that night in Diane's GLAM camp dorm room made Neve's stomach drop.

"And I want you to do it tomorrow."

The car slowed in front of Neve's house, dark except for the light over the front door. Not a single bit of incriminating audio had slipped from Diane's lips during their ride, and once again, Neve was dismayed at the fact that her nemesis was one step ahead of her.

"I won't," Neve said as she clutched her bag to her chest. "I won't kill anyone for you."

"This is your stop."

Once again, she'd failed. She'd begun opening the door when Diane stopped her with a hand on the arm.

"Oh, I almost forgot!" she squealed, the faux perkiness back on full display. "I got you something." She reached over and unlocked the glove compartment, pulling a wrapped box from inside and depositing it in Neve's lap.

"What is it?"

Diane grinned. "It's a reminder of our friendship."

Ugh. More games. Neve slid off the leather seat, leaving the box behind. "I'm not taking anything from you." Then she slammed the door in Diane's face.

The passenger window was down before Neve was off the sidewalk. "Oh yeah?" Diane leaned across the center console, snatched the box off the seat, and tossed it through the open window. "I think you should reconsider. Like I said, things could *always* get worse."

Neve kept her eyes locked onto the white BMW until it rounded the corner at the end of her block and disappeared. Even then, she didn't move from the sidewalk, half-convinced Diane would circle back. Five minutes later, standing in the glow of the nearby streetlamp, Neve slowly pulled her phone from her pocket and aimed the camera at the box that lay where it had fallen on the grassy median. Her phone was still recording.

She shifted the camera to selfie mode. "I don't know how much of that you caught, but I'm pretty sure Diane suspected that I was recording her. I know she didn't say anything that could make you believe that I'm telling the truth, but I swear to God, I am. Don't you think she'd be a little bit more shocked when I mentioned killing her stepbrother if it was the first time she'd ever heard the idea?"

Neve paused, shifting the camera back to the wrapped package as she crouched down beside it. She was going to document all of this. Just in case. "Here's what she gave me as I got out of the car: a book-size box wrapped in yellow-and-pink-striped wrapping paper." The cutesiness of the package was barf-inducing.

Neve used her free hand to open it, ripping the paper to shreds in the process.

Inside the box was a handgun.

"I hope you can see this," Neve said for the camera. "I don't know anything about guns, but this thing looks real."

Neve kind of sort of wanted to pick up the weapon, gauge the weight of it, and see if she felt any more like a killer with an actual lethal device in her hands, but she knew this was evidence, and she didn't want her fingerprints anywhere near it. Carefully, she replaced the lid, hastily pulled the shredded wrap around it, and shoved it in her bag before addressing the camera one last time.

"Diane Russell gave me a gun because she wants me to kill Javier Flores in payment for the death of Yasmin Attar, whom Diane murdered. She's been blackmailing me. My dad is completely innocent of this crime. And I'm going to prove it."

As she switched off the camera, Neve knew she meant it. She had no idea what she was going to do about this, especially since Diane had planned everything to perfection, always thinking one step ahead of everyone. But she had to try.

Someone had to stop Diane.

Buoyed by her own resolve, Neve stood and marched up to the

darkened, empty house. She'd call Inara when she got inside and tell her all about her dad's arrest. She needed a sympathetic ear, someone who would let her vent. Maybe together they could come up with a plan? She hurried to unlock the door and dashed into the entryway, only to freeze as she spun around.

Sitting at the entrance to the kitchen in one of their dining room chairs was Javier. His hand gripped a gun that looked eerily similar to the one Diane had just given Neve. And it was pointed directly at her.

"We need to talk."

THIRTY-SEVEN

NEVE STARED AT THE GUN, HER HAND TWITCHING ON THE strap of her messenger bag. She wasn't entirely sure whether having her own firearm would protect her in this situation or make it more likely that Javier might put a bullet in her chest, but standing there, unarmed, with a gun pointed at her, certainly didn't feel particularly safe.

"Talk about what?"

"My stepsister," Javier said, not moving a muscle. His body was rigid and tense in the chair and his eyes drooped with fatigue.

"Okay . . ." She wondered if he knew that his stepsister wanted him dead.

"Did she ask you to kill me?" *Yep, he knows.*

Neve relaxed, even though there was a gun still pointed at her. The fact that Javier already *knew* Diane was a psychopath meant they might be able to help each other. "*Ask* is a bit of a stretch."

Javier nodded his head once, conceding the point. "Blackmail?"

"Basically."

"And when you saved me from getting run over that day . . ." He let his voice trail off intentionally, which meant he wanted Neve to fill in the blanks.

"I was stalking you," she said, surprised by how easily the truth rolled off her tongue after almost a solid week of lying. It felt good. Freeing. She would have told him the truth even if he didn't have a gun aimed at her. "To figure out a good way to kill you."

He tightened his grip on the gun, and Neve realized that she was the only one who felt this newfound sense of camaraderie.

"I wasn't *actually* going to kill you," she said, eyeing the gun. "I was just trying to buy some time to figure out what to do."

She waited, hoping he'd let his guard down. He didn't.

"I think we're on the same side," she said.

"I doubt that."

Neve pursed her lips. This family. Living in their house must be a perpetual nightmare of suspicion and distrust. "You, presumably, don't want to be dead, and I certainly don't want to kill you. That makes us allies."

Javier paused for a moment, mulling over her words. "You'll have to forgive me if I trust you, like, not at all."

"Seems to run in your family."

"Yeah, we're a pretty fucked-up bunch."

The banter was cute—so Bogie and Bacall that Neve was tempted to add an *I don't like your manners* just for effect, but it wasn't getting them anywhere. "Look, I met your sister—"

"*Step*sister."

They were both so hung up on that label. "I met your *step*sister at GLAM camp this summer. I think she followed Charlotte Trainor there, hoping to use her for the murder swap, but Charlotte was suspicious, so she targeted me because I was obviously out of my element."

He still didn't relax. "So?"

"So I was the perfect victim for your sister's plan. I think she has a type."

"Usually," Javier said, which left Neve wondering if that meant she wasn't like Diane's past marks. And then wondering how Javier knew about past victims. She decided to take a stab in the dark.

"Like Pamela?"

Now it was Javier's turn to react. His chin shot up, his entire body suddenly on alert. "What do you know about her?"

"Not much," Neve said, which was the truth. "Only that Diane met her at school back in Massachusetts and followed her to Brown Ledge last summer, and then a few months later the guy Pamela had a crush on almost died in a hit-and-run. She apparently ended her own life soon after." Neve paused, waiting for Javier to confirm her story, elaborate, cry, laugh, *anything*. Instead, he stared at her in silence.

This was getting old.

"Did you know her?" Neve prompted. "Ever see her around?"

"She never sat in her car in a parking lot watching me take BP, if that's what you mean."

Okay. A hint of humor. "Funny."

"I like to think so."

The banter was a good indication that he wasn't going to put a bullet in her. Although with this family, who really knew for sure?

"How did you find out about Pamela?" Javier asked.

"My roommate at GLAM camp. Her ex-girlfriend was also at Brown Ledge last year and had told her the story. She put two and two together."

"Smart."

"I know. I should have listened to her."

"Why didn't you?" The edge had vanished from his voice.

That was a loaded question, and answering it would have laid all of Neve's deep-rooted insecurities bare for Javier to see. Although who cared? What did she have to lose at this point? She was already a former murder suspect and current school pariah whose dad was in jail and whose mom thought she had committed the crimes he'd been charged with. As Neve had said to Diane in the car, it wasn't really like things could get any worse.

"Because I had a crush on Diane and I didn't want to hear it." She blew out a breath through pursed lips. Stating her truth was easier than she thought it would be. "I'm bisexual. But I've never told anyone that until, like, yesterday and so I'm usually uncomfortable everywhere I go because I'm either hiding it or assuming that everyone who looks at me funny knows I'm hiding this secret. And your sister—sorry, *step*sister . . ."

Javier snorted a laugh but didn't interrupt her further.

"Your stepsister kind of knew somehow and I know she was just using me, I know she was only flirting to get me to do what she wanted, but she . . . she made me feel like I mattered."

The choke of a sob stopped Neve, cutting off her voice and threatening to explode through her mouth in a torrential downpour of tears, and she sure the hell didn't want Javier to see her ugly-cry. She squeezed her eyes shut and dug her fingernails into the palms of her hands, clenching her fists as tightly as her strength would allow, and hoped the sharp twinge of pain would force back the emotion that was threatening to erupt. She took a ragged breath, then let it out slowly through pursed lips. The sob that was lodged in her throat sank back down to the depths of her body. She relaxed her shoulders, which had migrated up toward her ears, and slowly peeled her eyes open.

Javier had risen to his feet, the gun that he'd held so steadily at her discarded on the dining-room chair. The lines of his face were no longer rigid and hard, and those haunting greenish-brown eyes reflected only worry and concern. Not anger. Not hatred. He crossed the entryway to her in four long, purposeful strides and for one gloriously confusing second, Neve imagined that he was going to wrap his arm around her waist, pull her body to his, and kiss her.

Instead, he stood there, ten inches away, gazing down at her. Then, as if he wasn't entirely sure what he was doing, he reached out his hand and awkwardly patted her on the arm. Like she was a puppy who'd just performed a good trick. Or one of his teammates who'd booted a play and needed to be consoled.

Ouch.

"I'm sorry," he said, dropping his hand back to his side. Even he recognized the weirdness of his gesture.

Neve shook her head. She didn't trust her voice with an answer.

"I suspected you," he said softly. "That day at Holy Name. I thought maybe the whole car-trying-to-run-me-down thing was a setup to gain my confidence."

"Oh."

He held up his hand, begging for silence. He obviously wanted to get something off his chest uninterrupted. "I wasn't sure, and that's why

I asked you to lunch. I wanted to see how you'd react if I brought up Diane."

Neve remembered being so satisfied when he'd mentioned his stepsister, because she'd been trying to figure out a way to get her into the conversation and hadn't managed to maneuver her in yet. Meanwhile, all along, *he* had been playing *her*.

"You're right about Pamela. She was Diane's experiment last summer. All of a sudden, this strange girl started showing up at my practices after school, trying to make conversation. I could tell she didn't really want to. She wasn't interested in me, and she looked terrified all the time, eyes darting over her shoulder like someone was following her."

Neve thought of all the times Diane appeared out of nowhere, or sent a text that proved she'd been watching Neve's every move. "That's probably because someone was."

"First Yasmin died," Javier continued. "And then you showed up at my school. Well, I kind of knew what was up. I'd heard your name—Yasmin would bring you up to Marisol all the time just so they could bitch about you—and I overheard all about how you'd been treated at school."

Neve rolled her eyes at the idea that Marisol, Luna, and Yasmin would sit around talking about that single stupid text ad nauseam. Like get the fuck over it already. Neve had already suffered a public shaming and total social ostracizing. Wasn't that enough?

"Seemed like you had a motive to kill Yasmin," he continued, "and I realized that Diane could use it against you. It was leverage she didn't have with Pamela."

Javier was savvier about Diane's craziness than she'd realized. "And now she's framed my dad for both murders."

Javier started. "Both?"

"Yasmin and Charlotte."

His jaw dropped. "Charlotte's dead?" Duh, of course he didn't know about her. Word couldn't have gotten out yet.

"Sorry," Neve said quickly. "I forgot you didn't know."

Javier shook his head. "Poor Charlotte."

"Yeah." Neve shuddered, flashing on an image of the giant knife sticking out of Charlotte's back.

"And your dad. I'm so sorry."

Neve didn't trust her voice to answer. Diane had threatened to send her "evidence" against Neve's dad to the police and his arrest would indicate that she'd followed through. How was Diane going to exonerate him now even if Neve did what she demanded? It seemed like Neve's only course of action at this point was to prove that Diane was the murderer.

"What are you going to do now?" Javier asked. He'd taken a step toward Neve during her silence.

She looked up at him, allowing herself to indulge in the warmth of his hazel eyes. "I wish I knew."

"Maybe . . ." His hazel eyes crinkled up as he smiled. "Maybe we can help each other."

THIRTY-EIGHT

NEVE TOLD JAVIER EVERYTHING. IT WAS LIKE VERBAL disembowelment, the tale of her friendship with Diane Russell pouring out of her so quickly she wasn't even sure Javier would process the facts. From the moment Diane introduced herself, through Annabelle's mysterious illness, the theater module, Confessional, rehearsals, the showcase, and that final night at GLAM. Neve felt a clawing sense of urgency to get her story out, as if she needed to make sure the truth was spoken in case Javier decided to pick up that handgun again.

Though she was pretty sure that he was no longer concerned with protecting himself. Not from her, at least. He stood close to Neve while she wove her tale, arms crossed over his chest, eyes focused on her face. Normally, that kind of intense, unceasing eye contact with a guy or girl she found attractive would have made Neve incredibly uncomfortable. She would have looked away—at the ceiling, at the carpet, down the hallway, anywhere but Javier's face. But his placid calmness encouraged her, his quiet strength emboldened her truth, and instead of retreating into herself at his unwavering gaze, she found herself matching it, holding on to it like a metaphorical lifeline as she raced through all her encounters with Diane since GLAM.

"Then she gifted me a handgun," she said, punctuating the last episode of her story. "It looks a lot like . . ." Her eyes drifted to the chair behind Javier.

"Like my dad's Glock?" Javier arched an eyebrow. "Can I see it?"

Neve hesitated as she wondered why an infectious-disease doctor would need to keep a handgun in the house, but then reached for her messenger bag. In for a penny, in for a pound, as Grandma K always said. She opened the box.

Javier whistled. "It looks a lot like my dad's because it's the exact same model. I wonder why Diane chose it?"

Neve carefully lowered the Glock back into its resting place and pulled the lid over it. She didn't know enough about guns or ballistics or weapon serial numbers to formulate an answer, but she knew Diane. "She's been a step or two ahead of me all along, so I would assume that if she gave me an identical gun to use, it's for a reason."

Javier ran his fingers through his hair, holding it all back from his face for a second before letting go. Instead of enthused or at the very least mollified by Neve's story, he looked baffled. "Have you told the police?"

Neve snorted. "I tried. They didn't believe me."

"What we need," Javier continued, his face more pensive than despairing, "is a confession."

"Good luck," Neve said with a shake of her head. "I tried that twice, and she definitely sniffed me out. Didn't slip up once."

"Have you told anyone else?"

"Inara," Neve said. "My roommate from camp."

"Did she believe you?"

"Yeah, she did." Neve smiled at the thought of Inara. "Even though she had no reason to. I wasn't very nice to her at GLAM."

Javier rolled his eyes slightly—enough that Neve noticed, but with a subtlety that hinted he was trying to hide the reaction.

"I know, I know. The camp name is awful." She paused, thinking of her time at GLAM. Even with Diane's betrayal, she remembered those two weeks fondly. Which was not something she had expected. "But the people were all right."

"Even though my stepsister tried to Svengali you into murdering a total stranger?"

Neve's smile faded. She might remember GLAM fondly, but her presence there had led directly to the deaths of two people. "Even though Yasmin and Charlotte are dead."

"Yeah." Javier let out a heavy breath. "Sorry. I didn't mean to make a joke of it."

Was this guy's sensitivity for real? Yasmin could never have deserved him. "It's not your fault. I'm the one to blame."

He gripped her arm lightly. "No, *Diane* is the one to blame. You're trying to fix things."

Neve met his eyes and for one exhilarating moment she had the urge to wrap her arms around his neck and pull him close. Instead she turned toward the window and gazed out onto the darkened street while she tried to hide the hot blush racing up her neck to her face. "We've got to stop her."

"Well . . ." Javier cleared his throat. "You've got this gun here."

She glanced at him over her shoulder, worried he actually meant that she could take vengeance into her own hands. Instead of murderous resolve etched into his features, he flashed Neve a sheepish grin.

"I'm kidding," he said. "I know you're not a killer."

"Thanks?"

"But maybe we could use the gun to force a confession out of her?"

Neve shook her head. Diane wouldn't have given her the gun if she didn't have a contingency plan for Neve using it against her. "She's planned for that. I can guarantee it."

"You're right, I'm sure." Then he laughed. "That's life. Whichever way you turn, fate sticks out a foot to trip you."

Neve gasped. The line was familiar. "Is that from *Detour*?" It was a deep cut, a creepy dark noir from the midforties that had become more of a cult film in recent years.

Javier's eyebrows shot up in surprise. "Yeah. How did you know?"

"Heh." Neve pushed back the hood of her sweatshirt and motioned to her pin curls. "I, uh, have a thing for film noir."

"Me too." He smiled warmly and Neve felt herself drawn toward him. She'd never met anyone else who appreciated *Detour*.

"Funny, huh?" Neve said. "That Diane would come up with this *Strangers on a Train* murder plot having never watched the movie."

"I was thinking the same thing." Javier shook his head. "And she's *such* a Bruno Antony."

"Spoiled, egotistical, single-minded."

"Single-minded on me." He laughed again, only this time it was sharp and devoid of amusement. "The only way we'd get her to admit to anything is if she thought I was already dead."

Already dead . . . Neve's eyes grew wide as she spun back toward Javier. "That's it!"

"Whoa." Javier held his hands up in front of him defensively, his eyes darting toward the gun. "I thought you *weren't* going to kill me."

"Not *actually* kill you."

Javier lifted his left eyebrow. "I'm pretty sure it's either dead or not dead. Nothing in between."

"Murdering you is not on the table."

"Thanks."

Neve's lips parted in excitement as a plan started to form in her mind. "But we'll have to make Diane believe that she watched you die."

"A faked death." Javier looked at her sidelong. "Just like *The Third Man*."

"You've seen it?"

"Of course," Javier said with a casual shrug. "It's the greatest crime movie of all time."

Why was Javier so perfect?

"Do you think we can pull it off?" he asked.

Neve nodded, suddenly excited. Diane thought Neve was a horrible actress, so she wouldn't believe for one red-hot second that Neve would be capable of faking her way through a murder. But Neve could. She knew she could. Kellie had told her that she had real talent.

Diane was about to witness the performance of a lifetime.

THIRTY-NINE

NEVE SLEPT LATE MONDAY MORNING. IT WAS A HOLIDAY weekend, so no alarm to wake her up, plus Deirdre being at Aunt Connie's cut the noise quotient in half. Even though the relative silence made it feel like the early hours, the sunlight slicing through a gap in her black-velvet curtains was robust and intense, a clue that it was well past morning.

It had been almost four a.m. the last time Neve had looked at her phone while tossing and turning in bed as the details she and Javier hashed out swirled in her mind. Four o'clock and her mom still hadn't come home.

Neve pictured her spending the night at the police station. She was that stubborn—the kind of woman who might refuse to leave until she had answers. Neve tried to suppress the anger and resentment bubbling up inside her as she pictured her mom's face last night, telling her daughter that this was all her fault.

Angry, hurt, scared . . . whatever. In that moment, her mom truly believed that Neve had killed those girls, and that her dad was taking the fall.

Neve knew that she wasn't always the easiest kid. She was angry a lot. She and her mom fought like crazy over everything from how Neve did her makeup to how she refused to fit in at LCC. *Refused.* As if it was somehow perfectly okay to ask your daughter to change the way she dressed and did her hair just so she'd meet the social standards of her new school. It was her mom's fault, after all, that they'd ended up in the closed-minded suburban hellhole of Carlsbad in the first place. She'd moved them there. She'd insisted they live in Grandma K's house. She'd uprooted everyone's lives.

No, she didn't.

The voice of logic overwhelmed the voice of emotion, drowning out the latter's high-pitched squeal with a paced, booming tone in Neve's head. The new voice was right. Neve's mom hadn't been selfish or arbitrary when she'd moved the entire family from the Bay Area to the San Diego suburbs. She'd been trying to protect her husband and his precarious mental health. By living rent-free in Carlsbad, he wouldn't have to go back to work.

If anyone is to blame, it's your dad.

Tears welled up in Neve's eyes. She'd been blaming her mom for so long. For the family's problems. For her dad's problems. But deep down, she'd always known her anger was misplaced. Her dad had refused help, refused treatment, refused to even acknowledge that he had a problem even after he'd lost his job, a promising IT career flushed down the toilet by his inability to admit he needed help. Neve's mom had kept the family from completely falling apart.

"I am such an asshole," she said out loud.

"What's wrong? What happened?" Javier's voice drifted through the shared bathroom. She heard a loud thud. "Shit," he said under his breath.

She pictured Javier trying to get his pants on in Deirdre's cluttered room plastered with posters of YouTube stars and some video game she was obsessed with. "You okay?"

"Great." Another thud and then some shuffling before Javier's disheveled face appeared in the doorway to the Jack-and-Jill bathroom. "What time is it?"

Neve checked her phone and saw that she had a missed call from Inara. "Eleven thirty."

Javier groaned, leaning against the doorframe. "Damn. Missed my Sunday workout."

"It's Monday."

He groaned deeper. "Then I'm really late for school."

Neve laughed. "It's a holiday."

"Oh." He straightened up and shrugged. "Then fuck it."

Neve had felt a mix of teen rebellion and parental concern when she offered to let Javier spend the night. His parents were out of town for the weekend and he hadn't wanted to go home, figuring it was best not to be alone with Diane, and he was going to sleep in his car. For a brief second, she thought about offering him the other side of her full bed but decided that was too much of a leap for their—well, whatever it was that was going on between them. So she offered Deirdre's room instead.

Neve swung her feet onto the floor and padded over to the bathroom door. "Towels are in the cupboard." She pointed. "You want some coffee?"

Javier reached up under his shirt to scratch his chest, exposing the cut lines of his abdomen. It was what she expected from an athlete who took his physical conditioning very seriously, and though Neve had never been the kind of girl who was impressed by the traditional six-pack, she found herself staring distractedly at the bulging diagonal line of his obliques as they disappeared down into his pants.

"That would be great," he said, jarring Neve back to reality. She prayed he didn't notice her perving.

"Okay." She closed the door on her side as Javier began to strip. "Meet me in the kitchen when you're done."

She leaned back against the door, taking a deep breath to steady the weird fluttering in her stomach, and noticed that Javier didn't lock the door before he turned on the hot water. Neve laughed to herself. Javier Flores, apparently the most drooled-after high school senior in the greater San Diego area, was naked in her bathroom. What would Marisol and Luna think? Judging by some of his playful touching last night while they were hashing out their plan, she could probably have waltzed into that bathroom and been welcomed into the shower with him.

Instead, she picked up her phone.

The camera app was still open from last night when Neve had recorded her car ride with Diane, and before she called Inara, she uploaded the long video to a share link and sent it to Inara's email. Someone needed to keep that video safe. Just in case. Then she called Inara.

"'Sup?" Inara said, answering within two seconds of the ring on Neve's end. "Found out anything else about—"

Before Inara could finish her sentence, the sound of a rich baritone singing voice filtered through the bathroom door, filling Neve's room. She recognized the song right away: "Sweet Caroline" by Neil Diamond.

"Um, who is that?" Inara asked.

"Javier." She immediately felt this odd panicky feeling in her gut and word-vomited an explanation. "He was here late because we were coming up with a plan to get Diane to confess, and he didn't want to go home to face her since their parents are in Cabo, so I offered him my sister's room because she's staying with my aunt who's not really my aunt, because my dad got arrested yesterday."

"Wow." Inara paused for a moment while Neve felt herself blushing with embarrassment for her incoherent verbal diarrhea. Just like she'd done with Javier last night. What was wrong with her? "Sorry about Mr. Lanier."

"Thanks."

"Have some info that might help," Inara said quickly, getting down to business. "On that Mitchell person."

Neve fought back an irrational annoyance at Inara's all-business tone shift. "Oh yeah?"

"Internet was no help," Inara continued, speaking quickly. "But Gina was pretty sure Pamela submitted a photo of Mitchell along with an original short story in creative writing class."

"Okay. Cool." Neve wasn't exactly sure how that would help her right now.

"Figured since Diane probably tried to run this Mitchell down the same as Mr. Neil Diamond Sleepover . . ." She paused, waiting for Neve to jump in with something, but Neve wasn't sure what she was expected to say, so she remained silent. "If Diane tried to run Mitchell down, maybe Mitchell could identify the driver. That's all."

She sounded annoyed and Neve wasn't sure why. "I really appreciate that," she said quickly. "But how can the photo help?"

Inara sighed loud enough for Neve to hear. "There are literally no photos of Mitchell on the internet. All social media on lockdown. Can't even find an email address. Thought maybe the photo could lead to more information."

"Awesome!" Neve said, trying to sound more enthusiastic than she felt. It was super sweet of Inara to go through all this trouble, but she and Javier had a pretty tight plan lined up for later in the day. "Maybe once we get a confession from Diane, Mitchell can help testify at her trial."

"Confession?"

"Long story," Neve said. She heard the water turn off in the shower, so she spoke quickly while dropping her voice. She wasn't sure why, but she didn't want to explain to Javier who she'd been talking to. "Javier and I have a plan to get a confession out of Diane. This afternoon at her house, so I have to go. But the photo thing really is awesome and I appreciate it."

"Yeah." Another pause. "Gina's going to dig up the photo from the creative writing teacher. Forward it on."

"Thanks. Oh, and I emailed you a video I shot last night. Nothing earth-shattering, but it might help us later."

"Okay." Inara dropped the gruffness in her voice. "Hey, Neve?"

"Yeah?"

"Be careful."

Neve smiled. It was the second time Inara had said it. "I will. Promise."

FORTY

"YOU TALKING TO SOMEONE?" JAVIER CALLED THROUGH THE closed door. "I don't want your mom to get the wrong idea."

Neve rolled her eyes. Her mom would do backflips of joy if she found a boy in Neve's bathroom. Anything that might indicate her daughter wasn't totally and completely antisocial. "The cat," she lied.

"Tell him to stop shedding all over the beds." Javier sneezed. "I give this Airbnb a six out of ten for pet hair."

"Bed-and-breakfast," Neve said, correcting him. "I'm going to the kitchen to scrounge up some food."

He cracked the door, poking out a head of wet hair. "And coffee. You promised."

Neve smiled. "Freeloader."

She continued smiling all the way down the hall and into the kitchen until she heard a familiar voice say her name.

"Neevy."

Her mom stood at the kitchen island, slowly stirring protein powder into a glass of almond milk.

Neve felt simultaneously relieved and guilty. Relieved that her mom was home from the police station and guilty that Neve had spent the first half hour of her day thinking of everything *but* her parents. She needed to stay focused on why she was doing all of this: to exonerate her father.

"How's Dad?"

Her mom's bloodshot eyes welled up with tears and the spoon fell to the bottom of the glass with a dull clank. Without a word, she rounded the island, stumbling over her own feet. Tears spilled down her cheeks as she cupped Neve's face.

Neve wanted to say something, to reassure her mom that she was going to fix everything, but the words caught in her throat. Instead, she felt tears forming in her own eyes as she watched her mom's silent weeping, streams tracing a path through the maze of freckles on her pale face. They held each other's gaze for a moment; then Neve's mom threw her arms around her daughter and hugged her tightly.

Neve wasn't entirely sure how long it had been since she and her mom had hugged it out. Months? Definitely. Years? Possibly. It might have been the one thing she and her mom had in common: a reluctance to initiate displays of affection. There were no words attached to the embrace—no apologies, no explanations—but the hug itself spoke volumes.

"About what I said yesterday," her mom said, wiping her cheek with her fingers as she broke away, "I didn't mean—"

"It's okay." Neve's voice was shaky. "It's okay."

"Officer Lee mentioned Charlotte's last texts from her phone were to you, and then after what he did with Yasmin . . ." She took a steadying breath. "I thought maybe your father was trying to protect you again."

Other way around, Mom. "Neither of us is a murderer."

"I know." Neve's mom pulled away, reaching for a paper towel to wipe her nose. "Aunt Connie's neighbor is a trial attorney. She mostly does real estate disputes, but she came to the station this morning and said that once the coroner's report comes in, she's going to ask for a dismissal. Seems that the girl—"

"Charlotte," Neve said, correcting her. It felt disrespectful not to name her.

"Sorry. It seems Charlotte had been dead at least four hours when you found her, but your father was with Deirdre at Maddox Malone's birthday pool party all afternoon, so there is no way he could have killed her."

Neve wasn't particularly religious, but she silently thanked God, the Virgin Mary, the saints, and anyone else with celestial powers who might have been looking out for her dad yesterday, making sure that he actually chaperoned Deirdre to the birthday party and wasn't home, alone, in bed all day per usual. "Why did they even arrest him if he has an alibi?"

"It appears that there is some DNA evidence in Yasmin's case," her mom said, shaking her head. "That led them to your father."

Fucking Diane.

"That's all we know. Hopefully not enough to prolong this beyond tomorrow when the courts reopen."

Neve prayed that her mom was right, but she couldn't get Diane's words from last night out of her mind. *Things could* always *get worse.* Did that mean she had another surprise in store?

Her mom took a deep breath, exhaling quickly, then she smiled, big and bright. "Enough. Everything is going to be okay. Now, there's practically no food in the house, so do you want me to run out and get some bagels and—"

As she was speaking, Javier rounded the corner into the kitchen. He was fully dressed, thank freaking God, with a bath towel draped over his head, which made it look more like he'd just come out of a locker room than from an illicit night of passion in Neve's bed. He stared at Neve and her mom, his eyes flicking rapidly back and forth between them, face growing paler by the second.

"M-Mrs. Lanier," he stammered, pulling the towel off of his head and stashing it behind his back, as if it was somehow disrespectful to even be using it in the first place. "I didn't know you were here. I was just . . . I mean, I took a shower." His eyes landed on Neve, his panic deepening. "Your daughter's bed is very comfortable."

Her mom raised an eyebrow. "Pardon?"

"Your other daughter!" The words exploded out of him. "Neve's sister. Who isn't here. I slept in her bed last night. Um, alone."

Right, like that was going to make this situation better.

Her mom probably should have freaked out. There was no reality in which the optics on this weren't horrible. But instead of flying into a protective rage and demanding that Javier leave the house before she called the police, Neve's mom merely smiled and extended her hand.

"You can call me Siobhan," she said warmly.

"Javier." He took her hand tentatively, like it was some kind of trap. "I'm a friend of Neve's."

"I should hope so. Otherwise this would be even more awkward." Her mom laughed. "Can I make you guys some coffee? That's about all I have in the house."

Neve could have hugged her again. She was one hundred percent sure she was going to have to explain this later, but at least there wasn't going to be a scene in front of Javier. So even though she had been about to go make coffee herself, she turned and hustled Javier out of the kitchen. "No, thanks, Mom. We need to go see a friend about a thing."

"Yes." Javier waved over his shoulder as Neve pushed him down the hall. "A friend. About a thing."

Her mom's voice trailed after them down the hallway. "Nice to meet you, Javier. Hope to see you around more often."

Neve cringed. Really? That practically confirmed whatever suspicions her mom had formulated about what they'd been doing in Neve's room that night. Ugh, explaining this later was going to be a pain in the ass.

But when she glanced back at her mom, instead of hitting her with raised eyebrows and a look of shock, her mother merely smiled softly before turning back to her protein milk.

FORTY-ONE

"I CAN'T BELIEVE SHE DIDN'T FREAK THE FUCK OUT," JAVIER said as soon as Neve closed the door to her room. "Or, like, call the cops."

"The last thing we need in this family is more cops around."

"Good point."

Neve sat down on the edge of her bed. There were so many emotions slithering through her, she wasn't sure how to process them, and having a hot guy in her room wasn't even at the top of the list. Aunt Connie's neighbor was going to get the charges against her dad dismissed. Or at least try to. That DNA evidence her mom mentioned as a throwaway was the part that worried Neve the most. She knew exactly what it was and exactly where it came from. Her dad might have an alibi for Charlotte's murder, but Yasmin's was still on the table. Still, if Aunt Connie's neighbor could get him released tomorrow, he'd be home. She smiled at the thought. It wasn't much, but it was something.

"It's nice when you smile." Javier still stood by the door, respectful of the fact that they were alone together in her room.

"Are you going to tell me I'm pretty when I smile?" Neve said, unable to contain the snark. "And should do so more often?" She really hoped Javier wasn't resorting to that sexist bullshit.

"You're pretty even when you don't," he countered without hesitation. "I meant that you looked happy just now. And I feel like you haven't been happy in a while."

Neve felt that familiar fluttering in her stomach. "I haven't."

He lingered by the door, fingering the handle absently. "That thing Yasmin did to you . . . I'm sorry it happened."

"I'm not." Neve couldn't believe what she was saying. The moment that had literally ruined her life, setting in motion a chain of events that led to the deaths of two people—didn't she wish every day that it had never happened?

"Really?"

"Yes." *Weirdly.* "I'm sorry I sent that text about Marisol. But I'm not sorry that I found out what kind of person Yasmin was. It helped me learn what real friendship means."

He paused before he replied, clearing his throat as he stepped closer. "I, uh, hope you consider me a friend."

"A new friend," she said cautiously.

He half smiled, shoving his hands deep into the pockets of his jeans. "Not that new. I've met you before."

Neve narrowed her eyes. "Yeah?"

"It took me a while to place you because there were a lot of people that night." He grinned sheepishly, resuming his slow trek across the carpet toward her. "But you don't exactly blend in. The night I met Yasmin at Marisol's party, you were there."

So he *had* noticed her.

Neve rolled her eyes, suddenly self-conscious. "I think half the party remembers when I picked a fight with the hostess."

"True." He was standing right in front of her and she had to tilt her head back to look him in those hazel eyes. "But before that. I saw you in your black dress, with your curled hair. I know you don't think anyone ever notices you, but I did."

"I don't *want* anyone to notice me," she said, angry at the note of breathlessness she detected in her own voice. "There's a difference."

"Is there?"

Neve arched an eyebrow. "Are you really going to stand there and psychoanalyze me?"

Javier shook his head. "I can honestly say that's the last thing on my mind." Then he placed one knee on the mattress beside her, lowering himself so his face was just above hers, grazed her cheek with his fingertips, and kissed her.

Neve closed her eyes as Javier pressed his lips to hers. She kissed him back, welcoming the contact, and breathed faster as she felt his arm slip around her waist. He gently lifted her, easing her farther back onto her bed, then lay on his side next to her.

He never even broke the kiss.

She wasn't stupid enough to think that this was Javier's first kiss— or first anything, for that matter—and the fluidity of his movements suggested that he was relatively skilled not only at maneuvering around the female body, but in doing so without coming across as threatening or forceful. The kisses were soft, and his body, though close, wasn't grinding against her or pinning her down from above. Though Neve had never made out with a boy, this was exactly how she'd imagined it.

Well, sort of. There was something missing. Something she couldn't quite put her finger on. That flutter in her stomach that Javier had ignited several times with his dreamy hazel eyes and kind, boyish charm had vanished, and instead of being replaced by the carnal burn Neve had expected, it felt empty.

She pushed herself up, rolling on top of Javier in an attempt to spark that *something*. He moaned into her mouth, threading his fingers through her hair as his mouth opened greedily for hers. Then Neve pulled away.

"What's wrong?" Javier panted, eyes half-closed. "Are you okay?"

"Yeah." Neve slid off him, crossing her legs before her on the comforter. "Actually, no."

Javier instantly sat up, lips parted, brows furrowed with concern. "I'm sorry. I shouldn't have done that. You've got so many heavy things going on, and I totally took advantage of the situation."

Neve held up her hand. "No, no. You're fine. I'm . . ." Not into it? Not into it *right now*? Not into *you*? She wasn't sure which.

He was quiet for a moment, sitting beside her, catching his breath. She let the silence linger, not really sure what she wanted to say and so was content to let him take the reins.

"Everything is super confusing right now." He stood up, hazel eyes sad but smiling. "But I want you to know that I'm still going to be here when this is all over. And I'll still feel the same way about you."

"Which is?" Maybe hearing him specify what they were would help her figure out her own feelings.

"Which is . . ." He smiled impishly. "Which is I don't really want you to murder me. So let's keep our heads straight, okay?"

Playful. That was an easy role to slip into with Javier. "Then you probably shouldn't have shoved your tongue down my throat."

Javier laughed. "Fair." He pulled his phone from his back pocket, checking the time. "I should also probably be heading home to get things set up."

Back to business. Good. They'd figure out the rest later. "Do you think you'll be able to set up the cameras without Diane noticing?"

"I think so."

I hope so. "Good."

Their plan depended on it.

It had taken them most of the night to figure out some way to get Diane to confess, based on Javier's innocent remark: *The only way we'd get her to admit to anything is if she thought I was already dead.* In the same vein as Harry Lime's faked death in *The Third Man*, Neve hypothesized that if Diane truly believed that Javier was dead, she'd let her guard down. Gloat in the triumph of not only getting what she wanted but getting someone else to do the dirty work. If Neve was a good enough actress, she should be able to manipulate a confession out of Diane.

But the first part was making sure that Javier's "death" looked convincing.

That part had been his idea, one that he'd seemed particularly excited about when he hashed it out at two in the morning. He proposed that Neve would show up at the Flores-Russell McMansion to find Javier alone in the kitchen-slash–family room. Unbeknownst to Diane, who would be home and presumably watching, Javier would have rigged the room with cameras to catch the entire scene, including Diane's confession. At some point, Neve would exchange the gun Diane had given her, the one with live ammo, for its identical twin, which Javier would have loaded with blank cartridges.

At Neve's request, he had opened Diane's gun and showed Neve the real bullets, explaining that the blanks were merely a cartridge without the projectile. Which made the danger of this plan feel that much more dire.

After switching guns, Javier would put the moves on Neve, but she'd pull away and go for her gun, then "kill" Javier, who would do his best to make the death look real. All Neve had to do was keep Diane away from the body until she got a confession on camera.

Easy, right?

Well, at least it was a plan. And she owed most of it to Javier.

"I couldn't do this without you," she said, standing up. Whatever complex romantic-adjacent feelings she had toward Javier, the warmth of gratitude she felt was real. Other than Inara, no one else had been able to give her hope that she could end this nightmare with Diane.

"Please"—he smirked as he typed something quickly into his phone—"you're helping me. I'm the one she wants dead, remember?"

"I'm pretty sure she wants both of us dead at this point."

He glanced up at her quickly. "You're okay to go through with this?"

"Absolutely." Diane had to be stopped. Even if Neve's dad was released from prison tomorrow, it wouldn't stop Diane from killing someone else. Too many people had suffered already, and if the police wouldn't listen to her, this was the only way.

"Okay." Javier reached out and touched her arm. "Be careful."

"Be careful yourself." Neve snorted, deflecting her discomfort with humor. "You're the one who has to load the blanks in the gun. I don't want to accidentally shoot you."

"I'll be careful." He held her gaze for a moment, and Neve wondered if he was contemplating kissing her again. Finally, he bent forward and pressed his lips quickly to her cheek, then turned, whipped open her bedroom door, and was gone.

FORTY-TWO

AFTER JAVIER LEFT, NEVE VENTURED BACK TO THE KITCHEN, her stomach rumbling, and was grateful to see that her mom wasn't there. She'd probably headed to the police station, if Neve knew her mom even a little, and would stay there as long as they'd let her.

Her mom hadn't been lying that there were no groceries in the house, but Neve was able to scrounge up some spreadable cheese and saltine crackers, as well as some coffee and a container of mushy leftover broccoli. Not great, but it was enough. She flipped through channels as she ate in front of the TV, the kind of indulgence that wasn't usually allowed in the

Lanier house, but she couldn't really focus on anything. Finally, she took a shower and got dressed, transforming herself into a real femme fatale.

Like an actress putting on a costume, Neve chose a black dress with cap sleeves and a plungier neckline than she normally wore, black fishnets, and her favorite stacked-heel Mary Janes. She spent a little extra time on her hair, curling and pinning it into place until she had the perfect sideswept Veronica Lake do, and topped off her look with red matte lips.

She looked the part at least. Now she just had to play it.

At three o'clock it was finally time to start the trek to La Jolla. She tried to act normal as she left the house and waited for her Uber, like she was going down to Starbucks to meet a friend and just happened to have the handgun Diane had given her tucked into her messenger bag. You know, totally normal. Even if there had been anyone around to see her, no one could possibly have known that she was carrying an illegally concealed firearm, yet she felt that it was conspicuous somehow. Like her bag had a flashing neon sign on it that said PACKING in bright pink script.

If the gun wasn't enough to make her paranoid, Neve couldn't shake the sensation that she was being watched, as if every single neighbor on the block were standing at the living room window, peeking through a crack in their blinds, thinking, *Is that girl driving off to murder someone?*

Of course, Neve knew where this paranoia came from: There probably *was* someone watching her, but it wasn't the Zhangs wondering when she was going to use their yard as an escape route again. As Neve ducked into the backseat of the ride share, she was one hundred percent sure that Diane was somewhere out there, watching.

Showtime.

Because that's what this entire afternoon was going to be: A scene. A performance. Diane thought that Neve was a horrible actress? Good. She was about to use that assumption to bring her down. All Javier had to do was plant the gun loaded with blanks and die convincingly. Neve would do the rest. And if things went sideways? She had Javier with her, lying "dead" within reach of the real gun. He wouldn't let anything happen to her.

Ugh, Javier. Neve groaned as the Uber driver changed lanes to let a speeding SUV race by. What was she going to do about him? She didn't allow herself to think for a moment that he was in love with her. They'd known each other for, like, a week and had only spent a few hours in each other's company, and it took more than a few glimpses and a single conversation to fall in love. But he did seem interested.

Ugh again. In the past few days, she'd absolutely had flutterings in her stomach caused by romantic or at the very least sexual feelings for Javier Flores, but somehow when they were actually making out, those feelings kind of fizzled. Neve couldn't understand why, but there it was. She wasn't into Javier, and eventually she'd have to tell him.

But not today. If something went wrong, she didn't want his last thoughts to be of rejection.

Not like there was a *good* kind of last thoughts. Rainbows? Cupcakes? Or was the best way to face death simply not to see it at all? Blindsided. Ambushed. Pros: no anxiety, no fear, and possibly no pain. Cons: You don't get to say good-bye to anyone. Or maybe that should have been in the pro category? Neve wasn't sure.

I wonder what Charlotte's last thoughts were.

Neve cringed as the car pulled off the freeway and began a twisted drive through the tangle of La Jolla streets. Poor Charlotte. Her eyes had been open when she died. Did that mean her last thoughts were of Diane as she watched the life slowly drain out of her victim? Had Charlotte tried to save herself? Claw her way across the floor toward the front door? Or had she reached for her phone to call for help? Maybe she'd been texting

Neve *when* she was killed, which meant Charlotte's last thoughts would have been of Neve.

Except . . .

Something wasn't right. Neve's mom told her that Charlotte had been dead at least four hours, giving her dad an alibi, but those texts . . . It had only taken Neve twenty minutes to get to the abandoned office. That timeline didn't match up at all.

Things could always get worse.

Is this what Diane had meant? Would the texts from Charlotte's phone contradict the coroner's estimated time of death enough that her dad's alibi would be a moot point?

Shit.

The Uber eased to a stop across the street from the opulent McMansion where Javier and Diane lived. As Neve hauled herself out of the backseat, her knees wobbled and the hand that grabbed the messenger bag visibly shook.

Why was she so nervous? She wasn't doing this alone. Javier was going to be right there with her the entire time. Two against one.

What if he's not here? What if he bailed on you and Diane is home alone?

Stop it. That made zero sense. She and Javier both needed Diane exposed for what she truly was—a killer and a psychopath. Neve was going to be fine.

"Hey!" Javier said as he opened the front door. Neve let out a slow, steady breath at the sight of him. She'd been betrayed by too many people over the last few months, but he wasn't one of them. His smile, happy but a little nervous, perfectly reflected her own state of mind, which instantly calmed her.

"Hey yourself."

He stepped aside, ushering her through. "Come on in."

Stepping over the threshold of Javier's home felt a little bit like Dorothy's first steps out of her house once it landed in Oz. Not that Neve was necessarily going from black-and-white to Technicolor, but she definitely felt as if she was stepping into a whole new world, literally and figuratively.

The figurative part was easy: Entrapping a killer was new territory in her life. The literal part was the house itself. The northern San Diego suburbs were littered with opulent mansions, but Neve, without rich friends, hadn't actually been inside one. The exterior of Javier's house was pretty generic—a single-story ranch, newer than Grandma K's house in Carlsbad, with the same Spanish touches: tile roof, stucco walls, arched doorway. But once inside, Neve felt like she was on one of those home makeover shows.

The expansive open-concept living room, sparsely decorated with mid-century modern lounge chairs and an oval teak coffee table, and crowned with exposed ceiling beams and lazily spinning ceiling fans, was all background noise to the floor-to-ceiling windows that stretched the entire width of the house, showcasing a panoramic view of the Pacific Ocean. Below, the coast curved northward, exposing sheer cliffs and inaccessible beaches, while palm trees lined the coastal road leading to the pier, jutting out into the waves. She felt like Joan Crawford at the beach house in *Mildred Pierce*, only without the two-piece swimsuit.

"Wow," she said, her voice low and reverent like she was in church. Neve understood that between living in La Jolla and attending Holy Name, Diane and Javier were in a totally different league of wealth and power than the Lanier family, but she'd never really internalized what that meant until she walked into their house.

"Nice, isn't it?" Javier closed and bolted the door behind her while she absently wandered toward the wall of glass. A moth drawn to the flame.

"*Nice* is a dandelion. *Nice* is a cloud. This view is mind-blowing."

Javier laughed, walking behind her to the kitchen. "You should see it at sunset."

"If I lived here, I don't think I'd ever leave the house." As if. This house must have cost millions.

"We probably take it for granted." He paused, and she heard his fingers tapping on the counter. "Can I get you anything?"

Neve turned, forcing her eyes away from the multimillion-dollar view. Javier's voice had sounded casual, but the look on his face was anything but. He stood at the far end of the kitchen, leaning back against the counter, eyes wide, lips wrinkled in frustration. When he was sure he had her attention, his eyes shifted down to his right and he tapped the marble countertop again with his middle finger, directly above a drawer.

Neve shook herself. The plan. Right. She needed to focus.

The drawer must be where Javier had stashed the gun, loaded with blank cartridges, that they'd use to fake his murder.

Her eyes met Javier's and she nodded slightly, acknowledging that she understood. He inclined his head almost imperceptibly, then turned and sauntered across the kitchen to the massive stainless-steel refrigerator. "We've got LaCroix, Perrier, or my stepmom's chardonnay, if that's your thing. Oh, and those mocha-coffee-drink things you love."

"Aw," Neve said, pulling her messenger bag in front of her as she moved toward the drawer. "You remembered."

"Gross sugary coffee it is!" He pulled a bottle out of the fridge along with a LaCroix for himself, then turned his back to her as he reached for glasses. "I don't know how you drink this junk."

She plopped her messenger bag on the counter above the drawer Javier had indicated and eased it open. The dummy handgun was there, just as Javier had promised. "And I don't know how you put those fake sweetener chemicals in yours. You know what that stuff does to lab mice?"

"You're adorable when you're socially conscious." She heard the pop of the lid as he opened her drink, then poured it into a glass.

"Is that the only time?" Neve glanced over her shoulder as she reached her hand into her bag, pretending to look for something. Her fingers closed around the cool metal of the handgun. In one fluid motion, she slipped Diane's gun into the drawer, grabbed the one Javier had planted, and shoved it back into her bag. Then, to justify rummaging around in her bag in case Diane could see her that closely, Neve removed her phone. What was more normal than checking your messages?

"Nope," Javier said. She heard the crack and fizz of the sparkling water as he opened the can. "But if I told you that, you'd accuse me of trying to flirt with you, and we know how that ends."

Neve laughed. Their plan was proceeding flawlessly so far, and Neve was beginning to relax. "With me rolling my eyes."

"Exactly."

She leaned against the counter as she looked at her phone, slowly closing the drawer with her hip, and noticed she had a text from Inara. Not something she should probably be distracting herself with at the moment, but she clicked on it anyway.

Gina found the photo. Pamela and Mitchell.

Neve scrolled down to the attached photo, and instantly she felt all of the air get sucked out of her lungs.

Staring back at her from her phone was a plain, nervous-looking brunette with limp hair and no makeup, and standing beside her, an arm snaked around her waist, was Javier.

FORTY-THREE

NEVE HAD TO SUMMON EVERY OUNCE OF PHYSICAL AND mental strength to keep from collapsing onto the hardwood floor.

No wonder there was no social media presence for the mysterious Mitchell. He didn't exist. And then all the strange, nonsensical pieces fell into place.

Charlotte's texts. She hadn't sent them to Neve, summoning her to the abandoned office four hours after she was murdered. The coroner was right: Charlotte was already dead. Diane had sent them.

Javier. When Neve ran into him while she was fleeing Yasmin's memorial, he was just arriving. Late. Neve had texted Charlotte right before she left for the memorial, saying she'd look for her there. That must have been when Diane and Javier decided to frame Neve for Charlotte's murder: Javier raced back to Carlsbad to provide Diane with an alibi while she staged Charlotte's body at her mom's old office and texted Neve from Charlotte's phone.

Yasmin's house. Of course the alarm at the Attar house hadn't been triggered by an intruder—Yasmin was ass over ankles in love with Javier and would have gladly, willingly let him in the night he killed her.

He killed her.

Yasmin's death. Even if she'd been asleep when it happened, Yasmin wouldn't have died instantly. She would have fought, moved, screamed, *something.* And yet in the photo Diane showed her, Yasmin looked utterly peaceful. Pamela had supposedly taken a bunch of sleeping pills *before* shooting herself. What if she'd been drugged? So that she wouldn't fight back when Javier or Diane pulled a gun on her. What if it hadn't been suicide at all? And these two psychopaths had drugged Yasmin, too?

"Your coffee, madam."

Javier's voice sent a shiver down Neve's spine. She could feel the warmth of his body against her back as he placed the glass of coffee on the counter. He stood right behind her. A killer.

Javier was twice her size and practically a professional athlete. Zero percent chance she'd even reach the door if she made a run for it now. Plus, she had no idea where Diane was. It was two against one all right. Only Neve was the one.

Shit!

Don't panic.

Right. Diane and Javier had a plan. There was a reason they had lured Neve to their house, a reason for the guns and the blank cartridges and the subterfuge. What it was, Neve had absolutely no idea, only that if things went according to *their* plan, it would probably end with Neve's death. How the fuck was she going to get out of this?

The gun. Right. The one in her bag was loaded with blank cartridges, but Javier had shown her the bullets in the gun Diane had given her. They definitely weren't blanks and she was pretty sure one of those bullets was meant for her. She needed to switch those guns back, that was for damn sure.

Inara. She could send help. Neve needed to get a text off to her, then maybe if she had the real gun, she could stall long enough for the police to arrive? It was her only chance.

"You okay?" Javier asked. Neve was pretty sure she detected an edge to his voice. If Neve was going to survive this day, she needed to keep playing along, pretending to be the same stupid, gullible girl she'd been thirty seconds ago.

Time to earn that standing ovation.

"Duh, fine." She hugged her phone to her chest as she turned to face him. Trying to stay in character, she mouthed the word *nervous*, then bit her lower lip to look fittingly so. Not really hard since she was barely holding her shit together.

He smiled and his body instantly relaxed. She hadn't even noticed that he'd tensed up.

It's okay, he mouthed back, then cleared his throat. "Drink this," he said loudly, nudging the glass toward her on the counter. "It always makes you feel better."

The glass. It had to be drugged. Something like the Norco in Pamela's system that would knock Neve out cold. She added a third item to her to-do list: switch the guns, text Inara, don't drink the goddamn coffee.

"Can I get a straw?" Neve blurted out. She needed Javier to turn his back so she could swap those guns. "Like on our date at the diner."

He tilted his head, watching her, then shrugged. "Sure."

The instant he turned away, Neve was at the drawer. She placed her phone on the counter, and she deftly swapped the guns as silently as possible while Javier rummaged through a drawer. He swung around, holding up a straw, just as Neve reached for her phone, using the movement to obscure the fact that she was closing the drawer with her butt.

"Found one!"

"Thank you so much," she said, plastering a smile on her face as her thumbs typed frantically.

That's Javier. 700 Hillside Dr.

"Who are you texting?" The edge was back in his voice as he moved quickly—too quickly—toward her.

"Inara," she said, slipping the phone into the pocket of her dress, cursing him silently for how quickly he closed the distance between them. No time to add *Call 911* before she hit SEND. She hoped Inara would understand her cry for help. "I told her I was on a date. Not sure if she'll get the hint or not, but whatever!"

Neve busied herself with unwrapping the straw, hoping the movement distracted Javier from the fact that her hands were shaking again. He was watching her closely, eyes sharp and alert, exactly as he'd been that day at the diner. *Play along.* She sank the straw into the glass and put it to her mouth, sucking in the brown liquid. But once the straw was full, she stopped it with her tongue, wrapping her hand around the glass to hide the fact that the level wasn't going down while pantomiming repeated swallows.

"Coooooool," he said, slowly drawing out the vowel sound. *Just like Diane.*

Neve swallowed one last time, mostly to force back the barf threatening to rocket up her throat.

"You wanna sit?" Javier asked, nodding his head toward the living room. The scenario they'd planned out—he wanted her to start. He was supposed to make a move on her and she'd be weird, then she'd go for her gun. Back-and-forth conversation about what Diane wanted her to do and why, then BAM.

Except this *bam* would, hopefully, have a real bullet attached instead of a blank. And if she didn't want Javier to figure out that she was onto him too soon, she needed somewhere for that bullet to go.

"Is it just me or is it kind of warm in here?" she asked, patting her cheek with the back of her hand.

Javier's brows drew tightly together. "I guess?"

"Do you think you could open the doors?" She fanned herself. *Don't overact.* "Get some of that ocean breeze in."

"Um, suuuure." Again with the drawn-out vowel. Javier looked at her with renewed tension in his face, obviously thrown by this change in the plan. Neve tried to assuage whatever suspicions might be festering in his mind.

"I . . . I guess I'm overtired," she said, remembering that Javier thought she'd swallowed at least some of the drugged coffee. "Feeling a little woozy. Like I might pass out."

"Yeah, we don't want that," Javier said, moving quickly to the sliding doors. He pushed one side all the way open; the window panels slid into one another like an accordion. "Better?"

You have no idea. "I think so." She staggered a little as if she were feeling the effects of the drug. "Maybe I should sit down."

"Good idea." Javier had a skip in his step as he rounded the sofa and sat beside her. Neve could barely contain her revulsion. Had he put the same moves on Yasmin? Had they been making out—or worse—when she fell unconscious from the drug?

Maybe Neve wouldn't aim high with the loaded gun. Maybe she'd put a bullet square in Javier's chest.

"Feel better?" He slipped an arm around her. Thank God their little planned scene required Neve to be fidgety and uncomfortable. Even though they'd been sucking face earlier, she couldn't have faked her way through another make-out session with him if she'd taken acting lessons with Bette freaking Davis. She couldn't stand it anymore. Time to start the show.

Neve twisted out of his embrace, grabbing her bag as she stood up.

"I'm . . . I'm sorry, Javier." She pulled out the gun, letting her bag drop to the floor.

He rocketed to his feet, a genuine look of fear flashing across his face. Neve shouldn't have been surprised at his acting chops, considering every single one of their interactions had been one big lie, but it still caught her off guard. "Whoa, Neve. What are you doing?"

"I'm so sorry. I have to."

Javier backed away, hands up in surrender. "You don't *have* to do this."

"I do," Neve said loudly. Somewhere, cameras were recording all of this. "But I don't want to. Your stepsister is forcing me."

"Diane?"

Neve nodded and took a few steps to her left, trying to line herself up so the bullet from her gun would land harmlessly in the bushes outside. She hoped. "She's blackmailing me."

"My Diane?" he said. "Why would she want me dead?"

My Diane? Neve narrowed her eyes. That wasn't the script they'd agreed upon. Neve thought of the audio recording Diane had spliced together from their last night of camp. She and Javier must be doing the same thing again, but why?

The answer made her stomach churn.

Once she was dead, they'd control the narrative. They wanted to make it look as if Neve had been the killer all along.

Keep going, Javier mouthed, sensing her hesitation. He was making it really fucking hard not to actually kill him.

Fine. If he was going off-script for his own agenda, she could do the same. "She framed my dad for the deaths of Yasmin and Charlotte," Neve said. "And she said she'd make it all go away if I killed you."

"My sister would *never* do that, Neve." Oh, *now* she was his sister. Gross. "Are you sure this isn't all in your head? Because I told you I don't feel that way?"

Then he angled his body away from the kitchen, held his hand up in front of him, and made the universal gun symbol with his thumb and forefinger. He wanted her to shoot him now, and he was hiding his hand from the camera that must have been in the kitchen.

Neve hesitated. This recording was going to look so bad for her— Javier was setting her up as an unhinged girl with an unrequited crush and access to a deadly weapon. Which meant there was no way he and Diane ever planned on letting her walk out of that house alive.

She had only one chance.

Neve aimed the gun at Javier and fired.

FORTY-FOUR

JAVIER HUNG FROZEN FOR A MOMENT, EYES LOCKED ONTO Neve's. His face was implacable. They'd both flinched at the explosive bang of the gun, and Javier's hands had flown up to his chest, gripping his shirt as if he'd been shot. But the pinched look around his eyes and mouth could have been from pain or stress, from amusement or triumph, and as he crumpled to the floor, Neve wasn't entirely sure if she'd shot him or not.

She still had the gun pointed at him when Diane rushed into the room.

"Oh my God! What did you do?" Diane wore black cropped jeans, a matching tank top, and ballet flats, with her hair perfectly coiffed in big beachy curls. She looked like a skinnier, less gothy version of Neve and her black dress and chunky Mary Janes as she wrung her hands together over Javier's immobile form. "You shot him!"

Did I? Neve swallowed. She'd never fired a gun before, and though she was pretty sure she'd aimed at the backyard, she wasn't certain. Was there a chance Javier was actually dead?

"Javi!" Diane cried. "Can you hear me? Please don't be dead. Please, please, please." She reached out and tentatively touched the body, as if checking to see if he was alive, and let out a little squeak of terror as her fingers touched his arm.

Neve rolled her eyes. Clearly Javier wasn't actually dead. Diane's reaction was way too over-the-top. Everything from the outfit to the hair to the fake terror played like a soap opera plot. Diane and Javier had planned all the details, set the scene, and she was now playing it out for the cameras.

Cameras that still might capture a killer's confession.

If Neve could get Diane and Javier to admit what they'd done, then keep them away from whatever laptop was currently recording the camera feed, she'd be able to exonerate both herself and her father. And put two psychopaths away for good.

"Please, God!" Diane said, looking up at the ceiling, her palms pressed flat against each other in prayer. "Take me instead. Anyone but my dear brother."

"Oh, for fuck's sake," Neve blurted out. "And you said *I* was a bad actress?"

To her credit, Diane didn't break character. She cleared her throat before slowly rising to her feet. "What are you going to do now, huh? Shoot me, too?"

I wish. She wanted to say a million things, but she didn't. She needed to string out the charade as long as she could. Neve remembered that she'd supposedly been drugged, so she slumped down into the nearest chair, careful to keep the gun firmly grasped in her hand, ready to use if needed.

The instant Neve lowered the gun, Diane took off. But instead of heading for a phone or the door, she sprinted across the room to the kitchen and yanked open the drawer that held the other gun.

Once she had it in her hands, she spun around, aiming it at Neve. "Drop it," she demanded, sounding like every cop drama Neve had ever watched on TV. "Now."

Neve held up the gun in her hand. "It doesn't have real bullets," she said, loud and clear so the cameras picked it up. "Your brother loaded it with blanks."

Diane, who clearly expected that answer, laughed, throwing her head back theatrically. "You're insane! Stop with your lies. You came here to kill my brother out of jealousy, just like you killed Yasmin. You loved her and she loved Javi. And then you killed poor Charlotte because she caught you stalking my brother. You . . . you murderer!" She paused as if waiting for something.

"Aaaaaand cut!" Javier sat up, applauding slowly. "Well done, Di. A fantastic performance."

Diane dropped the cop pose. "Do you really think so?"

Javier climbed to his feet, brushing off his jeans as if he'd been lying in the dirt instead of recently swept hardwood floors in his immaculate living room. "Absolutely. Your best yet."

Diane laid the gun on the counter and clapped her hands like a delighted child. "Yay!"

"What's . . . going on?" Neve said, faking a pant. She had no idea what the effects of the drug in her coffee were supposed to look like, but she figured fatigue and disorientation were a good bet.

Ignoring her, Javier strode across the room, scooped up Diane with an arm around her waist, and pulled her body to his. They fell into a passionate, sloppy kiss that was equal parts fascinating and horrifying.

The making out went on far longer than Neve cared to witness, and the gurgling and sucking noises were about to make her physically ill when Javier finally broke the embrace, snaking his hands up into Diane's hair and yanking her head away from his. "You're so fucking hot right now."

"No, you are."

"Yeah?"

"Oh yeah, baby."

Javier held her head back so she was staring up at his face. "Do you want me to throw you down on this countertop?"

"Yes," she moaned.

"And rip your clothes off?"

"Yes."

"And do whatever I want to you?"

Diane peeled off her shirt, exposing a lacy white bra. "Yessssss."

For fuck's sake.

Javier lifted Diane up and sat her on the marble counter beside the gun. "Beg me. Tell me how much you—"

"Um, hello?" Neve said, momentarily forgetting she was supposed to be half-drugged and falling asleep. She wasn't going to sit there while the two of them got all *Flowers in the Attic* on each other within earshot. "What is happening?"

Diane scowled at Neve for interrupting, but Javier merely looked amused. "We should deal with that."

That. Like she was a thing.

Diane sighed and hopped off the counter. She didn't even bother to put her shirt back on. "I suppose." She picked up the gun and sauntered toward Neve. "This is the part where we kill you and make it look like self-defense."

Neve had to pin her upper lip down between her teeth to keep from smiling. Coaxing a confession out of these two was going to be easier than she thought. They were so arrogant they were practically begging for an audience to their brilliance.

"We?" Neve shifted her glance over Diane's shoulder to Javier.

"Sorry about that," he said, his eyes crinkling in faux sympathy as Diane squatted down beside her. "I want you to know it's nothing personal."

Shit, she didn't know who was crazier, him or Diane. "I . . . I don't understand."

Diane shook her head. "They never do."

"Let me explain." Javier sat down in the lounge chair opposite Neve and manspread his legs, slapping his right thigh, an invitation for Diane to perch on it. Which she did, dutifully straddling his leg. Neve wondered if Javier had been the one driving this crazy train all along and Diane was just one more stupid, lovesick girl who would do anything for her man.

Thank freaking God I'm into girls, too.

Javier waited until she was settled before he began. "You see, we had a bet, my dear stepsister and I, to see which of us could get you to commit murder first."

"What?" Neve didn't even need to fake her horror here. The idea was truly insidious.

"I know, right? Amazing idea!" Javier laughed. "Mine, of course."

"I helped," Diane whined. She was pitiful in the way she desired his attention. Like Harley Quinn before she ditched the Joker. Painful and sad.

"Of course you did." Javier stroked her hair.

Diane wasn't mollified. "I did! After Pamela, I was the one who suggested we make the bet harder next time, remember?"

"I guess you're right," Javier conceded. "But the *Strangers on a Train* bit was my idea."

Of course. Neve thought it was odd that Diane had come up with a plan almost exactly like the book and movie, without having read the one or seen the other, and that was because she hadn't. It had been film-noir buff Javier.

"Fine," Diane huffed. Was she seriously pouting about this?

"You stole it from Hitchcock," Neve said slowly, as if she were fighting for the words.

"I did!" Javier smiled. "Love those old movies."

Diane pursed her glossy lips. "Thief."

Murderer.

"Whatever," Javier said with a sigh. "All that matters is that I won."

"You did not!" Diane said, waving the gun around as she threw her hands up the air. "That was totally my doing."

"Was not."

"Was too!" Diane smiled sweetly. "Besides, she knew she was shooting you with blanks. That doesn't even count."

Javier sighed. "Then how did you win?"

"Fine." Diane pointed the gun at Neve. "Tell us who won. Which of us was closer to making you actually commit murder?"

"She probably can't even talk by now," Javier said before Neve could even fully process what she was being asked. "The drug's been in her system long enough."

Diane stood up and walked over to Neve, peering down at her. "She looks pretty awake to me."

"Does she?" Javier shrugged. "She must not have had enough coffee."

Or any, you asshole. "You drugged me?" she said, trying to sound as if every word required extreme effort.

"That's the only way to make your death look believable," Diane said.

"Like you did with Yasmin," Neve continued. "And Pamela."

"But not Charlotte," Javier said, smiling. "She was totally awake when I killed her." He smiled to himself as if remembering the moment with delight, and Neve recoiled in horror at the idea that she'd been making out with this psychopath a few hours ago.

"So what?" Neve asked. "You're just going to kill me and then . . . do this all again?"

"That's the plan!" Diane said. "And live happily ever after."

Neve curled her lip. "Well, I can only think of fifteen or twenty reasons why you two should never be happy."

Diane groaned. "Is that another one of her movie quotes?"

"Yep," Javier said, luxuriating on the sofa. "It's from *The Postman Always Rings Twice.* A classic. You'd like it."

"I doubt that," Diane whined.

Neve shook her head. What had she ever seen in this chick?

"Okay, places, everyone!" Javier stood up and ushered Diane back toward the kitchen. "We should get this moving. You have to be over there when you shoot, Di. For continuity. To match your position from earlier."

Neve thought of the camera recording this scene. They planned to cut this whole section out of the video and edit it together to make it look like Diane had shot her in self-defense.

"Like this?" Diane said, pulling her shirt back on before resuming her TV-cop pose in the kitchen.

"Perfect." Javier eyed the distance to Neve. "Do you think you can hit her from there?"

Diane steadied her aim. "Absolutely. I've been practicing." Yet she didn't pull the trigger.

"Awesome." Javier moved toward the windows, where he had a clear view of both of them. "Let's go, then."

Still nothing. Diane stood with hips squared, arms locked with the gun pointed at Neve, one eye squinted closed as she aimed, but she was frozen, unable or unwilling to pull the trigger.

"What are you waiting for?" Javier asked.

"Nothing." Her voice shook. Diane was struggling.

Javier walked up behind her and smoothed his hands down the sides of her body. "Do you know how fucking choice you look right now?"

Ew.

Diane's eyes shifted away from Neve. "I do?"

"Oh yeah." Javier rested his chin on her shoulder, lips pressed against her earlobe. "And the things I'm going to do to you when this is over . . ."

"You are?" Her voice was smaller, meeker.

Javier nodded. "All you have to do is squeeze that trigger." Then he backed away again.

This is so fucked-up. Murder as foreplay was definitely not going on Neve's dating profile.

"Right," Diane said under her breath. Then she swallowed, gave her body a shimmy, like an athlete shaking out their muscles, and resumed her TV-cop pose. "Good-bye, BFF."

FORTY-FIVE

THE EXPLOSION SOUNDED EXACTLY THE SAME AS WHEN NEVE
had fired her gun moments before, and for an instant, she wasn't sure
what had happened. She sat frozen, staring straight ahead. Javier and
Diane watched her acutely, his eyes wide in expectation, hers narrowed
from concentration. Meanwhile Neve was confident that she'd know it if
she'd actually been shot—blood and pain and life draining out of her—
and since she felt none of those things, she was pretty confident she was
okay.

Javier clicked his tongue in disappointment. "You missed!"

"No way." Diane aimed again and pulled the trigger once, then twice. "There's something wrong."

The game was up.

"Yeah, there is." Neve leaped to her feet, the real gun firmly grasped in her hands, and backed around the chair toward the front door, putting as much furniture as possible between her and them. "You've got the wrong gun."

Javier's face deepened to an irate shade of crimson. "No. That's not . . . How could you . . ."

"How could I know that you're full of shit?" she said, the anger that had been building up over the last half hour exploding from her.

"That's impossible!" he roared. "Last night. This morning. You totally believed me."

"And I'm not that good of an actress, right?" It was a lie, Neve realized. She'd only discovered Javier's duplicity after she'd arrived at his house, but she couldn't resist the opportunity to poke holes in their arrogant bullshit.

"But you shot him with that gun," Diane said, examining her own weapon. "I saw you."

"I shot over his shoulder," Neve said. "Out the open door and into the bushes."

"That's why you wanted the windows open." Javier shook his head. "I should have known."

"You really should have," Diane said. "Do you realize how fucked we are if she walks out of here?"

Javier smiled, his composure regained. "She's not walking out of here." There was something evil in those hazel eyes, something sinister and ugly and Neve couldn't believe she'd ever thought him handsome.

"I have the real gun," Neve said, trying not to sound as afraid as the look in Javier's eyes was making her. "With the real bullets."

"True." Javier took a slow step toward her. "But I'm guessing you've never held a gun before. Never fired one before today."

"I missed you, didn't I?" Neve said, trying to sound confident. "Shot the bullet exactly where I wanted it to go."

"But shooting to kill is something completely different." Javier smiled. "I know."

Neve backed toward the front door. "Don't come any closer." Had Inara called the cops? She didn't have a car outside, so even if she made it that far she'd have to run down the street screaming for help and hope that someone heard her.

"And I also know," he continued, "that you've never killed anyone."

"Javi, be careful." Diane, at least, lacked his confidence.

"The drawer where you got the gun, Di," he said without taking his eyes off of Neve. "There's a box of cartridges in the back."

Diane hesitated as if she was about to ask a question, but Javier cut her off.

"Do you remember how to load it?"

She nodded meekly.

"Good. Bring it to me when you're done."

Neve swallowed. Was there really a box of ammo lying around in a kitchen drawer? Or was Diane's hesitation a sign that Javier was bluffing? She couldn't see what Diane was doing, and even if she could, it wasn't as if she'd be able to recognize real bullets from blank cartridges at that distance.

"I *will* shoot you." Neve wasn't sure who she was trying to convince—Javier or herself.

An ugly smirk marred Javier's handsome, smug face. "Will you, really?" He moved forward again, slowly closing the distance between them. "It's easier than you think, taking a life. A squeeze, a slash, a push, and it's done. Shockingly simple."

"The cops will be here any second," she said, hoping it was true.

"Mm-hm." He nodded, still advancing. "You know, if you're lucky, you're close enough when it happens to see all the steps of death register on a person's face. Fear, that's usually first. Then pain, followed by this pleading they get in their eyes as they hope maybe you'll do something to save them. Finally, if you're really, *really* lucky and their eyes are still open, right before the end, this weird calmness overcomes them. Like they've accepted it." Javier was just on the other side of the coffee table when he paused and held out his hand toward Diane, snapping his fingers for the gun. "I hope your eyes are still open, Neve."

"Ready!" Diane rounded the kitchen island holding the gun up in the air like a kid waving around a soccer trophy. Neve had no idea if it was actually loaded this time, but she wasn't about to find out the hard way. She still had the coffee table as a barrier between her and Javier, so she quickly shifted her aim from him to his stepsister.

"Stop!" she barked. The sheer volume of her command caused Diane to hesitate. "Don't move, Diane."

"Give me the gun." Javier stood calmly in place, arm outstretched, but his voice held more urgency than before.

Neve needed to stall. Shooting either of them was a last resort, and while she'd much prefer to have the police show up and deal with it, she also wasn't about to let Javier and Diane win. Diane had been stone cold throughout all of this, but Javier . . . the way he described death, the way he relished it. She thought of Charlotte, dying with her eyes open. Neve hadn't seen any calmness reflected in them. Only pain and terror.

Javier had done that, not Diane. And the way she'd hesitated when Javier told her to shoot Neve . . . those weren't the actions of a killer. It had been Javier all along.

"You don't have to listen to him," Neve said, her words calm and measured, like the tone her mom used when Deirdre was a toddler having a dramatic, screaming meltdown. "You haven't done anything wrong yet. Haven't murdered anyone. You can tell Officer Hernández that Javier did it all."

Javier clenched his jaw. "Shut. Up."

Ah, so he knew Diane was a liability? Good. Time to pick at that scab.

"He's the one who drugged Pamela, right?" Neve pressed, speaking more quickly. "And killed her. He planned the near accidents, first when he was pretending to be Mitchell and then at Holy Name. He killed Yasmin. He killed Charlotte."

Diane's eyes shifted back and forth between Neve and Javier, noticeably rattled. Neve had finally found Diane's weak spot: her loyalty to Javier. "I . . ."

"The cameras, Diane," Javier said under his breath, lips hardly moving like a ventriloquist manipulating a dummy.

"Exactly," Neve said, pouncing on his words. "The cameras. He wanted *you* to kill me so that he'd have something on film. To blackmail *you* with. Or to throw you under the bus if things got too hot."

"He . . . he wouldn't."

"If it's a choice between you and him?" Neve laughed. "You bet your ass he'd turn you in."

Diane's face was pained as she turned to her brother-slash-boyfriend. "Javi?"

"She's trying to drive a wedge between us, babe," he said, eyes wide, in full charm mode. "Give me the gun."

"Don't do it," Neve said quickly, adjusting her grip. Was she really prepared to shoot? She wasn't sure she could shoot to kill, even if it meant saving herself.

Then she thought of Grandma K's words. A sense of calm came over her and she smiled.

"What's so funny?" Diane asked. She was nervous, edgy. Neve's argument was getting to her.

Neve's smile deepened. "Just a line I once heard. Don't ever let someone else dictate the terms of your life."

"What movie is that from?" Javier asked. "I hope it's a favorite, since these are some of the last words you'll ever speak."

Before she could answer, Neve heard a noise in the distance, the low but distinctive wail of a siren getting louder by the nanosecond.

"Is that . . . ?" Diane began.

"Yep." Neve nodded. "And that line isn't from a movie. It's from my grandma. This is my life, and I'm taking control of it by turning you two assholes in to the cops. It's over."

But Javier definitely did not see it that way. Instead of causing him to give up, the sirens jarred him into action. Without waiting for Diane to bring him the weapon, he sprinted toward her, wrenching the gun from her hand.

Everything seemed to happen at once. There was a crash from behind Neve, a rush of air, and then the sirens grew exponentially louder. She watched Javier's arm come down with the gun firmly gripped in his hand until the barrel was level with her eyes, realizing in that moment that Diane must have loaded real bullets into it. She heard the pounding of footsteps and the crack of gunfire, but those sounds all came from behind her. She heard some muffled poofs and then watched Javier's chest and shoulders collapse inward. He looked up at Neve just as she registered the red holes in his gray shirt, and then she saw that look he had described: pleading, like he thought perhaps Neve could save him.

Neve's eyes were locked onto his as he crumpled to his knees before toppling face-first onto the floor.

A police officer took the gun from her hand and put her in handcuffs, but her gaze never left Javier, and as Neve was escorted from the room, she smiled to herself, delighted.

No calmness for Javier in death. His hazel eyes held only rage.

WINTER

EPILOGUE

NEVE STOOD BEHIND INARA'S PRIUS, ARMS FOLDED ACROSS
her chest, as she watched a trail of students stream into the front entrance
of La Costa Canyon High School. It was an overcast January morning, a
far cry from the last time she'd walked through that parking lot with the
blistering late-summer sunshine bouncing off the gleaming front windows, but then, as now, Neve felt an odd sense of calm.

Back in August it had been a false positive—Neve had fortified herself
against what she expected to be a renewal of the harassment from the
previous spring—but now her confidence was real.

While she couldn't change the leaked text message that had made her the most hated person at LCC, the news about her that had spread like wildfire over the last couple of months was, at least, not as negative this time.

How Javier Flores, star athlete at Holy Name Academy, had killed Yasmin Attar and Charlotte Trainor, and possibly some other girl back in Boston, which was why the family had moved to San Diego in the first place.

How Neve and Inara had figured it out in time to save Neve's life. How she'd held off the killers by herself until the police arrived.

How she'd barely been saved from death by the SDPD officers who shot and killed Javier as he was pointing a loaded Glock at Neve.

And how all of it was caught on tape.

Diane had eventually caved. At first, she'd dissolved into hysterics over Javier's dead body, then tried to blame Neve as the actual perpetrator, who had been holding Javier and her hostage at gunpoint. Until Officers Hernández and Lee arrived on the scene. Officer Hernández immediately released Neve and placed Diane under arrest. Apparently, Inara had forwarded Neve's recording from the night before, then called Officer Hernández directly. Neve quickly explained the cameras and the video footage being recorded somewhere in the house, and Officer Hernández had confiscated the laptop. It contained the video feed of Diane and Javier admitting to the murders, and when she was confronted with her own words, Diane's story fell apart and she shifted the blame from Neve to Javier. She begged Neve to back her up, claiming that Javier had manipulated her into acting as his accomplice.

Which was half-true, Neve had to admit, but that would be for a judge to decide. Despite whatever feelings she'd had for Diane, she wasn't about to let her get away with murder, and channeling her best Sam Spade at the end of *The Maltese Falcon*, Neve turned her back on her former best friend.

Neve wasn't expecting her fellow students to high-five her in the hallway or invite her to eat lunch at the cool douches' table when she started back at school that morning, but she *was* expecting to be left alone without the hostilities and threats that had plagued her last spring.

"Gonna be okay?" Inara stood beside her, almost propped up against the car. "LCC has been rough."

She'd told Inara a lot over the last few months as their friendship developed. It was nothing more than that—just a regular old friendship—but it was exactly what Neve needed in her life. Someone who accepted her as she was and cared about her and her well-being.

And besides, you never know what friendship can turn into.

"I'll be okay," Neve said, exhaling long and slow.

"Scott and Vonny are worried."

Neve laughed. Somehow it felt perfectly normal that Inara referred to her parents by their first names. "They have every right to be, but things are different now."

"Yep."

"Thank you," Neve said, turning to Inara, who was going in late to her own classes in order to drive Neve to school. "For coming with me today. I appreciate it." Inara's long hair was tied back at the temples and hung down the back of her plaid jacket, and Neve noticed for the first time how much Inara's hair had grown since they'd met.

Inara smiled by way of a reply, then reached into the pocket of her jacket. "Got a gift here."

"For me?" Neve had gotten used to deciphering when Inara's lack of pronouns made things ambiguous.

"Yep." Inara handed her a small box wrapped in green tartan paper.

Other than Diane's gun, Neve was pretty sure this was the first gift she'd gotten from a non–family member since her mom stopped hosting birthday parties when she was twelve, and she was delighted, after prying open the wrapping paper and lifting the lid, to discover a pendant inside.

She lifted the pendant by the black cord threaded through its eye, and realized it was a bird. Not just any bird—it was a replica of the Maltese falcon from her favorite movie.

"Found this place on Etsy for custom pendants," Inara said, then smiled. "Since the real-life noir plot."

Neve laughed. She'd definitely lived the part. All those actresses who'd played femme fatales and damsels in distress would have been proud of how Neve had taken control of her own destiny. She smiled as she looped the pendant over her head. "I love it. Thank you so much."

The bell rang, signaling the five-minute warning until first period.

"Five more months," Neve said, staring at the school she hated so much. "Then I'm outta here forever."

"Forever?" Inara asked. "Never coming back to Carlsbad at all? For any reason?"

They'd shared their college plans—Neve's wish to go up north or back east, and Inara's desire to stay close to her family and go to a state school in either San Diego, Riverside, or Orange County—and though Spring Neve would have said, *I'm never coming back to this shithole* and meant it, Winter Neve didn't feel quite the same way.

"I'll always come back," she said, one hand clasping the new pendant. "For my parents. And Deirdre." Then she glanced up at Inara and smiled. "And to see my best friend."

And she knew she would. Forever.

THE END

ACKNOWLEDGMENTS

I'VE BEEN INCREDIBLY BLESSED TO HAVE SO MANY AMAZING people in my corner, both personally and professionally, through eleven novels, and it gives me a great deal of joy to be able to thank them each and every time.

To my longtime agent Ginger Clark, who has believed in this book idea since I first pitched it to her way back in 2015, and her fabulous colleague Nicole Eisenbraun, both of Ginger Clark Literary. Without them, I'd be a boat without a rudder.

To the awesome and awe-inspiring team at Hyperion, who have put so much love and work and support into our books together, it leaves me speechless: my lifesaving editor Kieran Viola; Cassidy Leyendecker, who keeps me on top of things; Marci Senders, whose cover designs never cease to amaze; publicity powerhouses Christine Saunders and Seale Ballenger; Dina Sherman, Sara Liebling, Guy Cunningham, Meredith Jones, Jenny Langsam, Holly Nagel, Andrew Sansone, Jerry Gonzalez, and Marybeth Tregarthen.

To my friend and fellow YA author Demetra Brodsky, whose Carlsbad expertise was invaluable.

To Mom for instilling an early love of black-and-white noir and all things Hitchcock.

To my husband, John, who has read every single one of my books and loves them all, bless his heart; and to my children, who theoretically will read my books one day and inevitably question their mother's sanity.

And last but very much not least, to Cecilia Ortiz and Veronica Rodriguez, without whom I would literally get nothing done. No working mom can stay sane while meeting deadlines without some help, and these two wonderful women have helped me more than they realize.